Ladybug Designs

LULU HART

Ladybug Designs

Cover Design by Hannah Reinhard of HannarchyStudios

Editing by L.D. Butler

First Edition

 Created with Vellum

Content Warning

Graphic Sex

Potential Triggers
Sexual Harassment

Playlist

"Summer Girls" by LFO
"Illegal" by PinkPantheress
"Fire Escape" by Call Me Karizma
"Falling" by Trevor Daniel
"Another Love" by Tom Odell
"Church" by Chase Atlantic
"Swear It Again" by Westlife
"Cradles" by Sub Urban
"Provider" by Sleep Token
"Sippy Cup" by Melanie Martinez
"Forever in Love" by A1
"Unstoppable" by Sia
"Mystical Magical" by Benson Boone
"Rockabye" by Clean Bandit
"Brahms' Lullaby" by Jewel

Contents

AMELIA

You'd think that I'd be turned on by the sight of my husband stepping out of the bathroom—naked, freshly showered—but I'm not.

At twenty-eight-years-old, Nick is dark-haired, undeniably attractive and the smug confidence that turns heads—for better or worse. He's charming when he wants to be, but mostly comes off as arrogant, self-absorbed and a little too obsessed with his own reflection. My husband is the textbook definition of a 'tool'—and he's totally fine with that.

He wasn't always like this, and after eight years of marriage, I couldn't tell you the moment he changed, just that it progressively got worse.

I turn a page in my book, trying to focus on the words, though I've read the same paragraph three times now. My mind is elsewhere—specifically on the living room, where my portfolio of designs sits untouched after I'd asked him to look at them earlier.

The mattress dips as he slides under the covers. I roll onto my side, facing away from him, keeping my eyes fixed on the page. The sheets rustle as he settles in behind me, his chest warm against my back. His arm snakes around my waist; his lips press against my bare shoulder.

"Mmm," he murmurs, his breath hot against my skin.

I continue staring at my book; the words blur together. His hand starts to wander, and I don't respond, don't lean into his touch like I normally would. My body remains rigid, the hardback clutched in my hands.

He pauses, then props himself on one elbow. "Are you still mad at me?"

"I'm reading."

"Is this about earlier? Because I didn't want to look at your stuff?"

"'Stuff?'" I place my bookmark between the pages and set the book on my nightstand. Designs, Nick. You didn't just 'not want to look' at them. You said, and I quote, 'I don't have time for your little drawings right now.'" I mimic his dismissive tone, still feeling the sting of those words.

He flops onto his back, dragging a hand down his face. "I'm sorry, Amelia. I didn't mean it like that." He sighs. "I'm just... frustrated. We've been in this house for two weeks, and there are still boxes everywhere. I can't find half my stuff, and work is killing me right now."

"I know," I say, softening slightly. "But we're both working professionals with full-time jobs. It's going to take us slightly longer to get settled. "Your stress doesn't give you the right to dismiss something that's important to me."

"You're right." His eyes meet mine. "I promise I'll look at

them tomorrow. Your designs aren't 'stuff' or 'little drawings' to me. I was being an ass."

I nod, accepting his apology but not quite ready to let go of my hurt feelings.

He shifts closer again, his lips returning to my shoulder, pressing soft kisses along my skin. His palm slides across my stomach, dipping lower beneath the covers. When his fingers find their way to my thighs, I sigh inwardly. His hand pushes up my nightdress, bunching the silky fabric around my hips as his fingers seek between my legs. I close my eyes and try to will myself in the mood. I should want this—we're married, after all—but instead, I lie here, my body unresponsive as he touches me, clearly expecting me to be ready for him despite the tension still lingering between us.

"You feel so good," he murmurs, though he must sense I'm not aroused at all.

I stare at the ceiling, wondering if he's really that oblivious or if he just doesn't care. His fingers continue to probe uncomfortably against dry skin. I wince. He pulls his hand away, and I hear a wet sound as he spits, presumably into his palm. The sheets rustle again as he reaches down to stroke himself.

This is exactly our problem lately—he wants the end result without putting in any effort. If he'd actually taken the time to kiss me properly, do some foreplay, to reconnect after our argument and make me feel desired rather than convenient, maybe I'd be into this.

He moves on top of me, pushing my legs apart with his knees. He presses against me, hard and insistent. There's an uncomfortable pressure as he tries to enter me, my body resisting the intrusion.

"Nick, I'm not—" I whisper.

He pushes forward with more force, and I wince as he finally manages to get in. The friction burns; my body is not ready for this at all. I turn my head to the side, fixing my gaze on the pale blue wall of our bedroom, counting the tiny imperfections in the paint as he moves above me.

The headboard creaks slightly with each thrust, his face buried in my neck. I lie motionless beneath him, feeling disconnected from my own body—from this moment—from him. The ceiling has a small water stain in the corner I hadn't noticed before—a faint yellowish circle that reminds me of a coffee ring. I focus on it, wondering if I should call someone about it tomorrow, before it gets worse.

"God, Amelia," he groans, his movements becoming more erratic, while his breathing grows heavier.

It can't really be that good, can it?

His eyes are closed, lost in his own pleasure while I lie beneath him, detached and waiting for it to end.

Three days later, I'm hauling garbage and broke down moving boxes to the bins on the side of our house, trying not to let the bag drag against the ground. It's Friday night, and I'm alone again. Nick texted an hour ago that he'd be working late—the third time this week. I gave up on showing him my sketches as he still hasn't looked at them like he promised.

The thump of bass catches my attention as I shut the lid on the trash can. Music pulses from the house next door.

I pause, listening to the laughter floating through the evening air. It sounds like... fun. Something I haven't had in a while. My curiosity gets the better of me as I drift toward the wooden fence separating our properties.

I step up to it and peek through a small hole in the wood. It's your typical college party—red cups scattered everywhere, string lights crisscrossing the backyard, music thumping loud enough to feel in my chest. The crowd is mostly late teens, early twenty-somethings, laughing and dancing, carefree.

That's when I notice him—tall and blond, shirtless despite the evening chill, leaning against the wall of the house. A beer bottle dangles casually from his fingers. I've glimpsed him a few times since we moved in, usually heading to his Jeep or checking the mail. Up close, through my little peephole, I find the definition in his chest and abs, the kind that comes from hard work and gym time.

A girl with long, wavy hair saunters to him. She's pretty in an effortless college way—cut-off shorts, crop top, glitter on her cheekbones catching the party lights. She places her hand on his chest, saying something I can't hear over the music. He smiles at her, then pulls her closer until their bodies press together. His mouth finds hers in a kiss that looks like it could devour her whole—it's consuming. His hand slides into her hair, tilting her head back as his mouth moves against hers.

He kisses her like she's oxygen and he's been underwater. Like nothing else in the world exists but her mouth against his.

God—I wish my husband would kiss me like that.

The thought hits me with such force that I almost step back. *When was the last time Nick kissed me with that kind of desire? Has he ever?* I search my memory, trying to recall a

5

moment when he looked at me the way this guy is looking at this girl, and I come up empty. Even in the beginning, his kisses were... pleasant. Comfortable. Never desperate or consuming.

A loud crash behind me makes me jump. I spin around to see the stack of flattened moving boxes I'd propped against the house has toppled over. Fantastic.

When I turn back to the fence, my heart stops. The blond guy is staring directly at my spying hole, his eyes locked with mine. His making out with the girl has ended, and now his full attention is on me, his neighbor, caught red-handed—spying. The corner of his mouth quirks up in a knowing smile. My cheeks flush hot, and I duck away from the fence.

I leave the boxes scattered on the ground and hurry back inside, mortified.

What are you doing, spying on your neighbors like some desperate housewife? You're twenty-eight years old, for God's sake, not some teenager with a crush.

In the kitchen, I fumble for a glass and fill it with water from the tap, gulping it down as if it might extinguish the fire in my cheeks. I set the glass down with a clink against the countertop, pressing my palms flat against the cool granite.

I'm not sure if I'm more embarrassed about being caught peeking through the fence or about the fact that watching that kiss affected me so much.

What's wrong with me? I'm married. I shouldn't be fantasizing about how some college guy kisses. But the image won't leave my mind—his hands in her hair, the intensity in his expression, the way his muscles tensed as he pulled her closer...

The doorbell rings.

Oh, God.

I do what any self-respecting adult woman would do in this situation: drop to the floor behind the kitchen island like I've been sniper-shot.

No warning—*just bam!*—full pancake mode on my hardwood.

It can't be. But it is. I know it is. It's him.

Why am I hiding? It's not like he can see through walls. Can he?

I consider ignoring it—but he already knows I'm home. The bell rings again, more insistently this time.

I take a deep breath, pull myself to my feet and smooth down my velour lounge pants, as if that is going to save my dignity, and make my way to the foyer.

When I pull it open, my suspicions are confirmed. It's him —the shirtless neighbor—standing on my doorstep with the same knowing smile from earlier. Up close, the guy is even more attractive than he appeared through the fence, with his blond hair somewhat tousled.

He reaches up, placing one hand on the top of my doorframe, leaning his body into the space as if he's about to share a secret. The casual position makes his abs flex, and I force my eyes to stay on his face.

"Hi," he says, his voice deeper than I expected.

I say nothing, my embarrassment from being caught spying still fresh. I cross my arms over my chest, trying to appear unimpressed rather than flustered.

"We're having a party next door," he continues, gesturing with his free hand toward his house. "Just wanted to say you should let me know if it gets too loud. And apologize for last weekend. Your—" he looks at my hand, which has a gold band on it. "husband—threatened to call the cops."

His eyes fix on me, expectant, waiting for a response I can't seem to form. The silence stretches between us, my tongue suddenly heavy in my mouth.

"Is he home?" he finally asks, glancing past me into the house.

I clear my throat. "No, he's not. Just me. He'll be home late, so..." I wave my hand vaguely toward his place. "You guys can be as loud as you want. For a while, anyway."

His smile widens, showing perfect teeth. "Well, in that case, why don't you come over? Much more fun than being alone on a Friday night."

"No, thank you," I say quickly, perhaps too quickly. "I have... things to do."

"What things?" he challenges, with his lopsided grin turning playful.

My thoughts are derailed when a female voice calls from the direction of his house. "Wes!"

I look past him to find the woman he was making out with. She's standing at the edge of our property line, with a hand on her hip, looking impatient. Her crop top sparkles under the streetlight; her legs are impossibly long in those tiny shorts.

He doesn't even turn around. His eyes remain fixed on me, as if her calling for him is merely background noise.

"You shouldn't keep your girlfriend waiting," I state, nodding toward her.

He laughs, a low rumble that I feel more than hear. "She's not my girlfriend."

"Right," I say, not believing him for a second. "Well, have fun with your not-girlfriend."

He backs away slowly, eyes still on mine. "Goodnight."

"Goodnight," I respond automatically before closing the door with a soft click.

I lean my back against it, my heart beating faster than it should be.

And that is how I met Wes Sullivan.

Chapter One

WESLEY

Two years later...

I'm three tequila shots in, two games up in beer pong, and already the reason two girls are fighting in the kitchen.

Typical Friday.

The music thumps through the walls like a second heartbeat, the air thick with sweat, cheap vodka, and whatever sorority girl has overdone her vanilla body spray. The living room of the team house is packed, red cups in the air, everyone shouting every line of every song like it's gospel.

This is what I do.

Parties don't really start until I show up, Dalton University's star quarterback, and they don't hit their peak until I pick who I'd spend the night with.

Tonight, I'd picked early.

Her name is... something. Ashley? Amber? She has fake eyelashes, a high ponytail, and a tight white top. She's been clinging to my arm since the second I sank my final pong shot, squealing like I had just cured cancer.

"Come on," I say, flashing her the grin that usually gets me whatever I want.

She giggles and stumbles after me, heels clicking on the hardwood floor as I lead her upstairs, dodging half-dressed bodies and beer puddles along the way. The third door on the right is my usual go-to—it has a decent lock, a bed that doesn't squeak (much), and a poster of Scarface that girls either find hilarious or intimidating. Either works for me.

Once inside, she goes straight for my mouth. I let her—for about all of thirty seconds. But yeah, nah—this isn't going to work.

Jesus Christ, it's like making out with a broken washing machine. Her tongue is everywhere—my teeth, the roof of my mouth, practically down my throat—while she makes these high-pitched moans that remind me of a chihuahua when it gets excited. She tastes like watermelon vodka and bubblegum, and her lip gloss is so sticky, it feels like I'm kissing a Jolly Rancher wrapped in duct tape.

"Mmm, you're so hot, Wes," she mumbles against my mouth, her hands fumbling with my belt. "I heard you're pierced."

I pull back, trying not to wince as I wipe actual saliva off my chin. My body isn't responding at all. Usually by this point, I'd be ready to go, but downstairs was decidedly uninterested.

She lunges at me again while attacking my neck with what feels like a combination of sucking and... was she nibbling? Jesus. This girl kisses like she learned everything from bad porn and wikiHow articles.

"Hey, hold up," I say, catching her wrists. "Maybe we should slow down." I step back.

My jeans aren't even tight. Nothing. Absolutely nothing happening down there—not a single twitch from my cock.

She pouts. "Don't you want me?"

Honestly? Not really.

I rest my hand on her hip as though I was still into it. She smiles at me, breathless, waiting for me to go in again.

I don't.

I can't stop thinking about how uninterested I am—like, soul-level bored, and slightly disgusted.

This was supposed to be fun. Easy. Instead, this was the fourth time this month. Fourth time I'd brought a girl upstairs, and fourth time my body had completely checked out of the situation. *What the hell was happening to me?*

A month ago, I would've been all over her. I would've had her screaming my name so loud the entire party would know exactly what was going on in this room.

Something about these hookups felt... empty.

She leans in again, and I tilt my head like I'm about to meet her halfway—

"You hear that?" I ask, pretending to hear something downstairs, frowning like I actually give a shit. "Sounded like someone broke something."

She blinks. "Really? I didn't hear anything."

I'm already reaching for the door. "Just gonna make sure they're okay."

I slip out before she can argue, closing the door behind me and exhaling the kind of breath you let out when you avoid a disaster.

Halfway down the stairs, I scan the crowd for Chase.

My brother was really the only reason I'd even shown up tonight. After what happened two weeks ago with the Los

13

Angeles Chapter of The Keepers, I'd wanted to stay home, but he had insisted this party would "get us back to normal."

I spot his blond head across the room, talking to some guy with a drink in his hand. Chase is nodding at whatever this dude is saying, looking more engaged than I've seen him all night. Typical Chase—he'd rather have one deep conversation than ten hookups.

I push through the crowd, dodging a girl who tries to grab my arm and ignoring someone calling my name from the kitchen.

"Hey," I interrupt, not bothering with introductions. "I'm out."

Chase's smile drops. "Already? It's barely midnight."

"I'm..." I run a hand through my hair. "Not feeling it tonight."

He frowns, excusing himself from his conversation and following me as I make my way toward the door. "What happened to the girl you were with? The one with the..." He gestures vaguely at his chest.

"Yeah, not happening."

He raises his eyebrow.

I shrug, keeping my eyes on the exit. "Just wasn't... into it."

He walks me to the door, and watches me with a concerned look he gets.

"Text me when you get home," he says, like I'm sixteen and not twenty-one.

"Sure thing, Mom," I mutter, but I nod anyway.

The walk to my off-campus house is only fifteen minutes, but tonight it feels longer. The cool night air clears my head a bit, but my thoughts keep circling back to what's happening

—or not happening—with my body lately. I've never had this problem before. Ever. Even when I was black-out drunk sophomore year, I managed to perform fine.

Maybe it's stress about the NFL draft. Or The Keepers.

By the time I reach our house, I've convinced myself it's just a phase. Temporary. It has to be.

The house is dark and quiet when I unlock the front door. I flip on a light, toss my keys in the bowl, and head straight upstairs to my bathroom. I need to get the taste of tonight out of my mouth.

I squeeze a fat line of sharp mint toothpaste onto my brush and scrub hard. I gargle with mouthwash after, swishing it around until my cheeks burn and my eyes water.

When I finally spit it out, I stare at myself in the mirror. Same face as always—the Sullivan golden boy, future NFL draft pick, Dalton U campus legend. But something in my eyes looks tired. Bored, maybe. Or just... done.

I flick off the bathroom light and step into my bedroom. As I walk by the window, a movement outside catches my eye. There's a shadow on the back porch of the house next door illuminated by the soft blue glow of a phone screen.

I stop and move closer to the glass.

It's her—Amelia. Ladybug, as I've started calling her in my head and to my brothers—though never to her face. I've had a schoolboy crush on my neighbor for two years.

Fuck. My body responds instantly, like it always does with her.

I close my eyes and lean against the window frame, already half-hard just thinking about her. It's pathetic, really.

It's been like this for months now. While girls my age with their perfect bodies and practiced moves leave me completely cold, the mere sight of my neighbor makes me harder than concrete. It's been her who's starred in every one of my late-night sessions with my right hand. Her, with those tight pencil skirts and high heels she wears to work. Her, in those ridiculously tight leggings she lounges in on nights and weekends. Her, with that sarcastic little smile she gives me when I'm being particularly annoying. And trust me—I try to be annoying, just to see that smile. I've lost count of how many times I've gotten myself off thinking about her.

But she's older—thirty now, I think—and married. And I'm just the college guy next door who she probably sees as some dumb jock who parties too loud on the weekends.

She sits outside with a fuzzy blanket, her legs tucked under her, staring down at her phone, her brunette hair falling around her face and over her back. Even in the dim light from her porch lamp, I can see the tension in her shoulders, the way she is hunched forward like she's protecting herself from something.

I study her features, how her lips press into a tight line as she scrolls. A small gold hoop glints in her left nostril, catching the light every time she turns her head. She wipes her eyes.

Fuck. She's crying.

What did that asshole husband of hers do now? I've seen him many times in the two years we've been neighbors. Always in a suit, always on his phone, always looking like he'd rather be anywhere else. Never once have I seen him look at her the way a man should look at a woman like Amelia.

She glances up suddenly, her eyes meeting mine through the window glass.

Shit. Caught. I freeze, staring like some creep. For a second, we just look at each other across the twenty feet of space between our houses. Should I wave? Pretend I was just closing the blinds? I think about raising my hand to wave, but her back door swings open.

A woman steps out—older—her mother? She says something to Amelia, who nods without breaking eye contact with me. She stands, gives me one last look—something complicated in her expression I can't read from here—before following the woman inside.

The porch light clicks off, leaving me staring at my reflection in the window.

I back away, feeling weird, like I've violated some kind of privacy. Which is rich, considering how many times I've caught her watching me mow the lawn shirtless, pretending not to look.

I strip to my boxers and fall into bed, looking up at the ceiling. My phone buzzes—probably Chase checking if I made it home—but I ignore it.

Why is she upset?

I roll onto my side, and punch my pillow into a more comfortable shape.

Why do you even care? She's just your neighbor. Your hot, married neighbor, with whom you've exchanged maybe fifty words with in two years.

Chapter Two

AMELIA

Everyone is saying Nick was a great guy, and I nod along—because it's rude to argue at your husband's funeral.

"Thank you, yes, he was wonderful," I say to Nick's Aunt Pam, taking yet another baking pan I don't have room for in my fridge.

They brought casseroles, condolences, and compliments—none of which I asked for.

They are all mourning the man they thought he was. *But if they knew what I knew, would they still be crying?*

I watch numb as my mother drifts away to comfort Nick's mom, Catherine, in the corner of my home's dining room, leaving me mercifully alone for a moment. The black dress I'm wearing feels too tight across my chest, like it's squeezing out what little air I have left. Ironic.

The murmur of conversations washes over me like static. Voices discussing their favorite Nick stories, reminiscing about his laugh, his generosity. I lean against the wall, nodding mechanically when someone catches my eye, but mostly I'm somewhere else entirely.

God, I just want this day to end.

A glass of water sits untouched in my hand. I stare at the tiny ripples that form when my fingers tremble. Ten years of marriage, and this is how it ends—with me standing in a corner, unable to conjure the appropriate grief everyone expects from a widow.

I should be sobbing into tissues, accepting hugs and sharing sweet anecdotes about my beloved husband. But the weight of my wedding ring feels strange now—like costume jewelry. A lie.

Mrs. Henley from down the street approaches, her face a mask of sympathy. "He was so young," she whispers. "Such a tragedy."

"Yes," I manage. "Thank you for coming."

When she walks away, I exhale.

Mourners finally begin to leave as the afternoon shadows lengthen across the living room floor. Nick's parents are the last to leave, their faces etched with grief that seems genuine—unlike mine.

Catherine clutches my hands, her eyes red-rimmed and swollen. "We'll get through this together, sweetheart," she whispers, pulling me into a hug that smells of floral perfume.

Richard stands beside her, his tall frame somehow diminished in his dark suit. He pats my shoulder awkwardly, his throat working. "If you need anything, day or night..."

"I'll be in touch," I promise, summoning a tremulous smile. "About Nick's things—I know there are some childhood mementos you'd like to have."

They nod gratefully and step out into the fading light, the door closing behind them with a soft click that echoes in the sudden quiet of the house.

I stand motionless in the entryway, listening to the silence. I can breathe without feeling like I'm performing for an audience.

The clinking of dishes from the kitchen breaks the spell.

Oh. Mom. She's still here. Probably puttering around in the kitchen like she always does when she feels helpless. I sigh and push away from the wall. The sound of plates clinking together grows louder as I approach.

My mother stands at the sink, sleeves rolled up past her elbows, methodically washing casserole pans people had kindly said not to return. The counter is already lined with neatly stacked containers, and she's organizing the refrigerator.

"Mom, you don't have to do that," I say, my voice coming out flatter than intended.

My mother turns, dishtowel in hand. "I'm trying to help, sweetie. You shouldn't have to deal with all this mess on top of everything else."

I prop myself against the doorframe. The sympathy in mom's eyes is almost too much to bear. Not because it hurts, but because it feels so undeserved.

"I think I need to be alone now," I say quietly.

My mother's hands still. "Of course, Amelia. You need space to process your grief." She hesitates. "But are you sure? I could stay the night. The guest room is—"

"I just want to be by myself for a while. Go join dad at the hotel."

Mom looks at me for a long moment, her brow furrowed with concern. Finally, she sighs and wipes her fingers on the dishtowel.

"If you're certain that's what you need..." She hangs the towel over the oven handle with the precision of someone stalling for time. "But promise you'll call if you change your mind. It doesn't matter what time."

I nod, relief washing over me. "I promise."

With obvious reluctance, my mother gathers her things from the counter and slips her cardigan on. She moves slowly, as if expecting me to change my mind with each passing second. When she finally picks up her purse, I feel like I could breathe again.

"I left some soup in the blue container," Mom says, pointing to the refrigerator. "And there's fresh bread in the breadbox. You need to eat, sweetheart."

"I will," I lie, guiding her toward the front door with a gentle hand on her back.

At the threshold, she turns and wraps me in a tight hug.

"I love you," she whispers against my hair.

"Love you too," I reply automatically.

After the door closes, I lean my forehead against the cool wood and exhale deeply.

I finally lock the door, sliding the deadbolt into place with a satisfying click. The house settles around me, creaking slightly as if acknowledging we're alone together for the first time in weeks.

The silence is deafening after constant murmurs, footsteps, and the careful voices people use around the newly widowed. For fourteen days, I've been passed between caregivers like a fragile package—Nick's parents staying the first week, then my mother. All of them watching me with worried eyes, waiting for the breakdown they're certain is coming.

I kick off the uncomfortable black heels I've been wearing all day and leave them where they fall. Moving through the living room, I turn off lights and lamps as I go, plunging the house into merciful darkness.

In the kitchen, I bypass the neatly organized leftovers and reach instead for the bottle of Cabernet Sauvignon hidden behind the flour. The cork makes a satisfying pop. I don't bother with a glass.

Wine bottle in hand, I pad down the hallway toward our —my—bedroom. The king-sized bed looks obscenely large with only my side turned down. After I set the wine bottle down on the nightstand, grab a pillow off the bed and bury my face in it, releasing a scream that had been building inside my chest all day. The cotton muffles the sound, but the vibration courses through my body, purging some of the tension I'd been carrying. When I finally pull my face away, I feel lighter somehow.

"That felt good," I whisper to the empty room. "Really good."

I put the pillow back in its place and take a long swig, the rich cabernet warming my throat and spreading through my chest. Setting it carefully on the nightstand again, I crawl under the covers and reach for the remote, not even bothering with pajamas.

The TV flickers to life, casting blue-white shadows across the bedroom walls. I click through channels until I find what I need—women with too much money arguing about nothing important. Perfect. The Real Housewives of Beverly Hills fills the screen with their designer outfits and petty conflicts.

"That's right, Dorit," I mutter as one woman gestures dramatically at a dinner table. "Tell her about her tacky shoes. That'll solve everything."

I sink deeper into the pillows, letting the ridiculous drama wash over me. These women's problems were so insignificant compared to mine. I take another lengthy drink from the bottle, feeling the wine's warmth spread through my limbs. The housewives' voices begin to blur together, their arguments about charity galas and friendship betrayals fading into meaningless noise.

I take another drink, and then another. The wine bottle grows lighter in my hand. My eyelids feel heavy, the TV screen becoming a smudge of colors and movement. I don't even care about who threw wine at whom anymore.

The remote slips from my fingers, landing somewhere in the tangle of blankets. I don't bother looking for it. My head sinks deeper into the pillow as my thoughts grow fuzzy around the edges.

I glance at the alarm clock, its red numbers glowing 7:04 PM in the dim room. It's ridiculously early, but exhaustion pulls at me like quicksand. The funeral, the people, the pretending—it's all drained me completely.

"Work tomorrow," I mumble to myself, taking one last sip before setting the bottle down. The architectural firm expects me back after "bereavement."

Chapter Three

WESLEY

"Shit!"

I look up from my mindless scrolling on social media to see thick gray smoke curling from the edges of the oven door. The lasagna! Grabbing the potholder from the counter, I yank open the oven's door. A billowing cloud of smoke rushes out, engulfing my face. I cough, eyes stinging, as the smoke detector above starts its piercing wail.

"What the hell, Wes?" Chase appears in the doorway, his expression shifting from annoyance to alarm. He lunges for the oven controls, twisting the knob to OFF while I grab a kitchen towel, flapping it desperately at the smoke detector.

"I got distracted!" I yell over the alarm. "Can you open a window?"

He throws open a window before grabbing another towel to help with smoke-clearing efforts. The detector finally stops its screaming, leaving an uncomfortable silence broken only by our coughing.

"Mom's lasagna recipe?" he asks, peering at the blackened

dish, removing it from the oven. The cheese, no longer bubbling but transformed into a charred crust.

"Ruined," I confirm with a sigh, as he sets the disaster on the stovetop. The smoke still hanging in the air makes my eyes water, bringing back unwelcome memories from two weeks ago.

"So what's with you trying to be Martha Stewart? Since when do you bake lasagna on a Sunday night?"

I grab a dishcloth, poking at the blackened edges of what should have been a perfect casserole. "It's for Ladybug." I feel a twinge of disappointment looking at my failed attempt. "Her husband died."

His eyebrows shoot up. "Wasp is dead? When?"

"Motorcycle accident, Halloween night. His little old grandma came to the door this afternoon asking if she could park in our driveway during the funeral reception next door. She wasn't big on details, and I didn't ask." I toss the dishcloth onto the counter. "Isn't this what you're supposed to do when someone dies? Bring casseroles? I've never done this before."

Chase nods, a flicker of sympathy crossing his face. "Yeah, but maybe not cremated ones." He pokes at the burnt mess with a fork. "Might send the wrong message."

"You think?" I say sarcastically, but there's no real heat behind it. I'm too disappointed in myself.

He tosses the utensil in the sink. "You should probably just go buy something at the store instead. Something pre-made."

"Yeah, you're right."

"Want me to come with you?" he asks.

"You don't have to. I can handle a grocery run."

He nods, scrolling through something on his phone.

"Grab some extra stuff while you're there. Luke texted that he's bringing Bebe home soon."

"Seriously? That's great news." I toss the potholder onto the counter. "How's she doing?"

"Better, I guess. Her brothers have been watching her like hawks since the whole incident. Making sure she gets the best doctors, treatments, everything." He runs a hand through his hair.

I grab my wallet and keys from the bowl by the door. "I'll get stuff for her homecoming too. Maybe some balloons or something."

"You're such a softie," he teases, but his smile is genuine.

I flip him off good-naturedly as I head out the door, the smell of burnt cheese following me. The evening air is cool against my face, a welcome relief from the smoky kitchen. My Jeep sits in the driveway, a little dusty but reliable as always. I climb in, tossing my wallet into the console before starting the engine.

The drive to Ambrose Market is short, just enough time to mentally kick myself over the lasagna disaster again. What was I thinking? I've never been much of a cook, and trying to impress Ladybug—Amelia—with homemade food was probably doomed from the start.

Inside the store, the fluorescent lights buzz overhead and make everything seem harsh and unappetizing. I stand in front of the refrigerated deli section, staring at rows of prepared meals. Rotisserie chickens spin slowly behind glass. Pasta salads that look like they're drying out. Pre-made lasagnas that look nothing like Mom's recipe.

None of it seems right. Not for someone whose husband just died.

"Fuck it," I mutter, turning away from the deli counter and heading toward the liquor aisle instead.

I grab a bottle of whiskey, the good stuff. The kind that burns on the way down but gives you a warm glow afterward. It reminds me of those dark days when Bebe was in the hospital, hooked up to machines, her skin pale as moonlight. We'd all taken turns sitting with her, Luke never leaving her side. I couldn't stomach much food—just coffee and whatever Chase forced on me. But the whiskey? It helped take the edge off, helped me sleep when my brain wouldn't shut up about how we all could've died or be in jail—framed for something we didn't do.

Ladybug must be feeling something similar now, but a hundred times worse. I never liked her husband. Wasp was always looking down his nose at us, like we were beneath him because we were college kids and he had some fancy job. Once, he called campus security on us for making too much noise at a perfectly reasonable hour. Another time, he "accidentally" sprayed me with the hose while I was washing my Jeep. Total dick move.

But she chose him. Married him. And now he's gone, just like that. And losing someone you love... I shake my head, trying to clear the image of Bebe's pale face when her brothers took her away... I can't imagine what she might be feeling.

I wander to the greeting card aisle next, where the rows of sympathy cards stare back at me with their somber fonts and watercolor flowers. So many variations of "With Deepest Condolences" and "In Your Time of Sorrow." I pick up a few, reading the inside messages, but they all feel too formal, too stiff for Ladybug.

That's when I spot it—a card with a cartoon bug on the

front wearing sunglasses. Inside it says, "Thinking about you... no special reason, no special rhyme, just wanted to reach out and say hi from time to time."

Perfect. Not a sympathy card, but not ignoring what happened either. Simply letting her know I'm around.

Not the standard funeral face, but something about it feels right for Amelia. She doesn't seem like the weepy, dramatic type.

I tuck it under my arm with the whiskey bottle and keep browsing. My eyes catch on a different section—the inappropriate humor cards. There's one with a woman on a hospital bed giving the middle finger that says, "Get Better Or Else." I snort out loud immediately thinking of Bebe. She'd love this.

I grab both cards and add them to my basket. For Bebe, I also grab a small stuffed bear wearing a football jersey—cheesy, maybe, but it'll make her smile. I head to the checkout, scanning the aisles one last time to see if there's anything else I should get.

The cashier, an older woman with gray hair pulled into a tight bun, eyes the whiskey bottle as she scans it.

"Big night?" She asks, her tone somewhere between judgment and concern.

"Not really," I reply, pulling out my wallet. "Just being neighborly."

She raises an eyebrow but doesn't comment further. I pay, grab my bags, and head back to my Jeep.

The drive home is quiet, only the low hum of the radio keeping me company.

I think about what I'll say to Ladybug when I see her. "Sorry your husband's dead, here's some booze"?

I turn onto our street, slowing as I approach our houses. Mine is lit up—Chase is probably still awake and gaming—but Ladybug's is completely dark. No porch light, no glow from the inside. Nothing.

I pull into my driveway and sit there for a minute, engine idling. My eyes drift to the whiskey and cards on the passenger seat.

I'll wait to give it to her in the morning.

Chapter Four

AMELIA

"Shut up!" I yell at the alarm clock, blindly reaching over to silence its insistent beeping, again.

Again?

My eyes snap open as my brain finally processes the time. I've been hitting the snooze button for—oh God—almost an hour? The blurry red numbers read 8:42.

"No, no, no!" I scramble upright, throwing the covers off with such force they slide completely off the bed. My head pounds from last night's wine, but there's no time to nurse a hangover. I have a 9:30 client meeting at the firm."

I stagger to my closet, yanking hangers around until I find my charcoal pencil skirt and a cream blouse that doesn't need ironing. No chance for a shower. I splash water on my face, brush my teeth in record time, and swipe on mascara and lipstick with shaking hands. My reflection looks pale and hollow-eyed, but professional enough.

"Keys, phone, portfolio," I mutter, shoving everything

into my bag. My stomach churns with hunger and anxiety, but breakfast isn't happening.

I hop to the door while putting my heels on, a ridiculous balancing act in this pencil skirt. I'm going to be so late. Somehow I manage to lock the front door without falling over, then brisk-walk down the path to my car, one hand clutching my bag and portfolio, the other trying to smooth my unwashed hair.

I reach my red Volkswagen Beetle and throw my stuff onto the passenger seat and slide behind the wheel, throwing my key fob into the cup holder.

I press the start button. The dashboard lights flicker briefly, then nothing.

"Come on," I mutter, pressing it again with more force, as if it would help.

Still nothing. Not even a struggling sound from the engine.

"This cannot be happening." My voice comes out as a strangled whisper. "Not today. Not now."

The pressure that's been building inside me since I woke up—since the funeral—suddenly becomes unbearable. I let my head fall forward onto the steering wheel, inadvertently pressing down on the horn. The blaring sound cuts through the quiet morning, but I don't lift my head. No—I let it scream for a solid five seconds while I sit here in defeat.

A sharp tap on my window jolts me out of my despair. I snap upright, my heart pounding wildly, and stare at the most perfectly defined set of abs I've ever seen, just inches from the glass. They're at eye level, tanned and sculpted like something from a fitness magazine.

For a disoriented moment, I wonder if I've died right here

in my defunct Beetle and this is heaven's welcome committee. God is ripped?

The abs shift as the man crouches, and suddenly I'm looking into bluish-green eyes under a sweep of tousled blond hair. A lopsided smile that's equal parts concerned and amused comes into view.

Wes—my neighbor. The football star who's always jogging shirtless when I'm trying to bring in groceries.

He mouths something I can't hear and makes a gesture toward the door handle. Right. I can't just sit here in my dead car staring at him.

I open the car door since the power is out. Once open, he crouches next to me still seated. I notice his large sneakers, the manly hair covering his legs—it's not a lot but enough to make me suddenly aware of how close he is. His running shorts reveal muscular thighs flexing as he balances on the balls of his feet.

"Battery dead?," he asks, his voice deep and surprisingly gentle. "I heard the horn and figured you were having car trouble."

I'm mortified that he's caught me having a meltdown. "I wasn't honking for help. I was... having a moment."

His eyes crinkle at the corners. "It looked like quite a moment."

"Just a minor setback in my already perfect day," I say, gesturing at the dashboard. "Of course it would happen today. I have a meeting in—" I glance at my watch and groan, "—forty minutes."

His eyes scan my face, noting my disheveled appearance. "Let me drive you," he offers. "I can pick you up later too, and we can take a better look at your car then."

"I can call a rideshare," I say, already fumbling for my phone. "I don't want to inconvenience you."

He leans one muscular arm against my car door. "Have you tried getting a rideshare in Ambrose lately? They're few and far between in this town. Could take twenty minutes just for someone to accept."

I glance at my watch again and feel panic rising. He's right. We're in an awkward not-quite-urban, not-quite-suburban area where rideshares are spotty at best.

"Come on," he says, that lopsided smile reappearing. "It'll be faster. Promise I'm not an axe murderer."

"Well, when you put it so reassuringly..." I sigh, knowing I don't have much choice. "Fine. Thank you."

"Gimme two seconds to grab my keys," he says, already jogging back toward his house in a perfect athletic stride, and I absolutely *do not* watch how perfectly his shorts frame his backside.

I make my way over to his driveway where his Jeep Wrangler sits, all rugged masculinity on wheels. Of course, he drives a Jeep. Open top, slightly lifted, with massive tires that make it sit higher than my little Beetle. I'm standing here contemplating the logistics of this situation when Wes emerges from his house, now wearing a simple gray t-shirt that does nothing to hide his athletic build.

"Sorry about that," he says, clicking the key fob to unlock the doors. "Ready to roll?"

I stare at the Jeep, the high step up to the passenger seat suddenly looking like Mount Everest. In my rush this morning, I chose possibly the tightest pencil skirt I own. The kind that looks professional but barely allows normal walking, let alone scaling the side of a vehicle.

"Um..." I hesitate, glancing down.

"Something wrong?" he asks, coming around to where I am.

"I can't get in," I admit, gesturing at my skirt. "Not exactly Jeep-climbing attire."

"Not a problem," he says, and there's that smile again— the one that probably makes cheerleaders swoon at Dalton University games.

He steps closer, gently pushing at my shoulder, indicating for me to turn around to face the Jeep, which I follow. His hands find my waist, and suddenly my feet are no longer touching the ground. He lifts me with such ease that I barely have time to gasp before I'm level with the seat.

"There we go," he murmurs, his voice close to my ear as he helps me settle into the seat.

I'm momentarily stunned by how effortlessly he handled my weight, like I was nothing more than a grocery bag. I'm taller than most women at 5'7—and have a little more meat on my bones too. The leather is cool against my legs as I adjust my skirt, trying to maintain some semblance of dignity.

He shuts the door with a solid thunk and jogs around to the driver's side, hopping in with an athletic grace that makes me feel even more awkward about my own undignified entry.

"Where to?" he asks, starting the engine. The Jeep rumbles to life, vibrating through the entire vehicle.

"Wheeler & Marks Architecture on Main and 5th," I tell him, checking my watch again. "And if you could possibly bend the laws of physics to get me there in twenty minutes, that would be great."

He grins, that crooked smile making something flutter in my chest that I immediately squash down.

"I'll do my best," he says, throwing the Jeep into reverse and backing out of the driveway.

As we pull onto the main road, he hits the gas, and the vehicle leaps forward. I grip the door handle, not expecting the sudden acceleration. The wind whips through the open top, instantly transforming my hastily arranged hair into what must look like a bird's nest in a hurricane. So much for those five minutes I spent trying to make myself presentable.

We don't talk during the drive. The roar of the wind and the rumble of the engine make conversation difficult anyway. I catch him glancing at me occasionally, and I find myself stealing looks at his profile too—the strong jawline, the focused eyes on the road. There's something oddly intimate about sitting in silence with a man I've barely spoken to before today.

The radio plays an indie rock song I don't recognize. He gestures toward it during a stoplight. "You like this? I can change it if you want."

"It's fine," I say, though honestly, I can barely hear it over the wind. The music is the least of my concerns right now.

We pull up outside the imposing glass-and-steel structure of Wheeler & Marks with eight minutes to spare. He expertly navigates into a loading zone, putting the Jeep in park.

"Thank you," I say, breathless with relief. "You've saved me from what would have been a very uncomfortable conversation with my boss." I gather my bag and portfolio, suddenly aware that I have no idea how I'm getting down from this monster vehicle in my skirt without flashing half of downtown.

The moment I attempt to figure it out, Wes is already out of his seat and opening my door. He offers his hand, and I take it, grateful for the help as I maneuver my way out. His palm is warm against mine, calloused in a way that speaks of his football career.

"What time should I pick you up?" he asks, still holding my hand even though my feet are now firmly on the sidewalk.

"Oh, that's really unnecessary," I say, withdrawing it and adjusting my skirt. "I can get a rideshare back. You must have plans or practice or... something." I wave vaguely at his athletic build, as if that explains everything.

His eyes look directly into mine with a seriousness that catches me off guard.

"Name the time and I'll be here," he says firmly. "I mean it."

Something about his unwavering gaze makes my chest tighten. The sincerity in his voice is so unexpected, so different from what I'm used to. I find myself thinking about Nick, imagining this exact scenario playing out with him instead.

He would have sighed dramatically, rolled his eyes and proceeded to put the blame on me—that I hadn't gotten the battery checked during my last service. Then lecture me about the cost to replace it, how it would set back our vacation fund.

He stands here, patient, waiting for my answer, offering help like it's the most natural thing in the world.

I blink, pushing away thoughts of Nick. "Um, five-thirty?" I manage to say. "If that works for you."

"Five-thirty it is," he says with a nod, checking his watch. "You'd better hurry. You've got about six minutes until your meeting."

"Right! Yes. Thank you again." I turn toward the building entrance, but pause and look back as he hops back inside the Jeep and pulls away.

Chapter Five

AMELIA

I hit the stairwell running, my heels clicking frantically against the concrete steps. The elevator would take too long, and I can't afford another minute of delay. My portfolio bangs against my thigh with each step, a rhythmic reminder of how thoroughly screwed I am if I mess up this meeting.

When I burst through the door to our floor, I'm breathing hard enough that several heads pop up from nearby cubicles. Great. Nothing says "consummate professional" like running through the office as if you're being chased by wolves.

I skid to a stop at my cubicle, dumping my bag onto my chair and frantically rummaging for the Barlowe presentation materials. My desk calendar mocks me with its neat red circle around today's date and the words "Barlowe MEETING - 9:30 - DON'T BE LATE" in all caps. Thanks, Past Amelia. Really helpful.

"There you are!" Cassie hisses from the neighboring cubicle. "Wheeler's been asking where you are for the last fifteen minutes. The Barlowes are already in the conference room."

"I know, I know," I whisper back, grabbing my tablet and the sample boards. "My car wouldn't start. Had to get a ride."

"Your hair looks like you rode here on the back of a motorcycle," she says, eyes wide.

I catch my reflection in my darkened computer screen— she's not wrong. The Jeep ride has transformed my hair into something that belongs in a horror movie. I attempt to smooth it down until the result is marginally better—I've gone from "recently exhumed" to merely "slept in my car."

"Cassie, help me out," I plead, grabbing a bobby pin from her desk. "Is there anything on my face? Toothpaste? Desperation?"

"You're fine," she says quickly, straightening my blouse collar. "Just act like you meant to be fashionably late."

I take a deep breath and stride toward the conference room, trying to channel confidence I definitely don't feel. Through the glass walls, I see them—Russell Barlowe and his wife Nina, sitting at our sleek table as though it's perfectly normal to have an NBA legend in our modest architecture firm.

My stomach does a nervous flip. Russell Barlowe isn't just wealthy—he's famous. My first celebrity client. The kind of client whose Instagram post about our work could change the entire trajectory of the firm.

I'm about to push open the door when my boss, Jeffrey Wheeler, spots me through the glass, his suit and salt-and-pepper hair looking professional and impeccable as always. His expression shifts from polite conversation to thinly veiled irritation in an instant. He excuses himself and intercepts me outside the conference room.

"Amelia," he says in that deceptively calm tone that always makes me feel like I'm back in elementary school. "So glad you could join us."

"I'm so sorry, Mr. Wheeler. My car battery died and—"

"This is our most important client of the quarter," he cuts me off, voice low but sharp. "You show up looking like you just rolled out of bed and expect me to—"

"Amelia?" Nina Barlowe's voice breaks through our hushed conversation as she appears in the doorway. Her expression softens when she looks at me. "I'm so sorry about your husband. We were devastated to hear the news."

Wheeler's reprimand halts mid-sentence as she approaches us.

"We could have pushed this meeting back another couple of weeks," she continues, reaching out to squeeze my arm. "Russell and I completely understand if you need more time."

I swallow hard, feeling Wheeler's eyes boring into me. Yesterday he'd left a voicemail insisting I needed to "move forward" and that the Barlowe project "couldn't wait for my personal issues to resolve." His exact words.

"Thank you, Mrs. Barlowe. That's very kind," I say, managing a smile I hope looks genuine. "But honestly, I've been eager to share these designs with you. The work has been... therapeutic."

It's not entirely a lie. The hours I've spent hunched over my tablet, sketching concept after concept for their mountain retreat, have been the only times my mind hasn't been consumed with thoughts of Nick and all the complications his death left behind.

"Well, we're excited to see what you've come up with," she says warmly. "And please, call me Nina."

She guides me into the conference room with a gentle hand on my back. Mr. Barlowe stands as we enter, extending his hand. He's even taller in person than he appears on TV, an imposing figure in an impeccably tailored suit. His handshake is firm but not crushing.

"Mrs. Campbell," he says, his voice resonant. "Thank you for making time for us today. We know it can't be easy."

I nod, trying not to think about how my hair probably looks like I stuck my finger in an electrical socket. "Please call me Amelia."

Wheeler clears his throat. "Shall we get started? Amelia has prepared quite the presentation for you both."

I set up my tablet and connected it to the room's display. As the screen comes to life, I feel a strange calm settle over me. This is my element. Here, I know exactly what I'm doing.

"So," I begin, "when we spoke about your vision for this mountain retreat, Nina, you mentioned wanting something that felt both grand and intimate. A place where you could host friends during the holidays but wouldn't feel empty when it's just the two of you."

The first image appears on the large screen—a sweeping exterior view of a modern mountain lodge with floor-to-ceiling windows reflecting snow-capped mountains nestled among towering pines. The structure blends natural materials with clean lines.

"Oh," Nina breathes, leaning forward. "That's stunning."

"I've designed a home that speaks to both those needs," I continue, swiping to the next image—a closer view of the entrance with its dramatic overhang and specialized ironwork on the front door. "I incorporated the iron detailing you admired from that resort in Aspen, but made it more personal with custom metalwork that includes subtle basketball motifs that only those who know would recognize."

Mr. Barlowe leans forward, his eyes narrowing as he spots the clever basketball-inspired patterns woven into the decorative ironwork. "That's incredible attention to detail," he says, nodding appreciatively.

I swipe to the next image—a floor plan of the main level.

"The house follows an open-concept design with the primary living areas flowing into one another," I explain, using my stylus to highlight different areas. "But I've incorporated architectural elements to create natural divisions between spaces without walls."

I move through the rooms methodically, watching their reactions. "The kitchen features dual islands—one for prep work and one for casual dining and entertaining. I remembered you mentioned how you love to cook together, so I designed it with two people in mind."

Nina reaches for her husband's hand, squeezing it as she smiles.

"Moving to the great room," I continue, "the twenty-foot ceilings create a dramatic space, but I've used warm materials —reclaimed timber beams, natural stone, and custom built-ins—to maintain that intimate feeling you wanted."

I swipe to a rendering of the master suite, complete with a sitting area and a spa-like bathroom with mountain views from the soaking tub.

"For the personal spaces, I focused on creating sanctuaries," I explain, clicking to the next image. "Each guest suite has its own unique character while maintaining the overall aesthetic."

I move through several more interior designs, noting how Nina squeezes Russell's hand when I reveal the home theater with custom leather recliners and the indoor basketball court with its polished maple flooring.

"And now," I say, feeling a flutter of excitement, "I'd like to show you how your home would look throughout the seasons."

I swipe to a summer view, the expansive deck bathed in golden light, then to fall with the surrounding aspens blazing in amber and crimson. When I reach the winter scene, I pause, knowing this is my strongest work.

"Here's the property during the holidays."

The rendering shows the lodge at twilight, nestled in pristine snow. Warm light spills from every window, and tasteful holiday decorations adorn the exterior—garlands of evergreen wrapped with tiny white lights frame the grand entrance, and a substantial wreath hangs on the custom iron door. The roof line is delicately traced with twinkling lights that complement rather than compete with the starry mountain sky. Through the massive windows, you can make out a towering Christmas tree in the great room, the family gathered around a crackling fire.

"I imagined your family traditions continuing here," I say softly.

Nina's eyes glisten with tears as she looks at the final rendering. Her hand rises to her chest, and she dabs at the corner of her eye with a perfectly manicured finger.

"This is..." she pauses, her voice thick with emotion. "It's perfect, Amelia. You've captured exactly what I was asking for.

I can see us there—Christmas morning with the kids, summer evenings on the beautiful deck." She reaches for Russell's hand again. "Can't you picture it, honey?"

Mr. Barlowe nods, his expression softening in a way you rarely see from the famously intense athlete. "You nailed it. You listened. Not just to what we said, but to what we meant," he says. "This is home."

The word "home" sends a flutter through my chest—that's exactly what I was going for. Not just a house, not just a vacation property, but a place where their family will build memories.

I turn toward Wheeler, feeling a surge of relief and pride replacing my earlier panic. He meets my eyes across the conference room, a genuine smile breaking through his usually stern demeanor. He gives me a subtle wink that says more than words could—I've knocked this out of the park.

This. This right here is why I love my job. Not the prestigious clients or the substantial commission this project will bring, but this moment—watching someone's face light up when they see their dreams transformed from vague ideas into something tangible. Something they can walk through in their mind before a single foundation stone is laid.

Chapter Six

WESLEY

I'm in my driveway before I even realize I've been smiling the entire way back from dropping Amelia off. Something about how she tucked her hair behind her ear when she said goodbye, all professional and flustered at once.

5:30pm can't come fast enough.

I kill the engine but don't get out right away. My eyes drift to her red Beetle parked dead in her driveway. The poor thing looks sad just sitting there, like a ladybug that's lost its spots. I drum my fingers on the steering wheel, thinking.

I've got three hours before my afternoon practice, and my first class isn't until tomorrow. I could go inside, play some Fallout, maybe grab a nap. Or...

Before I talk myself out of it, I'm out of the Jeep and walking toward her car, hands in my pockets, trying to look casual, even though no one's watching.

Dead battery. Such a simple problem with such an easy fix. I could fix it for her. Just being neighborly. Just helping someone who's going through a rough time.

Just wanting to see her smile again.

I peer through the driver's side window and spot the key fob sitting in the cup holder, right where she left it in her panic this morning. I try the door handle, half-expecting it to be locked, but it swings open easily. Some people would call this breaking and entering, but I prefer to think of it as surprise automotive assistance.

I grab the key, feeling a strange little thrill at holding something of hers in my hand.

"Alright, Sullivan," I mutter to myself. "Time to be useful."

Popping the hood takes a minute of fumbling—European cars always hide their release levers in weird places. But I eventually find it and prop it open. The engine compartment looks like a foreign country to me. I know the basics—this is where the magic happens, fuel turns into power, and the car moves. But ask me to point out specific parts, and I'm lost. That's Luke's department. Me? I simply drive them.

"Alright, the battery should be..." I mutter, scanning the tightly packed components. After a moment of squinting, I spot it—a black rectangular box with two terminals poking out. "There you are."

I tug experimentally at the battery, but it doesn't budge. Of course, it wouldn't be that easy. I notice it's held down by a bracket with a bolt. Back to the Jeep for my small toolbox from the trunk.

Five minutes and several colorful curses later, I've managed to loosen the bracket and disconnect the terminals—negative first, then positive, just like Luke taught me the one time I paid attention. The battery is heavier than I expected, and my hands are now smudged with grease.

"Look at you, Sullivan," I say to myself with a grin. "Regular mechanic now."

I wipe my fingers on my shorts—they're already dirty from my morning run anyway—and carefully lower the hood. I cradle the battery against my chest like a football.

I head straight to Larry's Auto Shop on Maple Street. It's a small, dingy place with an old-fashioned sign that's been there since I was a kid, but Larry knows his stuff. More importantly, he's the biggest Dalton University football fan in Ambrose.

The bell above the door jingles as I push inside, the familiar smell of motor oil and rubber hitting me immediately. Larry's hunched over the counter, his balding head reflecting the fluorescent lights as he squints at some paperwork.

"Well, if it isn't the arm of Dalton U!" His face breaks into a wide grin when he spots me. "What brings you to my humble establishment, Sullivan? The Jeep giving you trouble again?"

"Hey, Larry." I set the battery on the counter with a solid thunk. "Need a replacement for this."

He pushes his glasses up his nose and examines the battery, turning it in his grease-stained hands. "This ain't from your Jeep." He squints at me over his glasses, his bushy eyebrows raised. "Different size altogether. What're you doing with a European battery?"

I run a hand through my hair, suddenly feeling like I'm sixteen again, asking my dad if I could borrow the car. "It's, uh, for my neighbor's Beetle. Lady's battery died this morning."

"A lady, huh?" His face splits into a knowing grin, eyes twinkling. "Must be some special lady for you to be playing knight in shining armor with her car."

"Something like that," I mutter, feeling my ears go hot.

He examines the battery more closely, checking the specs on the side. "Well, this here's completely dead. Probably been on its last legs for a while." He punches some numbers into his ancient computer. "For a genuine VW replacement, you're looking at two hundred and thirty-five dollars, plus tax."

My smile drops faster than a fumbled pass. Two hundred and thirty-five dollars? I mentally check my bank account—there's most of it but not enough. My father's monthly allowance doesn't hit for another week, and even then, it barely covers food and gas. I can't exactly ask my brothers to use Bebe's rent money on this. I'd been hoping to do this for Amelia—something simple to help her out, to make her day a little better.

"Damn," I mutter. "That's steep."

"VW parts don't come cheap, son. European cars—they're like high-maintenance girlfriends." He chuckles at his own joke. "This model's a special order. Got lucky I even have one in stock."

I stare at the battery, disappointment settling in my chest. I'd had this whole scenario planned out—fixing her car before she got home, seeing the surprise on her face, maybe finally having a proper conversation with her instead of our usual awkward neighbor nods.

"Thanks for checking, Larry," I mention, trying to hide my discouragement. "I'll have to bring Amelia back later."

He holds up a grease-stained hand as soon as I start to grab the battery. "Hold on now. I didn't say that was the only way." He leans forward, elbows on the counter, voice dropping like we're discussing state secrets. "You've got a big game coming up against State, right?"

"Are you suggesting a trade?" I raise an eyebrow, leaning against the counter.

His grin widens. "Well, I hear those lower bowl seats are mighty nice this season. And I've been meaning to take the missus to a proper game—show her why I spend all Sunday afternoons yelling at the TV."

I can't help but smile. This is Ambrose in a nutshell—everyone knows everyone, and sometimes the economy runs on favors more than dollars.

I consider it for about half a second. The tickets are easy enough—I get a player allocation for every home game. Usually my brothers go, and I give any extra to whoever asks first.

"Tell you what," I say, leaning on the counter. "How about two pairs of tickets to the State game next weekend? Fifty-yard line. And I'll throw in signing the jersey of mine you've got hanging behind the register."

Larry smiles big, like I've just offered him the moon. "You'd do that? For real?"

"Consider it done." I pull out my phone. "I'll text my brother right now to set aside the tickets."

He practically bounces on his heels as he watches me type the message to Chase. "Hot damn! The wife's gonna flip!" He sticks out his hand, grease stains and all. "You've got yourself a deal."

As we shake on it, he leans in, his eyes crinkling with excitement. "You know what, Sullivan? When you make it to the NFL—and we both know you will—I want you to remember old Larry from Ambrose."

"Of course I'll remember you, Larry."

He shakes his head, still gripping my hand. "No, no. I

mean, really remember me. Like when they stick the microphone in your face after your first big game, and they ask who you want to thank." He puffs out his chest. "You say, 'I want to thank Larry from Ambrose, my biggest fan since high school!'"

I burst out laughing, picturing the scene—me in some NFL jersey, sweaty after a game-winning touchdown, dedicating my success to the local auto parts guy.

"You got it, Larry," I say, still chuckling. "First interview, prime time TV, I'll make sure the whole country knows about Larry from Ambrose, my number one fan."

"That's all I ask," he says with mock solemnity before breaking into another grin.

While he fetches the new battery and fills out the warranty information, I check my phone. There's a text from Chase confirming the tickets. I send back a quick thanks and check the time—still plenty before I need to pick her up.

He hands me the replacement battery, considerably heavier than the old one. "This'll get your lady friend back on the road. Need any help installing it?"

"I've got it," I say, though I'm not entirely confident. "How hard can it be, right?"

He snorts. "Famous last words."

Chapter Seven

AMELIA

At 5:30 on the dot, I step outside my office building to find Wes parked along the curb.

But he's not in the driver's seat as I expected. Instead, he's standing outside, leaning against the Jeep's passenger door with aviator sunglasses on, looking like he stepped out of a men's cologne commercial. The late afternoon sun catches his blond hair, making it appear golden. Several women walk past and slow their pace to get a better look at him, but his eyes find me immediately.

As I approach, he pushes off the Jeep with casual grace and slides his sunglasses off, tucking them into the collar of his t-shirt. The smile that spreads across his face seems genuinely pleased to see me.

My stomach does a little flip that I instantly attribute to hunger. I definitely didn't eat lunch.

"Hey there," he says, his eyes locking with mine. "How'd the big meeting go?"

I feel a rush of pride as I think about the presentation. "I absolutely killed it," I tell him, unable to keep the satisfaction from my voice. "The Barlowes loved my concept for their mountain retreat. Mrs. Barlowe said it was exactly what they'd been trying to articulate but couldn't put into words."

"That's awesome," Wes says, and there's something in his tone that suggests he's not just being polite—he sincerely means it. "I knew you'd blow everyone away."

"You did?" I raise an eyebrow, surprised by his confidence in me. "You barely know me."

He shrugs, his broad shoulders moving beneath his t-shirt. "I know enough. You seem like someone who doesn't do things halfway."

I'm not sure how to respond. It feels too accurate for a casual observation from a neighbor I've barely spoken to before today.

"We should probably get going," I say, glancing at my watch for no reason.

"Right this way," he says, gesturing toward the passenger side of the Jeep.

He opens the door for me and once again, places his hands on my waist and lifts me effortlessly into the seat. The sensation of being weightless for a brief moment sends an unexpected tingle up my spine.

As he shuts the door, I notice something on the center console—a bottle of Maker's Mark bourbon with a small card propped against it with my name on it.

"What's this?" I ask when he slides into the driver's seat.

"It's for you," he says simply, starting the engine.

I narrow my eyes at him before tentatively picking up the bottle, turning it in my hands. The whiskey catches the late afternoon sunlight streaming through the Jeep's open top.

"Are you serious?"

He shrugs, putting the Jeep in drive. "If you don't like it, we can go pick out a bottle of something else. Or I could grab you a casserole if you prefer? I noticed everyone bringing those over yesterday."

"God, no," I say, drawing out the word 'no' for emphasis. "I'm so tired of casseroles. They're still taking up half my fridge." I tap the bourbon bottle appreciatively. "This is perfect, actually."

"Good," he says, pulling out into traffic. "I figured after the weeks you've had, you could use something stronger than a sympathy lasagna."

I rest the bottle in my lap, oddly touched by the gesture. It's been days of people treating me like I might shatter at any moment, bringing food I don't want and saying things they think I need to hear. This simple acknowledgment that what I may need is a stiff drink.

I pick up the small card and open it to see a cute cartoon bug. I also find a simple message written in surprisingly neat handwriting:

FOR CAR TROUBLES AND TOUGH DAYS. — WES

"Thanks," I say softly, tucking the card into my bag.

"Picked it up last night," he says, merging into traffic. "I was going to bring it over, but your house was dark. Figured you might need some space after..." He trails off, not finishing the sentence.

"I went to bed early," I confess, running my finger along the bottle's seal. "Like, embarrassingly early. Around seven. The funeral was... exhausting."

"I bet."

We fall into silence as he gets on the freeway. The wind rushing through the open Jeep makes conversation difficult anyway. I rest my head against the seat and watch the city blur past, the bourbon bottle a comforting weight in my lap.

It's not until we exit near our neighborhood that he speaks again.

"By the way," he says casually, "I looked at your car after I dropped you off this morning."

"You did what?" I turn to look at him.

"You left the key fob in the cup holder. It was the battery." He turns onto our street, slowing down as we approach our homes. "I replaced it this morning. You're all set to go."

I stare at him, shocked. "You didn't have to do that. I could have called AAA or something."

"It was no big deal," he says with a casual shrug as we turn onto our street. The row of identical suburban houses comes into view, looking picturesque in the golden hour light.

"How much do I owe you for the battery?" I ask, already reaching for my purse. "Those things aren't cheap."

"Don't worry about it," he says, waving his hand dismissively.

"Seriously, Wes. I can't let you pay for that on top of everything else you've done today."

He glances over at me, that lopsided smile appearing again. After a moment, he lets out a small laugh. "Fine. I may have traded free Dalton U football tickets for a battery at the local auto parts shop. The owner is a huge fan."

"You're kidding," I say, genuinely surprised.

"Nope, not kidding. Being the quarterback has its perks." He pulls into his driveway and cuts the engine. "I figured we could check on your car first to make sure everything's running properly."

He hops out and comes around to my side, offering his hand. This time, I'm prepared for the lift, but it still feels strangely intimate when his hands encircle my waist. I clutch the bourbon bottle to my chest as he sets me down.

He leads the way across our adjoining lawns. I follow, watching as he strides confidently toward my car. It's been a strange day—waking up late, the meeting, and now this unexpected kindness.

He opens the driver's side door of my Beetle and gestures for me to get in. "Start her up."

I slide into the seat, setting the bourbon bottle carefully on the passenger side. When I press the start button, the engine purrs to life immediately.

"It works!" I say, feeling disproportionately relieved.

I stare at my car, then back at him. "I don't know what to say. Thank you doesn't seem like enough."

He shrugs. "It's just a battery."

"No, it's..." I trail off, struggling to articulate what I'm feeling. "It's everything. The ride, the bourbon, fixing my car. I just—" I take a deep breath, steadying myself. "I don't want anyone's pity, Wes. I probably don't even deserve it."

"Amelia, I don't pity you," he says firmly, his eyes locked on mine. "That's not what this is about at all."

"Then what is it about?" I ask, my voice barely above a whisper.

He runs a hand through his hair, seeming to search for the right words. "I just... I have an overwhelming need to see you happy. I can't explain it exactly." He shakes his head, looking almost surprised by his own admission. "When I saw you this morning, looking so stressed and defeated, something in me wanted to fix it. Not because I think you're broken or can't handle things yourself. But because I think you deserve happiness. I want to see you happy."

I stare at him, genuinely stunned by his words. There's no practiced sympathy in his expression, no careful tiptoeing around my feelings. Just raw honesty that catches me completely off guard.

"You barely know me," I say again, but this time it's not a challenge—it's wonder.

"Maybe that's why it's easier for me to see you. Not as a widow or someone to feel sorry for. Just as Amelia."

A lump forms in my throat. I turn my gaze to the bourbon bottle sitting on my passenger seat, then back to him.

"Would you..." I pause, gathering my courage. "Would you like to come inside and have a drink with me?" I gesture toward the bottle of Maker's Mark. "It would be a shame to drink it alone."

He hesitates, his eyes searching mine. For a moment, I think he might refuse—maybe he's just being neighborly and wants to get back to his own life. The silence stretches between us, and I'm about to retract the invitation when he nods.

"Yeah," he says finally. "I'd like to."

Chapter Eight

WESLEY

Amelia buried her husband yesterday morning, and here I am standing in her living room about to share some bourbon.

I shift nervously from one foot to the other, taking in the space. It's tastefully decorated—neutral colors, some art on the walls, a few plants that look like they could use some water. Nothing too personal is on display. No wedding photos. Interesting.

"Make yourself comfortable," she calls from down the hallway. "I'm going to change out of these work clothes."

I wander over to her bookshelf, scanning the titles. Architecture books, design magazines, a few novels. I run my finger along the spines, trying to get a sense of who she is.

The sound of a door opening pulls my attention, and I turn to see Amelia walking back into the living room.

Holy shit.

She's changed into gray leggings and a simple white t-shirt. Her hair is down now, falling in loose waves around her shoulders. The thin crescent of gold metal clings to her nostril like it belongs there—as natural as freckles. She looks younger, more relaxed, but somehow even better than she did in that work outfit.

Those leggings cling to her curves in all the right places. Her ass is perfectly round and tight in a way that makes my mouth go dry. I could bounce a penny off it. I force my eyes upward before she catches me staring. I didn't come here to ogle my grieving neighbor, no matter how attractive she is.

She appears in front of me, the bourbon bottle in one hand, two crystal tumblers in the other. She's got this half-smile that doesn't quite reach her eyes as she moves toward the coffee table.

"Let's sit," she says, setting down the bottle and glasses with a soft clink against the wooden surface.

I take a seat at one end of her couch; the cushions sinking slightly beneath my weight. The fabric is smooth, expensive-feeling. I reach for the bourbon and twist off the cap, the satisfying crack of the seal breaking filling the quiet room.

I pour a generous amount into each glass. She settles into the opposite corner of the couch, pulling her knees to her chest in a protective gesture similar to the other night. Her feet are bare, toenails painted a deep burgundy color.

I hand her one glass, our fingers brushing briefly during the exchange.

"Thank you," she says, taking a small sip. Her eyes close momentarily as she savors the burn. "God, I needed this."

"I'm glad I could help, Ladybug," I say before tasting a drink of mine, the bourbon warming my throat.

I freeze mid-swallow when I notice her eyebrows shoot up.
Shit. That slipped out.

"Ladybug?" Amelia repeats, tilting her head. "Do you have a nickname for me?"

Heat rises to my cheeks. Football players aren't supposed to blush, but here I am. "I, uh... yeah." I rub the back of my neck, suddenly feeling like a teenager caught passing notes in class. "I didn't actually know your name for a while when you first moved in."

She takes another sip, watching me over the rim of her glass. "So you've been calling me Ladybug? Why?"

"Your car," I admit, gesturing vaguely toward the window where her Beetle sits in the driveway. "Red with the black convertible top. It reminded me of a ladybug. Beetle—bug."

A slow smile spreads across her face and, for the first time since I've known her, it truly reaches her eyes. Something in my chest tightens at the sight.

"That's..." she pauses, taking another sip of bourbon. "That's really sweet."

"I thought it fit," I say, trying to downplay how much I've thought about her and her cute red car. "So you like the nickname then?"

"I do. That Beetle means a lot to me, actually."

"Yeah?" I take another sip, savoring both the bourbon and the way her face has softened.

"It was my first big purchase when my career started taking off." She looks into her glass, that half-smile growing more genuine. "I'd landed a major client, and instead of being practical and saving the money or paying off student loans, I bought that ridiculous red Beetle convertible."

"There's nothing ridiculous about celebrating your success," I offer.

"I was so proud of myself." She's alight with emotion as

she speaks, and I find myself leaning closer. "I'd worked so hard, and it was like... tangible proof I was making it, you know?"

I nod, understanding perfectly. "Like my first pair of custom cleats. It wasn't practical, but man, it meant something."

"Exactly."

She points to the picture hanging on the wall across from us. "That's the design that got me the car."

I stand to look at it closely. It's a collection of colored-pencil sketches of a home collaged together, drawn from different angles. The lines are clean and bold, with splashes of color highlighting certain architectural features. There's something both modern and timeless about it—innovative and inviting.

"You designed this?" I ask, genuinely impressed.

"My first major residential project," she says, coming to stand beside me. I smell her shampoo—a scent of citrus and clean. "The clients were a power couple from San Francisco who wanted a vacation home in Malibu. They'd gone through three firms before me."

"And you nailed it," I say, noticing how the sketches capture not just the structure but somehow the feeling of the space.

"I did," she says without false modesty. "The day they approved the final design, I went straight to the dealership." They loved it so much they referred me to all their friends. Within six months, I had a waiting list."

She sips again from her bourbon, her eyes fixed on the car outside, looking out the window. There's something in her expression—a mixture of pride and something darker.

"Nick hated it," she says under her breath, so quietly I almost miss it.

"Your husband?" I ask, though I already know the answer. "Why would he hate it?"

She shrugs. "Said it was silly and impractical."

I can't help it—a huff of disbelief escapes me. "Right, and his motorcycle was practical?" The words fly out before I can stop them.

The moment they leave my mouth, I feel like the world's biggest jerk. My eyes widen in horror as I realize what I've said. Her husband died in a motorcycle accident, and here I am, mocking his vehicle choice.

"Oh my God, I'm—I'm so sorry," I stammer. "That was incredibly insensitive of me. I shouldn't have—"

To my surprise, she waves away my apology, her expression unchanged. "Don't worry about it," she says as we head back to the couch to sit again. "You're not wrong."

I watch her carefully, trying to gauge if she's just being polite or genuinely isn't offended. Her eyes meet mine steadily, with no hint of tears or anger.

"Still," I say, "I shouldn't have brought it up like that."

"Wes," she says my name firmly, leaning forward. "It's okay. Really."

The silence that follows isn't uncomfortable exactly. She swirls the bourbon in her glass, staring into the amber liquid.

"Can I tell you something?" she asks suddenly, her voice soft but steady. "Something I haven't told anyone else?"

"Of course," I say without hesitation. "You can tell me anything, Amelia."

She takes a deep breath before downing the rest of her

bourbon. I watch her throat work as she swallows, the way her eyes close briefly against the burn.

"I'm upset that he's dead," she says, setting her empty glass on the coffee table with a decisive click. "I mean, obviously I wouldn't wish death on anyone, but..." She pauses, running her fingers through her hair. "I'm angry with him. So angry."

I remain silent, giving her space to continue. She looks at me, searching for judgment that I'm careful not to show.

"I know how that sounds," she continues. "Your husband dies, and you're supposed to be devastated, not bitter. But I can't help it. Every time someone tells me what a great guy he was, I want to scream."

"I think that's totally understandable," I say, keeping my voice gentle. "Grief is complicated. There's no right or wrong way to feel."

She looks at me, surprise flickering across her face. "You don't think I'm horrible?"

"Not at all. If anything, it seems honest. Yeah, I guess I would be mad too if a loved one left me suddenly."

She shakes her head. "No, I don't just mean I'm angry he died. I hate him right now, Wes. I actually hate him."

The venom in her voice catches me off guard. This isn't just grief talking—there's something deeper here—raw and painful. I can tell she means every word.

I want to tell her that my brothers and I never liked Nick. We'd see him around town sometimes, acting like he owned the place. Once at a local resturant—he'd been hitting on a waitress right in front of us while Amelia was in the bathroom. But this isn't about me or what I think of him.

"It's so much worse," she says, her voice dropping to a near whisper. "You know what he told me on Halloween night? The night he died? That he had to work late on a time-sensitive project, covering for a coworker who wanted to take his kid trick-or-treating."

"That sounds pretty nice," I offer cautiously, refilling her glass.

She lets out a laugh that's so bitter. There's not a trace of humor in it—just raw pain.

"Nice? Yeah, that's what I thought too." She takes the refilled glass from me. "Until the police told me exactly where the accident happened. He died at the intersection of Maple and 12th."

I nod slowly, not immediately seeing her point. "Okay..."

"His office is on Riverdale and 45th," she says, watching my face carefully.

I mentally map our town, trying to connect the dots. It takes me a moment, but then it clicks. Those streets are on completely opposite sides of town. There's no way he was coming home from work.

"Oh," I say, realization dawning on me.

"Exactly." Amelia's eyes glint with a hardness I haven't seen before. "And there's only one reason a man lies to his wife about working late."

"He was cheating on you," I state, not as a question but as a conclusion. My jaw tightens as anger rises in my chest. "What an asshole."

"At first I refused to believe it, making up excuses for why he'd be across town. But it gets so much worse." She sets her glass down and pulls her knees tighter to her chest. "When the hospital called me, I was in shock. I rushed over there, but... he was already gone by the time I arrived." Her voice becomes clinical, detached. "They gave me a plastic bag with his belongings—wallet, keys, wedding ring, and his phone. The screen was shattered, but it was still intact. The next morning I took it to one of those repair places to get it unlocked."

I lean forward. "And?"

"Wes, you wouldn't believe the stuff I found. Multiple women—he's been cheating since before we moved to Ambrose. Six of our ten years of marriage, at least. How could he do that to me? All those years I thought we were happy... he was lying to my face."

Chapter Nine

AMELIA

Telling someone about Nick—my lying, cheating husband —finally feels good.

"That son of a bitch," Wes mutters, shaking his head. "And all those people at the funeral talking about what a great guy he was?"

I nod, feeling a weight lifting off my chest. "Exactly. Everyone's telling me how sorry they are for my loss, and I'm standing there thinking they have no idea who he really was. I had no idea who he really was."

He leans forward, his elbows on his knees, bourbon forgotten in his hand. "Why haven't you told anyone? Your mom or his family?"

The question makes me pause. I've asked myself the same thing so many times over the past two weeks.

"I don't know," I say, tracing the rim of my glass. "Part of me doesn't want to tarnish what everyone thought of him. It won't change anything to tell them—he'll still be gone." I take another sip of bourbon. "And honestly? It feels like admitting

I failed him as a wife. What did I do wrong? Was I not enough for him? We were intimate, but like, was I not attractive anymore? Like I couldn't keep him happy enough to stay faithful."

His eyes flash with sudden intensity. He sets his glass down on the coffee table with a sharp clink.

"Don't," he says firmly. "Don't you dare blame yourself for this."

"But maybe if I had been more—"

"Stop." His voice is gentle but leaves no room for argument. He shifts closer on the couch, his eyes locked on mine. "Amelia, listen to me. You weren't the one sneaking around behind his back. You weren't the one lying about where you were."

Unshed tears threaten to spill despite my best efforts to hold them back. "But clearly I wasn't enough for him. If I'd been more attentive or—"

"No." The conviction in his voice makes my throat tighten unexpectedly. His hand reaches for my own, hovering just above it before making contact, like he's asking permission. When I don't pull away, his warm fingers wrap around mine.

I want to believe him. "In every marriage, there are two sides—"

"In cheating, there's only one. He made those choices completely outside of your marriage—your partnership," he continues, his thumb brushing softly across my knuckles. "That's on him. Only him."

I glance at our hands, his so much larger than mine. "You sound so sure."

"Because I am," he says without hesitation. "Look, I

played football my whole life, and you know what makes a good team great?"

I shake my head, curious about where he's going with this.

A gentle smile spreads across his face as he leans back slightly. "Communication. On the field, our success doesn't just come from talent or strength—it comes from talking to each other. We're constantly signaling, calling plays, adjusting when something doesn't work." There's a spark in his eyes when he talks about his sport, a passion evident in every word. "Even when things get chaotic, even when we're losing, we keep the lines open. That's what separates champions from everyone else," he continues. "Sometimes signals get crossed or plays fail, but we adjust and move forward—together."

I understand what he's saying now, and something inside me stirs. I can tell this matters to him deeply.

"The point is," he says, his voice softening, "if your husband wasn't happy in your marriage, he had a responsibility to communicate that to you. To give you both a chance to work on things together or decide to end it." He hesitates before asking, "Did he ever do that? Did he ever actually tell you he was unhappy?"

I slowly shake my head. "No." My voice comes out softer than I intended as I think back over our marriage. "We weren't perfect—no marriage is—but he never actually said he was unhappy with me."

Memories flood back now—subtle shifts I'd noticed but dismissed.

How many moments were real? Was he really happy? Was I?

We both started working late more often. His phone would always be face-down. He'd tense when I'd ask about his day. We'd had our arguments, sure—about his spending habits, and he'd point out that I'd gained weight. But he never once sat me down and said he was unfulfilled or wanted something different.

"There were red flags," I admit, more to myself than to Wes. "Little things I probably ignored because it was easier than confronting them. Times when he'd be vague about where he was going, or get defensive if I asked simple questions. I guess part of me knew there was a problem, but I didn't want to see it."

He listens intently, his eyes never leaving mine. There's something deeply comforting about his unwavering attention. When a strand of hair falls across my face, he reaches forward with gentle hesitation. His fingers brush my cheek as he tucks it behind my ear, the small gesture somehow more intimate than it should be, sending a slight shiver through me..

"Amelia," he says, his voice dropping to practically a whisper, "you didn't deserve any of this. Not the cheating, not the lying, not having to stand there and listen to everyone praise him." His eyes hold mine with such sincerity. "You deserve so much more—someone who appreciates your incredible mind and spirit. Someone who would never dream of looking elsewhere."

"God, I feel so stupid," I whisper. "I wasted so many years with someone who didn't even respect me enough to be honest."

"You deserve better," he says quietly. "You deserve someone who sees you—really sees you—and chooses you every day."

"Will anyone ever love me the way I deserve?" I ask.

I hadn't meant to ask it out loud. It was more of a thought

that escaped—a question I've been asking the universe since I found out about Nick's betrayal.

"Yes."

The word comes from him with such fierce certainty that my eyes snap back to his. There's no hesitation, no pause— just absolute conviction blazing in those sea-colored eyes.

The intensity in his gaze makes my chest tighten. I'm not used to this—this raw honesty, this validation without conditions. Nick made me feel like I had to earn his affection, like loving me was something he did despite my flaws rather than because of who I am.

I stare at him, this younger man sitting so close to me, looking at me with an intensity that makes me feel both vulnerable and seen in a way I haven't experienced in years— maybe ever.

"Thank you," I whisper, my voice catching slightly. "For saying that."

For the first time since Nick's death, someone is seeing me —not as a grieving widow to be pitied, but as a person worthy of something better.

A small silence stretches between us, charged with something. Wes might sense it too. His expression shifts, that familiar playful smile returning to his face while he glances in the direction of the window where my car sits in the driveway.

"You know," he says, a mischievous glint appearing in his eyes as he nods toward the window, "I've been meaning to ask —does your Ladybug have a name? All good vehicles deserve one."

I can't help but laugh, it bubbles from my chest. "Are you serious right now? You want to know if I named my car?"

"Hey, it's a legitimate question," he protests, holding his hands up defensively. "My Jeep's name is Brutus."

"Brutus?" I snort, grateful for the sudden lightness between us. "That's so... predictable for a football player."

"Ouch." He clutches his chest dramatically. "You wound me, Ladybug."

The nickname rolls off his tongue so naturally, and I find myself smiling despite everything. "If you must know, her name is Ruby."

"Ruby the Ladybug," he says, testing it out. "I like it. Classic, elegant—suits you both."

I roll my eyes but can't hide my smile. "You're ridiculous."

"Part of my charm," he winks, draining the last of his bourbon before setting it down. "I should probably get going. Early practice tomorrow morning."

My heart sinks a little at his words. I want to ask him to stay longer, but I know that's not a good idea. I've just buried my husband. Even if he was a cheating liar, even if this gorgeous, kind man sitting on my couch makes me feel more seen than Nick ever did—the timing couldn't be worse.

"Yeah," I agree, setting my glass beside his.

He stands, stretching, and I try not to notice how his t-shirt rides up just enough to reveal a sliver of toned stomach. I lead him toward the front door, suddenly aware of how small my entryway feels with his broad shoulders filling the space.

At the threshold, he turns to face me, and there's something in his eyes—a warmth, a question, maybe both—that makes my heart skip. The faint smile playing at the corners of his mouth is almost shy, so different from the confident quarterback I've seen all day.

"Thanks for the drink," he says softly. "And for trusting

me with all of that. I know it couldn't have been easy to talk about."

"Actually, it was the easiest conversation I've had all week," I admit. "It felt good to be honest with someone for once."

His eyes soften, and he steps forward. His arm slides around my shoulder, pulling me into a gentle half-embrace. My body responds before my brain can catch up, my arms finding their way to his sides, feeling the solid warmth of him through his t-shirt.

His chest is firm against mine, and I notice the faint scent of his cologne—something woodsy and clean that makes me want to breathe deeper. The embrace lasts only seconds, but it feels significant in a way I can't articulate.

Then I feel the gentle pressure of his lips against the top of my head, so light I might have imagined it if not for the way my pulse immediately quickens.

"Goodnight, Ladybug," he murmurs, his voice a low rumble I can feel as much as hear.

He steps back; his hand on the doorknob. With one last smile—that lopsided, devastatingly charming smile—he slips out into the night.

Chapter Ten

AMELIA

I close the door after Wes leaves, leaning against it as I try to catch my breath.

Is it hot in here, or is it just me? It's me.

My skin feels flushed, my heart racing from that brief embrace. His woodsy scent still lingers in my nostrils, and I can feel the ghost of his lips where they pressed against my hair. What is happening to me? I barely know this man, and yet...

"Get it together, Amelia," I mutter to myself, pushing away from the door.

The bourbon glasses sit on the coffee table, one with a faint imprint of his lips on the rim. I gather them, trying not to think about his mouth and how it would feel against places other than the top of my head.

As I walk to the kitchen, I replay our conversation in my mind, the way he listened without judgment, how his eyes stayed locked on mine when I confessed my darkest thoughts about Nick.

I place the dirty glasses in the sink, fanning myself with my hand. I'm still reeling from the closeness with Wes—the solid warmth of his chest against me, how small I felt in his embrace. It was innocent, just a goodbye hug between neighbors, but my body seems to have other ideas about what it meant.

How long has it been since I felt this kind of attraction? The awareness of another person who makes my pulse quicken and my thoughts scatter? Too long. Way too long.

I glance down the hallway toward my bedroom. My skin still feels hot, my body humming with a need I haven't felt in so long. Before I can talk myself out of it, I'm walking down the hall, drawn by a sudden memory.

Nick and I had been intimate. But I can't remember when it had become routine, mechanical—something to check off a to-do list rather than a genuine connection.

Most of the time there was no buildup, no foreplay, no bond. And five minutes later it would be over, him rolling away with a satisfied sigh while I stared at the ceiling, or the wall, hollow and unfulfilled.

I hadn't even bothered to fake it anymore toward the end of the marriage.

Other than that, he always had an excuse not to have sex when I initiated—too tired, too stressed, headache.

Now I know why. He was getting it elsewhere.

I enter my bedroom and stare at the closet door, wondering if my little box of toys is still buried in there or if Nick threw them out. I always thought it was ridiculous for a man to be jealous of sex toys like he was.

Taking a deep breath, I slide the door open and push aside hanging clothes. I kneel and pull out a few storage boxes—

winter sweaters, photo albums—before spotting the innocuous beige container tucked in the back corner. I reach for it with a triumphant smile.

"Hello, old friends," I whisper, blowing dust off the lid before flipping it off.

They're all still here—the vibrator, the handcuffs we used exactly once, and there, nestled among a paddle and lube, is my flesh-colored dildo. I pick it up and run my fingers over it, admiring how it has bumps and ridges and veins like a real one does. And suddenly I understand why Nick was jealous. It's bigger than he was and has given me more orgasms. The realization makes me laugh out loud in the empty bedroom.

"Well, that's a depressing thought," I say to no one.

I turn the silicone toy over in my hands, feeling its weight, the familiar texture. It had been my guilty pleasure, something I'd pull out on nights when Nick was "working late"—which now takes on a whole new meaning.

My mind drifts to Wes, to his firm grip lifting me into the Jeep like I weighed nothing, to his intense eyes as he listened to me. To his abs—ugh, he's so ripped. Heat floods through me again. I shouldn't be thinking about him this way. It's too soon, too complicated.

But my body doesn't seem to care about what's appropriate.

I stand, dildo and lube in hand, and move toward the bed, lying on top of the covers.

The bourbon is still warming my blood, making my skin hypersensitive.

I reach for the hem of my leggings, tugging them down over my hips along with my thong in one swift motion. The cool air of the bedroom kisses my exposed skin, sending a shiver up my spine. I kick the clothing away, letting it land somewhere on the floor.

I uncap the lube, squeezing a generous amount onto the silicone toy. I disperse it, watching it glisten in the soft light. I part my legs, heart racing as I bring the toy between my thighs.

I tease myself first, running the smooth head up and down the length of my pussy with slow, deliberate strokes, my breath catching at the cool sensation. My body responds immediately, with a rush of heat flooding through me. My eyes fall closed as I slowly press it forward, a gasp escaping my lips as it fills me.

"Wes," I say in a tone that's between a whisper and a moan. Very needy like...

His face materializes behind my eyelids—those intense blue-green eyes, that lopsided smile. I imagine his firm hands gripping my hips.

I push the toy deeper, imagining what it would feel like if it were him—his weight pressing me into the mattress, his breath hot against my neck. I slide the toy in and out, building a rhythm that makes my toes curl. With my free hand, I reach down, fingers finding the sensitive bundle of nerves above where the toy is working its magic.

"Oh God," I breathe, circling my clit with practiced fingers.

My imagination runs wild now, conjuring his voice whispering in my ear, telling me how beautiful I am, how good I feel. I picture his athletic body, those abs I'd seen this morning, the way his muscles would flex as he'd move above me.

The dual sensations—the fullness of the toy and the electric pleasure from my fingers—build quickly. My hips rise off the mattress of their own accord, meeting each thrust with growing urgency. I'm chasing something that's been missing for so long, something that feels dangerously close now.

"Wes," I moan again, louder this time. And still very needy...

My back arches as waves of pleasure crash through me, radiating outward from my core. My thighs tremble, my breath coming in short, desperate gasps. For a moment, the world narrows to just this—this perfect, blinding release.

My body clamps around the toy, muscles contracting rhythmically as I ride out the wave. I keep thrusting, prolonging the sensation as my inner walls pulse and grip, unwilling to let go. Each push sends aftershocks through me, making me gasp and shudder. It's been so long since I've experienced this—this complete surrender, this blissful release that leaves you breathless and boneless.

"Fuck, Wes, yes," I whisper, the words escaping between ragged breaths.

I slow my movements gradually as the intensity ebbs, but don't stop completely. My body is greedy for more, still sensitive but hungry. I haven't felt this alive in months, maybe years.

My breathing is hard as I come down, chest rising and falling rapidly. I close my eyes, savoring the lingering sensation, my fingers still lazily circling as I chase the last whispers of pleasure.

A floorboard creaks.

My eyes snap open. Something moves in my peripheral vision—a shadow by the door that shouldn't be in my empty house.

I turn my head and freeze. My heart, already racing from my orgasm, nearly stops completely.

Wes is standing in my bedroom doorway.

His eyes are wide, lips slightly parted, one hand still raised like he was about to knock. The shock on his face mirrors what must be on mine. Neither of us moves or speaks for what feels like an eternity.

I want to disappear, to melt into the mattress and cease to exist. I want to explain that this isn't—but the explanation dies in my throat as I realize the toy is still inside me, my legs still spread, my shirt hiked up exposing my stomach.

It is exactly what it looks like.

"I—" He finally breaks the silence, his voice strangled. He swallows hard, his Adam's apple bobs. "I forgot my phone," he stammers, his eyes darting between my face and the toy still buried inside me. "I knocked but... your door was unlocked. I heard... I thought..."

I can't move. Can't speak. I can't even pull the blanket over myself. I'm completely frozen, mortified beyond words as I watch his gaze travel my body again.

His expression shifts from shock to something darker, more intense. His eyes have turned a deeper shade of blue-green, pupils dilating as he watches me.

"Fuck it," he mutters.

Chapter Eleven

WESLEY

I shouldn't be here—shouldn't be in her bedroom. But yes, I watched as she got herself off and said my name while doing it.

And that's why I'm staying.

Two steps and I'm at the edge of her bed, my heart hammering against my ribs. I can't tear my eyes away from her —flushed cheeks, parted lips, the rise and fall of her chest.

"Wes..." she whispers, but doesn't move to cover herself or remove the toy. She watches as I grab the hem of my shirt and pull it over my head, tossing it somewhere behind me.

Her breathing changes, becoming deeper, faster. Her eyes widen as they rake over my chest, my abs, lingering on the trail of hair disappearing into my jeans. There's no mistaking the hunger in her gaze—it matches the fire burning through my veins.

"Tell me to leave and I will," I say, my voice rough with desire. "But I heard you say my name, Amelia."

She swallows hard. "I don't want you to go."

That's all I need to hear. I climb onto the bed; the mattress dipping beneath my weight as I crawl toward her. I kneel between her legs, taking in the sight of her—so exposed, so vulnerable, yet so unbelievably sexy. The toy is still inside her, glistening with her arousal. My mouth goes dry at the vision of her like this, spread out before me.

"You're beautiful," I breathe, unable to hold back the words.

I run my hands up her smooth legs, feeling the warmth of her skin beneath my palms. Her muscles tense slightly at my touch before relaxing as I continue my exploration. My fingers trace patterns to her hips, then back down to where her inner thighs meet.

"Can I?" I ask, nodding toward the toy.

She nods, her eyes never leaving mine. I hook my arms under her knees, pulling her closer to me. The position opens her more, giving me a perfect view. I wrap my fingers around the base of the dildo where her hand had been moments before.

Slowly, I pull it out, watching as her body clings to it. It's coated with the evidence of her pleasure—creamy and slick.

I ease it back inside her, observing her face as I do. The slight parting of her lips, the flush creeping up her neck, the way her eyelids flutter.

"Oh..." she gasps as I push it deeper, her back arching slightly off the bed.

A groan escapes my throat as I establish a slow, steady rhythm with the toy. Her face is mesmerizing—completely unguarded, every emotion playing across her features. There's something raw and honest in her expression that makes my heart pound even harder than my arousal.

"That's it," I whisper, transfixed by how she responds to each movement. "You're so damn beautiful like this."

My jeans have become a prison, my erection straining painfully against the zipper. I've never been this hard in my life. Seeing her writhing as I work the toy in and out of her slick pussy makes me dizzy with want.

Her eyes flutter open, meeting mine. "Take those off," she says, nodding toward the jeans I'm wearing.

I don't need to be told twice.

I shift my weight back onto my knees, my fingers still working the dildo inside her as I unbutton my jeans with my free hand. The denim slides down my hips, and I kick them off.

She sits up, her eyes travel downward, widening as they reach my erection.

"Oh my God," she whispers, her jaw dropping open. "Is that... are those...?"

I follow her gaze to the metal barbells piercing through the underside of my shaft—five of them in a vertical line. My Jacob's ladder. The silver gleams in the dim light of her bedroom, a stark contrast against my flushed skin.

"Holy shit," she whispers, a nervous laugh escaping her lips. Her gaze remains fixed on my piercings, fascination replacing her initial shock. "I've seen nothing like that before."

Despite her surprise, I see excitement in her eyes—her pupils dilated, breathing quickened. She grabs the hem of her t-shirt and pulls it over her head, tossing it aside.

Her breasts are perfect—full and round with dusky pink nipples that have hardened into tight peaks.

"You're gorgeous," I manage to say.

She leans back onto the pillows, her dark hair fanning out

around her like a halo. I can't believe this is happening—that I'm here with Amelia, the woman I've been thinking about for years.

I give her a few more deep thrusts with the dildo, watching as her back arches and her eyes flutter closed. Her breasts rise and fall with each quickened breath, and I'm mesmerized by the way her body responds to my touch. With deliberate slowness, I pull the toy completely out of her, leaving her empty.

The look on her face is a mixture of disappointment and anticipation—her brows furrow at the loss. I toss the toy aside and move up her body, one hand bracing beside her head while the other cups her cheek. Her eyes meet mine, and there's something vulnerable in them. I've imagined this moment countless times since she moved in next door, but the reality of having her beneath me, looking at me with those dark eyes, is overwhelming.

"I've wanted to do this for so long," I whisper, lowering my face to hers.

When our lips finally meet, it's like electricity shooting through my body. Her mouth is soft and warm, opening for me as I deepen the kiss. She tastes of bourbon and something sweeter, something uniquely her. Our lips move together perfectly, as if we've been kissing each other for years instead of seconds. Her hands slide up my back, nails lightly scratching my skin as she pulls me closer.

I could kiss her all day. The way she responds to me, the little sounds she makes in the back of her throat when I gently bite her lower lip—it's intoxicating. I never want to stop.

When we finally break apart, we're both breathing hard. I rest my forehead against hers, our ragged breaths mingling in the small space between us. Her eyes are dark with desire, pupils blown wide.

"Amelia," I whisper, my voice husky with need. I brush a strand of hair from her face, letting my fingers linger against her cheek. "Are you sure you want to do this? We can stop right now if you're not ready."

I need to give her this chance, this moment to back out if she wants to. As much as I want her—*and God, do I want her*—I need to know she's certain.

Her eyes lock with mine, clear and unwavering despite the bourbon we've shared. There's no hesitation when she nods. "Yes," she says firmly. "I want this. I want you, Wes."

Those words send a surge of heat through my entire body, but there's something else we need to address because I really don't want to put a condom on—not with her.

"I'm clean," I tell her, my thumb tracing the curve of her jaw. "I get tested regularly for football. The team doctors are pretty strict about it."

"I was tested recently too," she says. "I'm clean."

I capture her lips again, losing myself in the taste of her. My hand slides between us, positioning myself at her pussy. She's so wet, so ready for me.

I push forward, sinking into her. She cries out against my mouth, her body tensing around me. The sensation is incredible—her heat enveloping me, gripping me tightly. I stay perfectly still, giving her time to adjust to my size—I'm bigger than that fucking toy.

"Are you okay?" I whisper against her lips, fighting every instinct that screams at me to thrust into this woman.

Her eyes are wide, lips parted as she nods. "Yes," she breathes. "God, Wes... I've never felt so full."

I start to move, pulling back slowly before pushing forward again. Each thrust sends the metal barbells dragging along her inner walls, and the effect is immediate. Amelia arches off the bed, her fingers digging into my shoulders.

"Oh my God, yes!" she cries out, her voice echoing through the bedroom.

Her reaction fuels something primal in me. I grip her hips tighter, angling them upward as I increase my pace. The sight of her beneath me—head thrown back, breasts bouncing with each movement, face contorted in pleasure—it's a sight that could make a saint blush. Her body responds to mine as if we were made for each other, every thrust pulling sounds from her throat that drives me wild.

I can't get enough of her. I need more—need to see her completely lost in pleasure.

I slide my hands down to the backs of her thighs, pushing them up and back toward her chest. The move opens her completely to me, allowing me to slide even deeper.

"Oh, fuck!" she cries out.

The change in angle has my piercings dragging perfectly against her most sensitive spots. I feel her trembling beneath me, around me. But it's the way she's looking at me that makes my chest tighten—her eyes are dilated and vulnerable, filled with a mixture of pleasure and something deeper. Like I'm giving her something she's been missing, something she's craved but been denied.

"Wes," she whispers, her voice breaking. "Please don't stop."

"I won't," I promise, maintaining our connection as I thrust into her. "I've got you."

Her hands reach for me, pulling me in until our foreheads touch. Each stroke brings us closer together. She grips my biceps, nails digging into my skin. The slight pain intensifies my pleasure.

I seize her lips in a passionate kiss, my tongue sliding against hers as our bodies move in perfect rhythm. She tastes like bourbon and desire, and I lose myself in the sensation of her below me, as I drive into her with increasing urgency.

Without warning, her body tenses around me. She tears her mouth away from mine with a desperate cry, her back arching dramatically off the bed. I feel a rush of wetness around my cock as her inner walls clamp down, pulsing and fluttering with incredible force. Her orgasm is so powerful, so all-consuming that it triggers my own.

"Amelia," I groan, burying my face in her neck as my orgasm crashes through me. My hips jerk forward, balls tighten, pressing deep inside her as I cum, filling her completely. Wave after wave of pleasure courses through my body, my mind going totally blank except for the overwhelming sensation of her body milking every drop from me.

For several moments, we remain frozen in this position, both of us trembling and gasping for air. I'm lost in the moment, in her, in everything that just happened between us —her body beneath mine, our heartbeats gradually slowing to normal.

I lift my head from her neck, taking in her flushed face, her parted lips, her half-closed eyes. Something swells in my chest that feels bigger than just physical satisfaction. I lean and press my lips to hers in one final, tender kiss. I try to pour everything I'm feeling into it—desire, reassurance, comfort.

When I finally pull away and slide out of her, there's an immediate sense of loss at the broken connection.

Her eyes are closed, her chest rising and falling with each deep breath. Her skin glistens with a light sheen of sweat, and her dark hair is splayed across the pillow in wild disarray. She's never looked more beautiful to me.

As I gaze at her, my attention drifts downward. Between her still-spread thighs, I see the evidence of what we shared. My cum is seeping from her pink, swollen slit, a thick stream that slowly drips onto the dark sheets beneath her. The contrast is striking—her flushed pale skin, the creamy white of my cum, the navy blue of her bedding. The perfect creampie. I've always used condoms before so I've never seen anything so erotic in my life.

Her face is glowing with a contentment—a lazy, satisfied smile spreads across her lips as she looks at me through heavy-lidded eyes. She looks younger, unburdened. Something about seeing her like this—happy, relaxed, free from the weight she's been carrying—fills me with a warmth that has nothing to do with physical pleasure.

"That was..." she breathes, trailing off as if words aren't sufficient.

"Yeah," I agree, collapsing next to her.

Chapter Twelve

AMELIA

Do you know that feeling when you go to work the next day after having great sex and you feel like the most powerful woman in the world? That's me—right now.

I strut through the office like I'm walking on a runway. My heels click against the polished floor as I make my way past the reception desk. My pencil skirt feels a bit tighter today, but in the best possible way—like it's hugging curves I suddenly feel proud of. I swear I can still feel Wes's hands on my waist, the ghost of his touch lingering on my skin even through the fabric of my blouse.

"Morning, Amelia," calls Denise from reception. "You look... different today."

I toss my hair over my shoulder with a confidence I haven't felt in years. "Just had a good night's sleep," I lie, though the opposite is true. He and I barely slept at all.

"Well, whatever it is, keep doing it. You're glowing."

Glowing. That's exactly how I feel—like I'm radiating light from the inside out. Last night replays in my mind on a continuous loop: His lips on mine, his hands exploring every inch of me, those piercings that made me see stars. And more than just the physical—the way he looked at me like I was the most fascinating creature he'd ever encountered.

The office is already buzzing with activity—phones ringing, the soft hum of conversations, the occasional burst of laughter from the break room. I navigate between cubicles, nodding hello to coworkers who glance up from their monitors. For once, I don't feel the weight of their sympathy. The "poor widow" cloud that's been following me seems to have dissipated overnight.

Because last night changed everything.

I pause at my desk, setting down my coffee cup and portfolio. My hand lingers on the leather case, and for a moment, I'm not thinking about the Barlowe project or the staff meeting I have in an hour. I'm thinking about how twenty-four hours ago, I was dreading coming to work, dreading facing people's sympathetic glances, dreading the weight of grief I was supposed to be carrying.

But now? Now I feel weightless.

For the first time since Nick's accident—no, if I'm honest, for the first time in years—I can see possibilities stretching out before me. Not just surviving day to day, but actually living. Actually wanting things again.

I have a life to live, with or without Nick.

I slide into my chair, powering up my computer while a smile plays at my lips. Last night with Wes wasn't just mind-blowing sex (though it absolutely was that). It was like someone flipped a switch inside me, illuminating all the dark corners where I'd stored away my hopes and desires.

"You're in a great mood," Evan says, peering over the

divider between our workspaces. "The Barlowes must have loved your designs."

"They did," I reply, unable to stop the smile spreading across my face. "But I think I'm just going to have a good day."

He leans in closer, lowering his voice conspiratorially. "Well, it's about to get even better. I overheard Wheeler talking in the conference room earlier."

"About what?" I was suddenly intrigued by his tone.

"About you." His eyes sparkle with excitement. "Word is, you're being considered for the senior design position. The promotion, Amelia."

I freeze, my coffee halfway to my lips. "What? Are you serious?"

"Dead serious. They were discussing who to promote after Simon leaves next month and how impressed they've been with your work, especially with the Barlowe account." He grins widely. "Sounds like someone's moving up in the world."

I set my cup down before I drop it, my mind racing. Senior designer. The position I've been working toward for the past two years. After everything that's happened—Nick's death, the funeral, the emotional rollercoaster—this feels almost surreal.

"I can't believe it," I whisper, more to myself than to him.

"We should celebrate!" he says, giving my shoulder a congratulatory squeeze.

The idea never gets a chance to settle. Gina pokes her head around the corner of my cubicle, her blonde bob swinging with the movement.

"Breakfast has been delivered and set up in the kitchen. The partners ordered in for the quarterly meeting prep."

"Perfect timing," Evan says, rubbing his hands together. "I skipped breakfast this morning. You coming, Amelia?"

"Sure," I reply, grateful for the distraction. The promotion news has my mind spinning, and I could use a moment to process.

We walk down the hallway toward the kitchen, Evan chatting animatedly about the upcoming quarterly presentation.

"I think your Barlowe designs are exactly what they're looking for to showcase our innovative approach," he says. "If they feature your work prominently, the senior position is practically yours."

"I hope so," I reply, feeling a flutter of excitement. "Some good news would be—"

The moment we step into the kitchen, the smell of eggs and bacon hits me like a brick wall. My stomach lurches violently, bile rising in my throat. I press my hand to my mouth, my eyes watering as I stumble backward.

"I—excuse me," I choke out, turning on my heel and practically running.

I make it halfway down the hallway before I have to stop, leaning against the wall as I take deep, measured breaths. The nausea rolls through me in waves, but the farther I get from the smell, the more it subsides.

What the hell was that? I've never had such a visceral reaction to breakfast foods before.

I close my eyes, focusing on my breathing. In through the nose, out through the mouth. The queasiness fades as I put more distance between myself and whatever unholy combination of grease and eggs they've got in there.

"Amelia? Are you okay?"

I open my eyes to find Evan standing a few feet away, concern etched across his face.

"Yeah," I say, straightening my posture and smoothing my skirt. "Sorry, I got dizzy suddenly."

His brows knit together. "You don't look so good. Are you sure you're alright?"

"I think so," I say, attempting a reassuring smile that may look more like a grimace. "Maybe I need to eat something. Probably low blood sugar."

"Do you want me to make you a plate and bring it to the conference room for the meeting?" He offers, glancing back toward the kitchen. "Might help you feel better."

The thought of those eggs makes my stomach flip again. "A plain bagel if they have it," I tell him gratefully. "Thank you."

"Plain bagel it is," he says with a nod.

As he disappears, I lean against the wall once more, trying to make sense of what just happened. I've never been sensitive to smells before. Maybe it's stress? The emotional rollercoaster of the past week, coupled with last night's... activities with Wes, could be catching up with me physically.

I push myself off the wall and make my way to the conference room, settling into one of the plush chairs. The room is still empty—I'm early for the meeting. Deciding to make use of the quiet time, I set up the conference room laptop and connect it to the projector. Might as well get set up while everyone is in the kitchen fawning over bacon and eggs. The thought makes my stomach lurch again, but I push through it, focusing instead on opening presentation files.

I arrange materials meticulously on the table—design boards, material samples, and portfolios. There's something calming about organizing everything just so, creating order when my personal life feels anything but orderly. I'm flipping through my notes when the door opens.

"Amelia! The woman I wanted to see."

I look up to find Wheeler striding into the room. As the founding partner of Wheeler & Marks, he rarely interacts with anyone below senior management, except for dealings with high profile clients such as Russell Barlowe. My heart immediately kicks into a higher gear.

"Good morning, Mr. Wheeler," I say, standing quickly. "I was just setting up for the meeting."

"Always ahead of the game," he says with an approving nod, his eyes taking in my organized display. "That's what I like about you, Amelia. The team is looking forward to seeing the Barlowe project today," Mr. Wheeler says, leaning against the conference table.

My heart skips a beat at his praise. "Thank you, Mr. Wheeler. I put a lot of thought into it."

He clears his throat, a small smile playing on his lips. "I should also mention that a little bird might have already told you about potential changes in our staffing structure." He raises an eyebrow. "Evan has never been one to keep exciting news to himself."

"I heard something about the senior designer position," I admit. "If I'm truly being considered, I'm incredibly honored. This firm has been my professional home, and I'd be grateful for the opportunity to take on more responsibility."

"Well, nothing's official yet," he says, straightening his tie, "but I will say your name is at the top of a very short list. The Barlowe project has showcased your abilities."

"That means a lot to me."

Mr. Wheeler shifts his weight, taking a step closer to me. His cologne—something expensive and musky—fills the space between us as he lowers his voice to just above a whisper.

"I was thinking we could discuss the position in more detail outside the office. We can grab a drink after work one day this week? I could answer questions you might have about the role... expectations, compensation." His eyes hold mine a beat longer than feels professional. "I find conversations flow more naturally away from fluorescent lighting, don't you?"

I blink, caught off guard by the invitation. *Would it be a business meeting or something else?* The way he's looking at me feels... different from our usual interactions. My mind races, trying to decipher his intent.

I open my mouth, but no words come out. I hesitate, unable to formulate a response to the awkward suggestion.

The conference room door swings open and Evan appears, holding a plain bagel on a napkin.

Thank God, right on time.

"Here you go, Amelia," he says cheerfully, oblivious to the tension in the room. "Last plain one they had."

Mr. Wheeler straightens, taking a small step back. His professional smile returns as he nods at Evan. "Good morning, Evan. Just giving her the news she already knows."

I take the bagel from Evan's outstretched hand. "Thanks," I murmur, sliding back into one of the conference chairs. The soft leather does nothing to ease the sudden tension in my shoulders. I focus on tearing small pieces from my bagel, grateful for something to do with my hands.

Just when my day was going so well—the amazing night with Wes, the confidence boost, the potential promotion—

now I'm sitting here wondering if my boss tried to ask me out. Great.

"We'll continue this conversation later, Amelia," Mr. Wheeler says, his voice carrying a weight I'm not sure I like. "I think you'll find the senior position comes with many benefits worth discussing."

Yeah, I'm sure...

Chapter Thirteen

WESLEY

"Wes, you're crushing her." Luke's voice cuts through my excitement as I engulf Bebe in what must be an overly enthusiastic bear hug.

I loosen my grip and step back with an apologetic smile. "Sorry! I just—I'm so glad you're okay, little roomie." My voice catches a little at the end. "We missed you around here."

She looks thinner, her normally vibrant complexion still carrying a hint of pallor, but her smile is genuine. She adjusts the strap of her overnight bag on her shoulder.

"I've missed you and Chase both," she says, reaching out to squeeze my arm. "It's good to be home."

Luke stands behind her, arms crossed but expression soft. He's been her shadow since the toxin injected in her nearly killed her, and I see the exhaustion etched into the lines around his eyes.

"The doctors say she needs rest," Luke says, but there's no real authority in his voice.

"I've had nothing but rest," she protests, rolling her eyes.

She spots the stuffed bear sitting on the coffee table. "Is that for me?"

"Yeah, I saw it at the store and thought of you." I nod, watching her smile brighten as she crosses the room to pick it up. "The card too."

Chase emerges from the kitchen, wiping his hands on a dishtowel. "Hey, welcome home, Beebs." Beebs? He's never called her that before, but I guess it works. He gives her a considerably gentler hug than mine. "Need anything? Water? Tea? I can make you something to eat if you're hungry."

Luke guides her toward the couch with a gentle hand at her elbow. "Come on, sit. You shouldn't be on your feet too much."

She lets out an exasperated sigh as she sinks into the cushions, clutching the stuffed bear to her chest. "Guys, I love you all, but please stop treating me like I'm made of glass. The doctors cleared me. I'm not going to break if I stand for more than five minutes."

"Sorry," Luke mumbles, but he still hovers nearby, ready to spring into action if she so much as sneezes.

He crouches next to where she sits and whispers to his recently hospitalized girlfriend like they are in some tragic love story.

"I'll only be gone for a couple of hours," he says, brushing hair from her face. "I'll return to check on you after my lecture," he continues, his voice cracking with emotion as he presses his forehead against hers. "I promise you, Bebe. I'll never be far away. If anything happens—anything at all—I'll sense it. I'll feel it in my heart and come running back to you."

I exchange a look with Chase, who's trying not to laugh.

Luke's been like this since the hospital—like he's auditioning for a role in some tragic romance movie.

She gives him a patient smile, though I notice the corners of her mouth twitching. "Luke, I'll be fine for two hours."

"I know, I know," he says, kissing her hand like she's royalty. "But my heart stays here with you."

"Dude," Chase interrupts, "she's not dying. She'll be sitting on the couch watching Netflix."

Luke shoots him a glare but finally stands. "Call me if—"

"—if I need anything," Bebe finishes for him. "I will. Now go before you're late."

Luke kisses her forehead like he was leaving for a year, not a class. "Okay. I'll be back before you even miss me."

"You already said that," Chase mutters through a mouthful of sour cream and onion chips.

Finally, the front door shuts behind him, and the air in the room lightened as if someone had cracked open a window. The intense energy left with him. Chase leans back, swinging one leg over the arm of the chair.

"So..." I say. "you gave us quite a scare."

She pulls the blanket tighter around herself. "Yeah. Not my best moment."

"Are you feeling better? Honestly—now that Luke is out of the room," I ask.

She nods. "I am."

"I'm sorry about Luke," I say, sinking onto the couch beside her. "He's been like that since the hospital. I know it's a bit much, but... he really thought he'd lost you." I fiddle with the edge of the blanket, remembering that terrifying moment when the mercenary injected her with the honey toxin. "We all did."

Bebe's eyes soften, and she reaches out and squeezes my hand. "I know. And honestly, I wasn't sure either." She looks at our joined hands, her voice dropping. "Even though I took the antidote, I didn't know if it would be enough. That stuff was... powerful. More than I expected." She shakes her head. "Luke and I have talked about this, and I... I feel I need to apologize to you both." She takes a deep breath, looking between us. "I should have told you who I was when I found out you were Keepers," she continues, "and that your dad had set a trap specifically for me—for The Killer Bee. Pushing Luke away seemed like the only option at the time."

"That's why you suddenly broke up with Luke?" I ask, the pieces clicking into place. "You found out?"

She nods, eyes downcast.

Chase leans forward, elbows on his knees. "You were put in a pretty awkward position, Bebe. Roommates with the sons of a man that played a part in trying to trap you."

"That's the thing," she says, finally looking at us. "I knew your family was good. Deep down, I always knew that. If I'd been honest—"

"That's not true," I say, moving closer to her on the couch. "You can't know that things would have gone differently if you'd told us sooner."

She looks at me with those eyes that still carry shadows from her ordeal. "But I should have trusted you all from the beginning. If I had come clean about who I was—maybe we could have figured it out together. Maybe I wouldn't have had to take the toxin at all."

"Or maybe my dad would have found another way to get to you," I point out gently. "The L.A. Chapter of the Keepers had dad under their thumb. There's no guarantee that honesty would have changed the outcome."

Chase gets up from his chair and comes to sit on Bebe's other side, the couch cushions dipping under his weight. Without hesitation, she reaches for his hand, holding it along with mine. He links their fingers together. It's a small gesture, meaningful—connecting the three of us in this moment of truth.

"Thank you both," she whispers, looking between us. "For still being here. For accepting me, even after everything."

He squeezes her hand, his expression serious. "You don't need to thank us. You're family." His voice is gruff with emotion. "Family sticks together, no matter what."

"He's right," I add. "Killer Bee or not, you're one of us."

Her eyes glisten with unshed tears as she smiles and leans her head against Chase's shoulder. After everything we've been through—the lies, the secrets, the near-death experiences—we've come out stronger on the other side.

"So," she says after a comfortable silence, lifting her head. "What have you guys been up to while I was away? Luke hasn't said much about anything."

My mind immediately flashes to Amelia—the whiskey I bought—our conversation, the amazing sex.

I hesitate, the news about her hovering on my lips. But something holds me back—maybe it's because what happened with Ladybug feels too new, too private to share just yet.

"Nothing much," I say with a shrug. "Just the usual—classes, football practice, a couple of parties at the team house."

Chase shifts uncomfortably on the couch. "Dad's trying to set me up with this girl who's visiting town next month.

Daughter of his old Dalton U buddy. Apparently she's Keeper royalty or something."

My head snaps toward him. "Wait, what? Since when?" This is the first I'm hearing about any setup, and from his casual tone, it sounds like old news.

"Since last week," he says casually, as if this isn't completely new information. "He keeps sending me these not-so-subtle texts about how she and I should 'connect' since we're the same age and she's also studying law." He makes air quotes with his fingers, rolling his eyes.

She looks at him curiously, tilting her head. "Why aren't you interested? She sounds perfect for you on paper—in law school—royalty and all that."

He and I exchange glances before bursting into laughter. She looks between us, confusion written across her face.

"What's so funny?" she asks.

I wipe a tear from my eye. "Keeper women are basically like 1950s housewives, Bebe. They're raised to be these perfect little supporters with zero personality and even less fun." I shake my head, thinking of the few I've met at family gatherings. "Taught to be demure, agreeable, and essentially just arm candy for men."

"Exactly," he adds, leaning forward with a smirk. "And in case you haven't noticed, we like to have fun." He gestures between us. "Can you imagine me with some boring girl who gasps if I say 'damn' and whose idea of rebellion is wearing red lipstick instead of pink?"

She laughs, the sound warming the room. It's good to hear her laugh again. "Fair point."

"We're kind of the black sheep of the Keeper world," I explain, grabbing a handful of chips from the bowl. None of us Sullivan brothers have ever been seriously interested in Keeper women. It's not our thing."

"Well..." Chase interjects with a knowing look.

I roll my eyes. "Okay, Luke tried dating one once. About two years ago. Dad was practically doing backflips of joy."

Her eyes widen. "No way. Luke? My Luke?" She sits straighter, suddenly fully invested.

Chase chuckles. "Kendall Hartwell. She was actually pretty sweet."

"Too sweet," I correct him. "Like, sickeningly sweet. She followed him around campus like a lost puppy. Always had homemade cookies or some crap. She knitted him scarves. Would call him every hour just to say she missed him."

Bebe laughs, her hand covering her mouth. "What happened?" she asks, eyes dancing with amusement.

"Luke lasted two weeks before he broke it off," he says. "Dad didn't speak to him for a month."

"Did he have any other failed Keeper romances?" she asks, leaning forward with interest, her eyes sparkling with a liveliness I haven't seen since before the hospital.

Chase perks up immediately, sitting straighter. "Oh, you want Luke stories? I've got plenty."

"We both do," I add, feeling a grin spread across my face. There's something about the way Bebe is looking at us—eager and amused—it makes me want to keep that expression there.

"Please," she says. "I would like to hear everything embarrassing about my boyfriend that you're willing to share."

"Where to begin?" Chase cracks his knuckles dramatically. "Oh! What about the time Luke tried to impress that girl in his philosophy class by pretending he could speak French?"

I burst out laughing. "Oh God, I forgot about that! He memorized this one phrase from Google Translate—"

"And he kept saying it over and over," Chase continues, "except he was pronouncing it so badly that when an actual French exchange student overheard him—she straight up told him he was actually asking if her grandmother's nipples tasted like blueberries!" He finishes, doubling over with laughter.

Her eyes widen, her mouth falling open before she erupts into uncontrollable giggles. The sound fills our living room, bright and genuine.

"No way," she gasps between laughs. "Please tell me that's not true."

"Hand to God," I say, placing my palm over my heart. "Luke turned so red I thought he was going to spontaneously combust. He avoided the French department for the rest of the semester."

"What about the Halloween party sophomore year?" Chase prompts, a mischievous glint in his eye.

I groan, remembering the disaster. "Oh man, the Superman incident."

For the next hour, Chase and I share embarrassing and funny Luke stories—in the name of Bebe's happiness.

Chapter Fourteen

WESLEY

Suicides. I hate suicides.

My lungs are burning, my thighs screaming in protest as I sprint back and forth across the field. The grass beneath my cleats is a blur of green, the sidelines seeming farther away with each pass. Coach Daniels stands at midfield, whistle between his lips, eyes tracking our movements like a hawk watching prey.

"Faster, Sullivan! You're lagging!" he barks when I hit the line and pivot.

I push harder, legs pumping, sweat pouring down my face and soaking through my practice jersey. The sun beats down mercilessly, turning the field into an oven. My teammates grunt and gasp around me, all of us suffering through this torture together.

The shrill sound of Coach's whistle pierces the air again, signaling another sprint. My heart hammers against my ribs as I dig deep for another burst of speed. *One more. You can do another.*

"Move it, move it! You think Clemson's defense is going to wait for you to catch your breath?" he yells.

The whistle screams again. And again. Each blast feels like a physical blow, drilling into my skull. *If I hear that damn thing one more time—*

The whistle blows once again, but this time it's different—longer, more sustained. The end signal. Thank God.

I collapse onto the grass, chest heaving, arms spread wide like I'm making a sweat angel. The blue sky spins above me as I gasp for air, my heart pounding so hard I swear I can see my practice jersey jumping with each beat.

A shadow falls across my face. I squint to see Coach standing over me, clipboard tucked under one arm, his expression a mixture of amusement and something else—pride, maybe?

He lets out a bark of laughter, offering me a hand. "If you're feeling it now, Sullivan, wait till you get to the pros. Those boys will eat you alive if this is your conditioning level."

I take his hand and let him pull me to my feet, my legs wobbling slightly. "I'll be ready," I manage between breaths.

Coach stands just shy of six feet, his stocky build under a windbreaker a testament to years of weight rooms and long-forgotten two-a-days. A weathered ball cap—bearing Dalton U's logo, the dragon—seems permanently attached to his head, shielding his receding hairline and a sunburned forehead. His face is creased from years of squinting across sunlit fields and shouting over roaring stadiums, with a voice that always sounded half-hoarse.

He gives me a long, appraising look. "Come see me in my office after you shower. Got something to discuss with you."

My stomach tightens. Coach wanting a private meeting

could mean anything. I'm still riding the adrenaline high from practice, but anxiety starts to creep in. Is he going to bench me for the next game? Did I mess up during drills without realizing it? Or maybe it's about my academic standing—I've been letting my economics class slide a bit this semester.

"Yes, sir," I nod, trying to keep my voice steady. "I'll be there."

As I trudge toward the locker room, my mind races through possibilities. Coach Daniels isn't the type for small talk or casual meetings. If he wants to see me, it's really good news or really bad news—there's no in-between.

The shower helps clear my head, the hot water soothing my aching muscles. I scrub quickly, not wanting to keep Coach waiting. Around me, my teammates joke and laugh, their voices echoing off the tile walls. They don't have mysterious meetings hanging over their heads.

I dress in record time, throwing on a clean Dalton U t-shirt and athletic shorts. My hair is still damp as I make my way down the hallway to Coach's office, my heart rate picking up with each step.

The door is ajar; I knock lightly on the doorframe. "Coach? You wanted to see me?"

He glances up from his desk, papers spread out in front of him. "Sullivan. Come in."

He waves me in, and I close it behind me before taking a seat in one of the worn leather chairs facing him. My stomach twists with nerves as I watch him shuffle some papers together, his expression unreadable.

His office smells of old coffee and the leather-bound playbooks that line his shelves. Game balls from significant victories are displayed in a glass case behind him—silent witnesses to whatever's about to happen.

"Wes," he begins, leaning forward and folding his hands on his desk. "I don't know how to tell you this..."

My heart drops. Shit. This is it. I brace myself for the worst.

Then, unexpectedly, his serious expression cracks. A smile spreads across his weathered face, growing wider by the second.

"I've received more inquiry phone calls about you from NFL scouts than I have for any player in my entire career as a coach."

I blink, the words not fully registering. "Wait, what?"

He laughs, the sound booming in the small office. "You heard me, Son. My phone's been ringing off the hook. NFL, Wes. The big leagues. They're not just interested like we initially thought—they're fighting over you."

I sit back, my mind reeling. I've dreamed about this moment since I was a kid throwing a football in my backyard, pretending to be Tom Brady in the Super Bowl. But now that it's happening, it feels surreal, like I'm floating outside my body watching someone else's life unfold.

"Seriously?" I manage, my voice sounding distant to my own ears.

"I mean it." He nods, his expression softening. "You've earned this, Sullivan. Your work ethic, your leadership on the field—it's all paying off."

A grin spreads across my face as reality sinks in. NFL scouts. Actually fighting over me. Holy shit.

His look shifts, becoming more serious. He leans forward, clasping his hands together on the desk.

"There is something else we need to discuss, though." His tone changes, becomes more measured. "Your father has been calling me. Repeatedly."

My smile fades instantly. Of course he has. The excitement drains from my body faster than sweat during suicides.

"My father?" I repeat, attempting to maintain my neutral tone even as my jaw tightens. I should have expected this. Dad's always been quick to insert himself whenever an opportunity arises. "What does he want?"

Coach sighs, leaning back in his chair. The leather creaks under his weight. "He wants to represent you. Says he's got connections with some top agents, that he can negotiate the best deal for you." His eyes study my face. "He's called six times this week."

I run a hand through my still-damp hair, a knot forming in my stomach. Of course, dad would do this. The moment he catches wind of NFL interest, he swoops in to take control. Just like always.

"I appreciate you telling me," I say, choosing my words carefully. "But I think I'd prefer to look for my own representation." I hesitate, guilt immediately creeping in. "Though it's complicated. He is my dad, after all. I feel some kind of obligation there."

Coach's eyes soften but his jaw sets firmly. He leans forward. "Let me tell you something, and I want you to really hear this." His voice takes on the tone he uses during crucial half-time talks—direct, no bullshit. "This is your career. You earned it. Every touchdown, every hit you took, every damn suicide I made you run—you earned this moment."

I nod slowly, processing his words.

"And because you earned it, you need to feel comfortable

with who you let manage it." He taps his finger on the desk for emphasis. "I've seen too many promising careers get trashed because the wrong people were involved. Players who took the best offer without considering the consequences."

"You mean the most money?" I ask.

He shakes his head. "It's not always about money, Son. Sometimes the largest checks come with the greatest headaches. I've watched players sign with agents who didn't have their best interests at heart, who pushed them toward endorsements that didn't fit, or teams that weren't right for their playing style."

Everything in my dad's world revolves around control and dollar signs. Every decision, every relationship, even his own son's future. For him, it's always about the money.

"You're right, Coach," I say, sitting straighter. "I need to think about this carefully."

I take a deep breath, my mind racing through options. I don't want to burn bridges with my father, but this is my future we're talking about. My career. My life.

"Would it be possible for you to run interference with my dad for a bit?" I ask. "Just until I can figure out the best approach? I need some time to research agents on my own, and make some calls."

His face relaxes into a smile. "Consider it done. I'll tell him you're focused on finishing the season strong, that we've agreed not to discuss professional matters until after championships." He leans back, crossing his arms. "It should buy you at least a few weeks."

Relief washes over me. "Thank you, Coach. For everything—not just this, but for pushing me to be better.

Those suicides might have nearly killed me, but they got me here."

We both laugh, and he stands, extending his hand across the desk. I rise to meet him, gripping his calloused palm firmly.

As I leave his office, my mind is racing faster than I did during those drills. NFL scouts. Multiple calls. Fighting over me. This is happening—I'm going into the NFL.

I should be sprinting down this hallway, whooping and hollering like I just scored the game-winning touchdown. But instead, my thoughts immediately turn to Amelia—the strange urge to tell her first. Not my teammates, not my brothers, but her.

When did she become the person I most want to share good news with? We've had sex—once—then talked for hours.

I grab my gym bag and check my phone. No messages. It's been four days since that night—since I walked back into her house and found her moaning my name... I feel heat rising to my face thinking about it. The way she looked, the sounds she made, how it felt to have her beneath me. It was incredible—better than any fantasy I'd had about her over the years.

But I haven't reached out since. Not a text, not a call, not even a casual knock on her door.

I've been deliberately giving her space.

I grab my keys and head to my Jeep, tossing my gym bag in the back.

The urge to drive straight to her office and share my news is almost overwhelming. I can picture her face lighting up, those dark eyes widening with excitement.

But I hold back. This thing between us—whatever it is—it's complicated. Her husband just died. Literally weeks ago.

I'm not an idiot; I know how this looks from the outside. The young neighbor swooping in before the body's even cold.

But they don't know what I know—that her husband was a cheating asshole who didn't deserve her. They have no idea that I've watched her from next door for two years, noticing how her smile never quite reached her eyes when she was with him.

I drive through campus with my windows down, the crisp fall air relatively warm and whipping through the Jeep. Despite the excitement coursing through me about the NFL scouts, my mind keeps circling back to Amelia.

Is four days enough space? Too much? What's the protocol here? There probably isn't one for "sleeping with your recently widowed neighbor who you've been crushing on for years."

I drum my fingers against the steering wheel at a red light, replaying that night in my head for the thousandth time.

The light turns green and I accelerate, trying to focus on the road instead of the memory of her naked beneath me.

What's the appropriate amount of time for someone to be dead before you start a relationship with their widow? A month? Six months? A year? There's no guidebook for this kind of situation. And the fact that he was cheating complicates things even further. Does it change the timeline? Make it shorter?

I shake my head, forcing myself to pump the brakes on that train of thought. I'm getting way ahead of myself.

What was I truly thinking? A relationship? We had sex—incredible, mind-blowing sex—but that doesn't mean she wants anything more. Maybe for her it was just a release, a way to forget her problems for a night. The rebound guy next door, who happened to be in the right place at the right time. And if it was, I'm okay with that—because *she* needed me.

Chapter Fifteen

WESLEY

I take the exit toward my neighborhood, slowing as I approach the familiar streets.

When I park in my driveway, I notice her red Beetle sitting in hers. She's home. My heart does that stupid little flip it always does when I know she's nearby. My hand actually twitches on the door handle. But I hesitate. Four days of silence between us feels like an eternity, but is it enough? Does she even want to see me?

I sigh, choosing not to go over there. Not yet. Better to give her more time, or let her make the next move. The last thing I want is to pressure her when her life is already complicated.

I grab my gym bag from the back seat and head inside, the screen door banging behind me as I enter. To my surprise, the dining room table is covered with textbooks, laptops, and scattered papers. My brothers look up as I walk in.

"Look what the cat dragged in," Luke says, leaning back in

his chair. "How was practice?" He takes a bite of what looks like leftover pizza.

I drop my gym bag with a heavy thud. "Suicide day," I groan, collapsing into the chair across from them.

Both of my brothers wince simultaneously.

"Damn," Chase says, pushing his laptop aside. "Coach must be in a mood."

"Those are brutal," Luke adds with genuine sympathy. "That's one thing I don't miss about baseball practices."

I reach over and steal a slice of pizza from the box between them. "He had us going for what felt like forever." I take a bite, suddenly realizing how hungry I am. "But that's not even the big news."

They both look at me expectantly.

"Coach called me into his office after practice. NFL scouts have been calling about me. Like a lot of them, apparently. He says they're fighting over me."

Chase's eyes widen. "Holy shit, Wes! That's incredible!"

Luke punches my shoulder, grinning. "Wow, you knew there were a couple, but this sounds promising. Like a done deal, you're going to be drafted."

"That's not all," I say. "Dad's been hounding Coach for their contact information. Called him six times this week, apparently."

Luke groans, throwing his head back dramatically. "God forbid someone else handle your career."

"Are you serious?" Chase's expression darkens. "After everything that happened with the L.A. Chapter of The Keepers, he's still trying to control things?"

I nod. The excitement of the NFL news is now tainted by my father's interference. "If anything, it's made him worse.

Like nearly dying and being framed gave him some kind of renewed purpose."

The memory of what took place just weeks ago sends a chill down my spine. Our family's secret society—The Keepers —has been a Dalton University tradition for generations. And another Chapter decided to frame our family—our dad specifically for their own drug manufacturing and distribution.

"Dad's been on a power trip ever since the incident," Luke says, leaning forward. "You're not the only one he's trying to control. He's been hounding Bebe's brother."

"Gabriel?" I sit straighter, suddenly more alert despite my exhaustion.

Chase rolls his eyes. "Trying to dictate the terms of the alliance between The Keepers and the Laurents. Acting like he's in charge even after Gabriel saved all our asses."

"Gabriel shut him down fast though," Luke adds with a smirk. "Told dad in no uncertain terms that any alliance would be on equal footing or there wouldn't be one at all."

I let out a low whistle. "I would've paid good money to see dad's face when Gabriel put him in his place."

"It was pretty epic," Luke confirms.

"Speaking of the Laurents," I say, leaning forward, "how's Bebe doing? She's back at school?"

Luke's expression softens at the mention of his girlfriend. I've noticed how his face changes whenever her name comes up—like someone flipped a switch from cool guy to lovesick puppy. "She's doing really well. Determined as ever to get back into her routine. The doctors wanted her to take it easy for at least a week, but she's already insisting on attending all her classes."

"Sounds like Bebe," I chuckle, shaking my head.

"She's already caught up on most of her assignments," Luke adds. "I want her to slow down, but at the same time I'm proud of her for challenging herself and not using what happened as a crutch."

"That girl is something else," Chase says, grabbing another slice of pizza.

I watch Luke's face as he talks about Bebe, how his eyes light up and his entire demeanor changes. It's like he becomes a different person—softer, more open. The way he smiles when he mentions her name is something I've never seen from him before. My brother is completely head over heels in love.

In a short amount of time, Bebe has become such an integral part of our lives—of our family. She fits with us, with Luke especially, like she was always meant to be here. The way they look at each other, how they've created this little bubble of happiness despite everything they've been through.

It hits me then, watching my brother talk about the woman he loves. I want that. I want what they have—that connection, that certainty that you've found your person in this world.

And immediately, Amelia's face flashes in my mind. But the timing is all wrong. She's grieving, even if her husband was a cheating asshole, even if what we shared was incredible, everyone would see it differently. They'd judge her—judge us. I don't want to put her through that. She needs space to process everything that's happened. And I'm about to enter the NFL draft, my whole life potentially uprooted depending on which team picks me up.

Chase suddenly raises his hand, cutting off Luke mid-sentence. "Do you guys hear that?"

We all go quiet, listening. There's a sound coming from outside—muffled at first, then growing louder. Like two women raising their voices.

"Is someone's TV on?" Luke asks, glancing around.

The voices get louder, more distinct. One of them sounds familiar—too familiar.

It hits me— "Amelia," I say, already pushing back from the table.

Before my brothers can respond, I'm on my feet and moving toward the front door. I yank it open and step onto our porch, my eyes immediately finding the source of the commotion.

Amelia is standing on her front porch, hands gesturing wildly as she faces off with a blonde woman in a sleek business suit. Even from this distance, I can see her tear-streaked face, hands shaking.

"You need to leave!" Amelia's voice carries clearly through the afternoon air. "You have no right to be here!"

The woman steps closer, her voice lower but insistent. "Please, just five minutes. That's all I'm asking. There are things you should understand—"

"I already know everything I need to about you," Amelia cuts her off. "What part of 'get off my property' don't you understand?"

I'm moving before I even realize it, something protective surges through me—an instinct I can't ignore. The woman sees me approaching and hesitates, her perfectly made-up face showing a flicker of uncertainty.

"Is everything okay here?" I ask, climbing the couple steps up the porch.

The moment Amelia sees me, something changes in her

posture. She practically launches herself toward me, her body colliding with mine as her arms wrap around me, burying her face against my chest. I feel her trembling against me, my arms automatically encircling her protectively.

"It's her," she whispers, her voice breaking. "The one from his phone."

The realization hits me like a linebacker. This polished blonde woman with her expensive suit and perfect makeup is the one her husband was cheating with. The other woman. The one who helped destroy Amelia's marriage before the accident even had the chance to expose it.

"Look," I say, keeping my voice firm but controlled as I address the woman. "You need to leave. She clearly doesn't want to talk to you."

The woman's perfectly manicured hand clutches her designer purse tighter. "Fine," she says, taking a step back. "He lied to us both."

Amelia stiffens against me, her whole body going rigid at the woman's words.

She shoots one last venomous look at Amelia before turning on her heel and striding down the porch steps. Her designer heels click against the concrete walkway as she gets to her car—a sleek silver Lexus parked at the curb. The engine purrs to life, and she peels away with more speed than necessary, the tires squeal on the pavement.

With her gone, Amelia's body sag against mine. Her fingers grip my t-shirt tightly, and I feel the dampness of her tears soaking through the fabric. Instinctively, my hand moves to stroke her hair, my fingers gently combing through the soft strands.

"It's okay," I murmur against the top of her head. "She's gone now."

She doesn't respond, just burrows deeper against my chest. I continue to hold her, my hand moving in slow, soothing patterns across her back and through her hair. The scent of her shampoo—something floral and delicate—fills my senses.

A movement from the corner of my eye catches my attention, and I glance toward my house. Shit. My brothers are standing on our porch, watching us with identical expressions of surprise and curiosity. Chase raises his eyebrows at me in silent question, while Luke crosses his arms, a knowing smirk playing at the corners of his mouth.

I haven't told them anything—so when I go home, I'll have some explaining to do.

Chapter Sixteen

AMELIA

I thought I'd seen her face only in the digital glow of Nick's phone screen. A ghost haunting our marriage from a distance. But the woman who just left my porch is devastatingly real. She was stunning. Tall and willowy with sleek blonde hair that looked like it belonged in a shampoo commercial. Not a single strand out of place, even in the afternoon breeze. And that suit—tailored to perfection on her slim frame, probably cost more than my entire wardrobe.

Next to her, I felt... small. Disheveled. Inadequate.

Standing in Wes's arms, I can't stop the comparison my brain insists on making. She's everything I'm not—polished, sophisticated, the kind of woman who likely never has to clean mascara smudges from under her eyes. I bet her underwear always matches her bra.

"You okay?" he asks, his voice rumbling against my ear where it's pressed to his chest.

I pull back, suddenly aware I've been clinging to him. "No." I admit.

He guides me inside my house, his arm protectively around my shoulders as I try to stop my hands from shaking. The encounter with Nick's mistress has left me feeling hollow and raw, like someone scraped out my insides with a dull spoon.

"Let's get you something to calm your nerves," he says, leading me toward the kitchen.

I let him guide me, grateful for his steady presence. My mind is reeling from seeing her—the audacity to show up at my house. The nerve of her to say he lied to us both, as if we're equals in this situation.

He pulls out a stool for me at the island counter. "Sit," he says softly. "I'll get you something."

I sink into the chair, watching as he moves around my kitchen with surprising familiarity, opening cabinets until he finds the one with glasses. He pulls down a tumbler and reaches for the bourbon bottle we'd been drinking from previously.

"I think you could use a drink," he says, unscrewing the cap.

"No!" I shout, the word erupting from me with startling force.

He freezes, bottle mid-air, his eyes wide with surprise at my outburst. The bottle hovers over the glass, his expression a mixture of confusion.

"Sorry," I say, my voice softer now. "I'd prefer water, please."

His eyebrows furrow with concern as he carefully sets the bourbon bottle back on the counter.

I consider telling him the real reason I asked for water, but the words stick in my throat.

The tap runs as he fills a glass. My fingers drum anxiously against the countertop while I try to process what happened on my front porch. The woman from Nick's phone— standing there in the flesh, trying to create some twisted bond between us as his victims. As if we're supposed to commiserate together.

He slides the glass across the counter to me, his eyes never leaving my face. I take it gratefully, my hands still trembling slightly as I bring it to my lips. The cool liquid soothes my throat, which feels raw from yelling.

"Small sips," he says gently. "You're still shaking."

I nod, following his advice, taking careful sips while trying to steady my breathing. He leans against the counter opposite me.

"Thank you for stepping in like that," I say quietly, setting the water glass down. "She caught me completely off guard. I told her to leave at least five times, but she wouldn't take no for an answer."

He pushes off from the surface, his expression softening as he moves toward me. I swivel my stool to face him as he steps close, close enough that I can see the different flecks of color in his blue-green eyes.

"I'm sorry you had to go through that," he says, his voice low and sincere. "It was incredibly inappropriate of her to show up here like that."

"I didn't think I'd ever have to see her face in person," I admit, looking at my hands wrapped around the water glass. "It was bad enough seeing her in those photos on Nick's phone, but having her here, in my space..."

Wes places his hand over mine, his palm warm and comforting.

"I recognized her immediately," I acknowledge. "She looked exactly the same—perfect hair, expensive clothes."

"You handled it better than most people would have."

"Did I? Because it felt like I completely fell apart."

"You stood your ground," he insists.

His eyes hold mine, and I see genuine concern there—not pity, just pure empathy that makes my chest tighten. He's standing near enough for me to smell his clean, sporty scent.

"I don't care what she has to say," I blurt out, the words tumbling from my lips. "Whatever she wanted to tell me about him—it doesn't matter anymore. Nothing she says is going to change anything."

He squeezes my hand gently. "Then you don't have to listen. You don't owe her a thing, Amelia."

He shifts closer, his other hand coming to rest on my knee. The warmth of his palm seeps through my jeans as his fingers slide upward along my thigh, the touch both comforting and electric. My breath catches in my throat.

"You get to decide who gets access to you," he continues, his voice dropping lower. "Your time, your attention—it's all yours to give or withhold."

I find myself leaning toward him, drawn by some invisible force. My hands reach out of their own accord, fingertips connecting with the soft cotton of his t-shirt. I feel the firm contours of his chest beneath the fabric, the steady rhythm of his heartbeat.

"I missed you," I whisper, surprised by my admission but unable to hold it back. Four days without seeing him, without hearing his voice, feels like an eternity.

His lips curve into that lopsided smile that excites me.

"I missed you too, Ladybug," he says, his voice a low

rumble. "I wanted to give you space. After everything that happened between us... I didn't want you to feel pressured or rushed."

I nod, appreciating his thoughtfulness. "I figured that's what you were doing. Thank you for that." My fingers trace small circles on his chest.

His eyes soften as he tucks a strand of hair behind my ear.

"I have some news," I say, suddenly remembering the bright spot in my week. "Wheeler and Marks were so impressed with the Barlowe presentation that they're considering me for senior designer."

His face lights up. "Seriously? Amelia, that's incredible!" His enthusiasm is so genuine it warms my chest. "That's a big deal, right?"

"Huge," I confirm, unable to contain my smile. "It means more responsibility, but also a significant pay bump and my own office."

"That's amazing, you deserve it," he says, his hands squeezing mine. "Actually, I've got some news too."

There's something in his expression—a boyish excitement that makes him look even younger than his twenty-one years. His eyes are practically sparkling.

"Coach called me into his office after practice today," he continues, unable to contain his grin. "NFL scouts have been calling about me. Like, a lot of them."

"Wes! Congratulations!" I exclaim genuinely thrilled for him. I reach up to cup his face, feeling the slight stubble against my palms. "I knew you were good, but wow—it's happening!"

"He says they're fighting over me," he adds, a hint of disbelief in his voice. "I mean, I've always dreamed about it, worked for it, but to hear that multiple teams are interested? It's surreal."

"Of course they're interested in you! You're amazing."

He pulls back slightly, his eyebrows raising as a teasing smile plays on his lips. "Amazing, huh? How would you know? You've never been to one of my games."

Heat rushes to my cheeks as I realize my slip-up. I bite my lower lip, suddenly feeling caught.

"Well..." I hesitate. "I may have watched a couple on TV."

His smile widens into a full grin, eyes lighting up with delight. "Really? You've been watching me play? This whole time?"

I roll my eyes, trying to downplay my embarrassment. "Don't let it go to your head. I was just flipping channels one day and happened to see Dalton U was playing. And then maybe I watched another game... or two."

"Or three?" he teases, his hands settling on my waist.

The solid warmth of his body against mine feels right somehow—I can't explain.

"I definitely did not watch the recap of last season on YouTube," I admit with a laugh. "And I might have Googled a few of your highlight reels."

His smile grows impossibly wider, his eyes crinkling at the corners. "Now you're trying to flatter me."

"Maybe a little." I tap my index finger against his chest playfully. "But it's also true. You're talented, Wes."

He captures my hand, holding it against his heart. The steady thump beneath my palm sends warmth spreading through me.

"Go out with me," he says suddenly, his voice low but certain. "Tomorrow night."

The request catches me off guard, and I blink at him. "A date?"

"If you want, or it can be an outing," he says, his thumbs tracing small circles where his hands rest on my waist. "But I'll pick you up, take you somewhere, and bring you home afterward."

There's a flutter in my stomach when I think of a "date"—something I haven't experienced in so long. The thought is both exciting and terrifying.

"A date," I repeat, testing how the word feels on my tongue. "I'd like that."

"So that's a yes?" he asks, as if he needs confirmation.

"Yes," I say, it comes out more breathless than I intended. "I'd love to go out with you."

"Tomorrow at seven? I'll pick you up right here."

"What should I expect? Where are we going?" I ask, curiosity getting the better of me.

His lips curl into a mischievous smile. "That's a secret. I want to surprise you."

"Not even a hint?" I push.

"Dress casually and comfortably."

"I can do casual and comfortable," I nod, smiling at him. The excitement of a date with Wes makes my heart flutter in a way I haven't felt in years.

His eyes drift to my lips, his expression softening. He leans in, closing the distance between us. When his mouth meets mine, it's gentle—not the desperate passion from the other night, but something deeper. His lips move against mine with such sweetness that my chest aches. One of his hands cups my face, thumb stroking my cheek as he kisses me with a reverence that leaves me feeling precious.

When we finally part, I keep my eyes closed for a moment, savoring the lingering sensation of his lips on mine. When I open them, he's watching me with a soft expression that makes me feel both exposed and cherished.

"Do you want to stay and watch some TV with me before bed?" I ask, my fingers playing with the collar of his shirt.

"Yeah."

My heart is pounding against my ribs, but not just from the excitement of Wes's news or even the lingering shock from the confrontation with Nick's mistress. There's something else —something I've been avoiding thinking about, something I confirmed yesterday morning with a drugstore test and again at my doctor's appointment this afternoon.

The words are right there, perched on the tip of my tongue.

I'm pregnant.

Nick's baby. Eight weeks along.

Wes is looking at me with those beautiful blue-green eyes, so full of hope and happiness about his future. His hands are still on my waist, warm and steady.

The truth swells inside me, pressing against my ribs like a physical thing. I know I should tell him—now, before this goes any further. But as I look at his face, I can't bring myself to do it. The NFL. Scouts fighting over him. His whole life is about to change in the most incredible way.

And mine? Mine is about to change too, but for entirely different reasons.

I touch my stomach unconsciously, thinking about the tiny life growing inside me. A baby that will never know its father.

My mind races with the implications. It's one thing for

Wes to comfort his widowed neighbor, to have what could be written off as a grief-fueled fling. But a pregnant, widowed neighbor? With her dead husband's baby? That's an entirely different situation—one with complications no twenty-one-year-old should have to deal with.

He gazes at me with such tenderness that my heart aches. I imagine his face when I tell him about the baby—confusion first, then that careful politeness people use when they're trying to hide their true feelings. Maybe even pity. The thought makes my stomach clench.

He has his whole life ahead of him—a brilliant future unfolding—travel, fame and money. *How could I possibly ask or expect him to take on someone else's child?* A reminder of a marriage that ended in betrayal and tragedy. He deserves better than to be saddled with my complicated life when his is just beginning to soar.

So, I make a decision in this moment, looking into his hopeful eyes. I'll keep this secret a little longer. Give us both these stolen moments of happiness before reality crashes in. It's selfish, maybe, but I want this—*want him*—right now. Even if it's just for a while.

Chapter Seventeen

AMELIA

"I swear to God, if Ramona says one more passive-aggressive thing to Bethenny, I'm going to lose my mind!" Wes shouts, his hand gesturing wildly at the television screen. "How does she not see that she's the problem here?"

I bite my lip to hold back laughter as I watch this six-foot-two quarterback get worked up over *Real Housewives of New York*. His face is flushed with genuine outrage, blue-green eyes narrowed at the screen as the women bicker over cocktails at some ridiculously lavish Hamptons party.

"You know she can't hear you, right?" I tease, tucking my feet under me on the couch.

He shoots me a look of mock offense. "I'm aware, Ladybug. But someone needs to call her out on her bullshit."

"And that someone is you? The football star watching from my living room?"

"Damn right." He reaches for the bowl of popcorn balanced between us, never taking his eyes off the screen. "Oh, come on! That's such a low blow!"

I can't help it—I burst into laughter at his outrage and lean into him.

"What's so funny?" he asks.

"You," I manage between lingering chuckles. "I never would have pegged you as a Real Housewives superfan."

"I am not a superfan," he protests. "I'm simply invested in the narrative."

"The narrative?" I raise an eyebrow. "You called Ramona a 'delusional narcissist with wine-induced amnesia' and threatened to write a strongly worded tweet about it."

"Well, she is!" he insists, wrapping his arm around me and pulling me closer.

I snuggle into his side, feeling the solid warmth of him against me. His cotton t-shirt is soft beneath my cheek, and I can hear the steady rhythm of his heartbeat. It feels so natural being here with him like this, watching ridiculous reality TV and sharing a bowl of popcorn.

"This is nice," I murmur, resting my head against his shoulder.

"Yeah, it is," he agrees, his voice soft. His fingers trace lazy patterns on my arm.

We watch in comfortable silence for a few minutes as the episode reaches its dramatic conclusion. As the credits roll, Wes grabs the remote and quickly switches to ESPN, glancing at me with sudden seriousness.

"You know this stays between us, right?" he says, lowering his voice conspiratorially. "If any of the guys on the team or Coach found out I've been binge-watching Real Housewives, I'd never hear the end of it. They'd probably make me wear a tiara during practice or something."

I press my lips together, pretending to consider this. "I

don't know... I was thinking of hiring one of those planes with the banner messages to fly over the stadium at your next game. 'Wes SULLIVAN: TEAM BETHENNY FOREVER' in giant letters."

His eyes widen in mock horror. "You wouldn't dare."

"Or maybe I could get the cheerleaders to incorporate some Real Housewives quotes into their routines?" I tap my chin thoughtfully. "I bet they could work 'Who gonna check me, boo?' into a cheer."

He groans, dropping his head onto the back of the couch. "My reputation would be destroyed."

"Your secret's safe with me," I assure him, patting his chest lightly. "I'm just enjoying having some dirt on you."

On the TV, the sports channel shows highlights from a recent NFL game. Wes's attention shifts, his whole body leaning forward as a quarterback launches a perfect throw downfield. The receiver catches it in stride and sprints to the end zone.

"Yes!" He pumps his fist, suddenly animated. "That's how it's done! Perfect read of the defense, beautiful spiral, and look at that separation the receiver got!"

His face is a beacon of joy, his passion for the game radiating from him. There's something adorable about how quickly he transitions from Housewives drama to football analysis without missing a beat.

"Wow, nice home run," I state casually, reaching for more popcorn.

His head swivels toward me so fast I'm surprised he doesn't get whiplash. His expression is one of pure, unfiltered horror, like I've just committed some cardinal sin against humanity—or rather—sports.

"What did you say?" he asks.

I blink innocently. "What? I said, nice home run. The guy ran really far with the ball across the line."

His jaw literally drops.

"It's called a touchdown, Amelia. A touchdown." He enunciates each syllable like he's explaining something to a small child. "Not a home run. That's baseball. And the 'line' is the end zone."

"Oh," I say with exaggerated innocence, fighting to keep my expression neutral. "A touchdown. Got it."

The highlight reel continues, showing the kicker coming onto the field for the extra point. The ball sails perfectly between the uprights, and I can't resist.

"GOOOOOAAAAALLLL!" I scream at the top of my lungs, throwing my arms up in the air like a soccer announcer.

His eyes narrow as he studies my face. I try to maintain my innocent expression, but the corner of my mouth twitches, and that's all it takes for him to see right through me.

"You..." His voice is low, dangerous. "You're messing with me."

I erupt in laughter, unable to hold it in any longer. "Your face! You should have seen your face!"

"Oh, you think it's funny?" In one swift motion, his fingers are at my sides, tickling mercilessly. I squeal and try to squirm away, but he's too quick. His fingers find every sensitive spot along my waist and under my arms, sending me into fits of breathless laughter.

"Wes! Stop!" I gasp between giggles, trying to catch his hands.

"Not until you admit you know the difference between a

touchdown and a home run," he says, grinning wickedly as he continues his assault.

I laugh so hard tears form in my eyes, writhing beneath him as he follows me down onto the couch. My back presses into the cushions as he hovers above me, his weight supported on one arm while the other keeps tickling me relentlessly.

"Fine! Fine!" I surrender, gasping for breath. "A touchdown is football, a home run is baseball!"

He pauses, looking at me with mock seriousness, his face just inches from mine. "And what's a goal?"

"Soccer," I manage between breaths, my chest still heaving from laughter.

"And basketball has...?" He raises an eyebrow, fingers poised threateningly at my ribs.

"Baskets," I answer.

"We're going to have a huge problem if you don't know basic football terms, Ladybug," he says, his voice dropping to a low, husky tone. "Especially since I plan on being around for a while."

His lips capture mine in a searing kiss that steals what little breath I had left. My hands instinctively slide up his chest and around his neck, fingers threading through his soft blond hair. His body presses against me, solid and warm, as his tongue traces the seam of my lips, asking for entrance. I open to him willingly, eagerly, meeting his tongue with mine.

The playful atmosphere from moments ago transforms into something far more heated. Wes's hand slides beneath the hem of my shirt, his palm skimming over my ribs, leaving goosebumps in its wake. I arch into his touch, a small moan escaping me as his thumb brushes the underside of my breast. My breath hitches at the sensation, heat pooling low in my belly as his mouth moves from my lips to my jaw, then down the column of my throat.

His weight settles more fully between my legs, and I feel him hard against me. I instinctively roll my hips upward, creating delicious friction that makes us both gasp.

"Amelia," he groans against my neck, his voice strained.

I thread my fingers through his hair, tugging gently to bring his mouth back to mine. Our kisses grow more desperate, more hungry, his hands exploring my body with increasing boldness. My own hands slip underneath his t-shirt, mapping the ridges of his abdomen, feeling the muscles contract beneath my touch.

When he breaks away suddenly, I make a small sound of protest.

"God, I want you so bad," he confesses. "But I'm trying to be good here. I don't want to rush things."

His words pull me back to reality, even as my body still thrums with desire. I place my hands on his chest, feeling his heartbeat racing beneath my palm. The intensity in his eyes makes my breath catch—there's such naked longing there, but also restraint. He's holding back for my sake.

"You're right," I whisper, trying to steady my breathing. "We should slow down."

He nods, though the tension in his jaw tells me it's taking considerable effort. He shifts his weight, moving to sit beside me instead of hovering above me. I sit too, smoothing my rumpled shirt.

"I want to do this right," he says, taking my hand in his. "You deserve better than rushed moments on the couch."

I smile, touched by his consideration, but there's something gnawing at me—a question I need to ask even though I'm afraid of the answer. My fingers tighten around his as I gather my courage.

"Wes?" My voice comes out smaller than I intended.

"Yeah?"

"Are you... seeing other people? Or planning to while we... ?"

Surprise flickers across his features. I immediately regret asking. *What right do I have to question his dating life when we haven't even defined what this is between us?*

I'm certain I don't want to just jump into a relationship out of pain or because he treats me better, rather than a genuine connection, especially if the attraction feels too good to be true.

And maybe it's my trust issues talking. Nick's betrayal has left me wary, waiting for the other shoe to drop. I know I have no right to ask him not to see other people, but I need to know where I stand. I need to protect myself from being blindsided again.

His expression softens as he looks at me, his thumb tracing gentle circles on the back of my hand. "No," he says firmly, his eyes never leaving mine. "I'm not seeing anyone else. I haven't been with anyone in months, actually."

Relief washes through me, though I try not to show just how much his answer means to me.

"And I'm not interested in anyone but you, Amelia," he continues. "Not even a little bit."

I swallow hard. "Really?"

"Really." He brings my hand to his lips, pressing a soft kiss against my knuckles. "I know this is complicated. You're working through a lot right now, and I respect that."

His words warm me, but a wave of guilt immediately

washes over me. I'm not being honest with him. Here he is, laying his feelings bare, while I'm keeping a secret that would change everything between us.

I pull my hand away, suddenly feeling unworthy of his touch. "Wes, I..." I start, but the words catch in my throat.

His eyes search mine, concern evident in his expression. "What is it?"

I shake my head, looking at my lap.

How can he be so sure about only being interested in me when he doesn't have all the information?

I'm being completely selfish, and I know it. Leading him on when there's this massive complication he knows nothing about. My hand instinctively moves to rest on my still-flat stomach. Pregnant with Nick's baby. A permanent connection to a man who betrayed me, who's no longer here. A baby he doesn't know exists.

"What are you thinking about?" he asks. "You suddenly looked a million miles away."

I quickly move my hand back to my lap. "Just... processing everything. It's been an intense day."

His face softens with concern. "Between that woman showing up and now this conversation, and what happened on Real Housewives..." His eyes crinkle at the corners as he smiles.

I can't help laughing at his attempt to cheer me up.

He tucks a strand of hair behind my ear, his touch so tender it makes me want to cry. "We can take this as slow as you need."

"I know," I say softly. "And I appreciate that."

As I look at him—this kind, thoughtful man who's crashed into my life at the most complicated time—I'm overwhelmed by conflicting emotions. I want to stay in this bubble with him, where everything feels simple and good. Where I can pretend that my life isn't about to completely transform in ways he can't possibly imagine.

"You look tired," he says, brushing his thumb across my cheek.

I nod, suddenly aware of the bone-deep exhaustion settling over me. The confrontation with Nick's mistress, the emotional roller coaster of reconnecting with Wes, and the constant weight of my secret—it's all catching up to me.

"I should probably let you get some rest," he says, starting to rise from the couch.

I reach for his hand. "Stay a little longer? Just until I fall asleep?"

"Of course."

Chapter Eighteen

Wesley

"Busted."

I hear Chase's voice and freeze in my tracks halfway through the front door. The living room is dark except for the soft glow of the TV, illuminating my brothers' faces with blue light. He's sprawled across the couch, a bowl of popcorn balanced on his chest, smirking, while Luke sits in the recliner, one eyebrow raised as he looks at me.

I sigh, closing the door behind me. So much for sneaking in unnoticed. "What are you guys still doing up?"

"Watching game highlights," Luke says, gesturing toward the TV where SportsCenter is playing quietly. "The better question is what are you doing? Where have you been?"

I shrug, trying to be casual as I drop my keys on the side table. "Just out."

Chase snorts, tossing a piece of popcorn into his mouth. "Yeah, 'just out' next door with Ladybug."

I shake my head. They saw me go over there; they're not stupid.

"You're sleeping with her," Luke says. Not a question.

"I am," I admit. No point in denying it when they've clearly figured it out. "I did—once, earlier in the week."

Both my brothers exchange a look—that silent communication thing we've perfected over the years. It's not quite judgment in their eyes, but definitely concern.

"I knew it," Chase says triumphantly. "The way you rushed over there today like a knight in shining armor when she was fighting with that woman—dude," he sits straighter and sets the popcorn aside. "Her husband's been dead for what, two weeks?"

"Almost three," I correct him automatically before wincing at how that sounds. "Look, I know how it looks, okay? But it's not what you think."

Luke leans forward in the recliner, his expression serious. "What is it exactly? Because from where we're sitting, it looks like you're taking advantage of a vulnerable widow."

"Jesus, Luke," I mutter, dropping onto the couch beside Chase. "It's more complicated than that."

"Then uncomplicate it for us," Chase says, muting the TV.

I take a deep breath, trying to organize my thoughts. "Wasp was cheating on her," I say, using our old nickname for him. "Not just cheating—multiple women over the years— taking them on vacations when he claimed to be on work trips," I say, watching my brothers' eyes widen. "Amelia found pictures and messages on his phone after the accident. She feels like their entire marriage was a lie—like she never really knew him at all."

Chase lets out a low whistle. "Damn. That's messed up."

"And that woman today?" Luke asks, leaning forward.

"The most recent one," I confirm, my jaw tightening at the memory of Amelia's tear-streaked face. "She had the nerve to show up at Amelia's house, trying to talk to her about Nick. Claiming he lied to them both or some bullshit." I run a hand through my hair, feeling the weight of everything she's been dealing with. "Look, what happened between us... it wasn't planned. I went over there with a bottle of bourbon because I'd made her a lasagna and burned it to hell."

Luke raises an eyebrow. "You cooked for her?"

"Tried to," Chase admits to Luke. "He nearly burnt the house down trying to recreate mom's lasagna."

"She didn't need another damn casserole, you know?" I say with a sheepish grin. "She needed someone who would just be real with her, not walk on eggshells or treat her like she was made of glass." I pause, remembering how her face broke into a radiant smile when I gave her the bourbon instead of food. "She didn't want pity or sympathy. She just needed someone to see her as a person, not a tragedy."

"And that person was you," Luke says, his tone softer now.

I nod, staring at my hands. "Yeah. I guess it was. She opened up to me—about Nick, about how she felt like a fraud at his funeral pretending to grieve when she was really just angry."

"So you two bonded over bourbon and her dead husband's infidelity," Chase summarizes. "And then...?"

Luke leans forward. "Wait, if you clicked that night, does that mean she made the first move?"

"Kind of," I admit, wincing.

My brothers exchange glances again, clearly sensing there's more to the story.

"Define 'kind of,'" Luke presses.

I drag a hand over my face. "I forgot my phone at her place and went back to get it. I knocked, but she didn't answer. The door was unlocked, so I went in and called her name."

"And?" Chase prompts when I pause.

"And I found her in her bedroom... touching herself."

The words hang in the air for a moment. Chase's eyes widen, and Luke nearly chokes on his water.

"I was going to leave—I swear I was—but then she said my name as she came and I couldn't move. When she realized I was standing there she didn't cover up or anything. She... looked at me with embarrassment but there was something else..."

"Holy shit," Chase whispers, a grin spreading across his face. "That's straight out of a porno."

I throw a pillow at him. "It wasn't like that, not entirely."

"So wait," Luke says, leaning forward with renewed interest. "You're telling me you walked in on your neighbor getting herself off while fantasizing about you, and then what? You just happened to fall into bed together?"

"Pretty much," I admit, unable to keep the small smile from my face as I remember that night. "It was... intense. Like nothing I've ever experienced before."

Chase makes a whoop that's so loud I reach over and punch him in the arm.

Luke studies me for a moment, his expression shifting from amusement to something more serious. "You like her, don't you?"

"Yeah," I say, failing to suppress the emotion out of my voice. "I do like her. A lot."

Luke nods slowly. "I'm happy for you, Wes, honestly. It's good to see you finally connecting with someone real instead of those party girls who only care about dating the football star. But," Luke continues, his voice taking on a more serious tone, "you need to be careful. She's grieving, even if she's mostly angry at her husband. People process loss in complicated ways, and the last thing you want is to be her rebound—the guy she uses to work through her feelings."

I open my mouth to protest, but deep down, I know he's right. The timing of all this is... problematic at best.

"I know," I admit reluctantly. "I've thought about that too. But it doesn't feel like a rebound. It feels..." I struggle to find the right words. "It feels like something that was meant to happen, just with unfortunate circumstances."

Before either of my brothers can respond, a light flicks on from the stairway. We all turn to see Bebe standing there in flannel pajama bottoms and Luke's Dalton U navy sweatshirt, her reddish-brown hair piled messily on top of her head.

"Are you two still interrogating him?" she asks, leaning against the banister with a sleepy smile. "It's after midnight, you know."

"We're just looking out for our brother," Chase protests.

She rolls her eyes. "Leave Wes alone. So he's sleeping with the hot widow next door."

"Bebe!" Luke exclaims, though he can't hide his laugh.

"Thanks for the support, I think?"

She descends the last few steps, crossing the living room to perch on the arm of Luke's chair. "Seriously though, if you like her, that's what matters. Timing is always going to be complicated with something like this." She runs her fingers through Luke's hair absently. "Life's too short."

Her words are heavy with meaning. *Life is too short.* I know she's right—after everything that happened with the

Laurents, with how close we came to losing her, we understand better than most how quickly everything can change.

Luke catches Bebe's hand and brings it to his lips, pressing a soft kiss against her palm. Their eyes meet, and I'm struck by the simple intimacy of the gesture, the quiet understanding that passes between them.

"We should head up," Luke says, not taking his eyes off her. "It's late, and I've got an early class tomorrow."

Bebe nods, sliding off the arm of the chair and into Luke's lap for a moment. He whispers something in her ear that makes her smile, and I feel a pang of something—not quite jealousy, but longing. I want that kind of connection with someone. With Amelia.

"Night guys," Luke says, standing and stretching. "Try not to stay up all night gossiping about Wes's love life."

"Chase groans and flops back dramatically on the couch, throwing an arm over his eyes. "I need to find a girlfriend. Seriously. This house is becoming couple central."

I smirk, unable to resist the opportunity to mess with him. "Maybe you should look for someone within the Keepers society," I suggest with a playful smirk. "Maybe the one dad wants you to be kissy-face with…"

He throws the pillow I tossed at him earlier, back at me. "Are you kidding? Those girls are the most boring, uptight people. They make church socials look like raves." He flops back dramatically. "I'd rather stay single than date someone who thinks a wild night is drinking chamomile tea past 9 PM."

I can't help but laugh at his reaction. It's too easy to tease him. I push myself off the couch. My body feels heavy with exhaustion after the long day, but lighter somehow after talking with my brothers. Even with their teasing, I know they have my back.

"Your loss," I say, heading toward the stairs. "Some of those Keeper girls are pretty hot."

"Yeah, until they open their mouths," he mutters, grabbing the remote and unmuting the TV. "Hey, before you go—does Ladybug have any friends? You know, maybe someone who's not recently widowed?"

I shake my head, climbing the first few steps. "Goodnight, Chase."

Chapter Nineteen

WESLEY

The park is quiet except for the crunch of gravel under our shoes. We continue walking, the evening air growing cooler as the sun dips lower behind the trees. The path curves ahead, winding deeper into the greenery. I've always loved this place at sunset—the way the light filters through the leaves, the gradual quieting as day transitions to night. But having Amelia here beside me makes it feel new, like I'm seeing it all for the first time.

Her fingers lace through mine, small and delicate against my much larger hand. It's such a simple thing, holding hands, but there's something about the way her palm fits perfectly against mine that feels right. Natural. I run my thumb across her knuckles, marveling at how soft her skin is compared to my calloused hand, rough from years of catching footballs.

She didn't know yet, but we were heading toward the little clearing I'd claimed earlier in the day, tucked away from the main path. I'd been planning this all day. My stomach is a mix of nerves and something close to excitement I hadn't felt in... a long time. I can't recall the last time I'd taken a woman on a date. High school probably.

"Are we lost?" She teases, glancing at me from the corner of her eye.

When we reach the clearing, I stop and gesture ahead. Candles—small glass jars with flickering tea lights—lined a blanket I'd spread over the grass. A picnic basket sits in the center with a bouquet of a dozen pink roses.

"No," I smile, watching her eyes widen as she takes in my surprise setup. "We are exactly where we're supposed to be."

I flick the small remote in my pocket, and suddenly the old oak tree to the right of our picnic spot comes to life. Hundreds of tiny golden lights twinkle between the dark branches. Amelia actually gasps, her free hand flying to her mouth. The soft light reflects in her eyes, making them shimmer as she stares at the tree in awe.

Her lips part slightly. "You... did this?"

"Yeah," I breathe, taking it all in. The scene is something out of a movie—a romantic gesture I'd never done before.

I nod to a freshman standing nearby, signaling he can go.

"You had help," she says with wonder in her voice, her eyes following my teammate as he jogs away down the path.

"A little," I admit, rubbing the back of my neck. "I couldn't exactly leave all this unattended in a public park. He was happy to stand guard while I picked you up. And... make sure I don't burn the park down."

Her fingers reach for mine, intertwining them as she steps toward the blanket. "It's perfect. I can't believe you went through all this trouble."

"It's no trouble when it's for you," I say softly. "I'd do this every night if I could."

Her cheeks flush at my words, and a warmth spreads through my chest. There's something about making Amelia blush that feels like winning the championship game.

I kneel beside the picnic basket, flipping open the lid to reveal several neatly packed containers. "I hope you like Japanese. There's this amazing place downtown—best in Ambrose."

"I love Japanese food," she says as she settles onto the blanket, smoothing her dress beneath her.

I grin, arranging the containers between us.

We sit cross-legged, close enough that our knees occasionally brush. I open each container, explaining the contents as I go—gyoza, teriyaki chicken, yakisoba and steamed rice.

"This smells delicious," she says, her eyes widening at the spread.

I reach for a pair of chopsticks, handing her one set before taking my own. "I was thinking—we've spent all this time together, but there's still so much I don't know about you."

She picks up a piece of gyoza, dipping it delicately in sauce. "What would you like to know?"

"Where were you before Ambrose?"

She smiles, a soft, nostalgic expression crossing her face. "Northern California. A small town called Auburn, about forty minutes from Sacramento. It's nestled in the foothills of the Sierra Nevada mountains—a beautiful place, especially in spring when the wildflowers bloom."

"That sounds amazing," I say, genuinely interested.

"It was. I grew up there, stayed for college too—went to UC Davis for design." She bites into her food, chewing thoughtfully before continuing. "After graduation, I landed an internship at this boutique firm in San Francisco. It was brutal hours, barely paid anything, but I learned so much. I loved that internship. When it ended, I was devastated—thought I'd have to move back to Auburn. But I was hired and spent a few good years there before the owner retired. He called me a week later and said Wheeler & Marks in Ambrose was looking for a junior designer. He'd recommended me." She smiles at the memory. "I drove down for the interview the next day, got the job on the spot."

She takes a bite of the yakisoba, making a small sound of appreciation that does things to my insides. When she looks up, there's curiosity in her eyes.

"What about you? Have you always lived in Ambrose? In that house?"

I shake my head, setting down my chopsticks. "Born and raised in Ambrose, but the house is relatively new. My brothers and I moved in about a year before you came to the neighborhood." I take a sip of water from the bottle I brought. "My parents bought it as an investment—my dad owns and manages multiple properties around town."

"And what about your brothers? Do they go to Dalton U too?"

"Yeah, it's a family tradition," I say, reaching for another piece of teriyaki chicken. "The Sullivan men have been attending Dalton U for generations."

I consider telling her about The Keepers, about how the men in my family have been part of the secret society since its founding, but I stop myself. Luke had been so nervous about telling Bebe, spending weeks agonizing over how to bring it up without sounding like he was in some weird cult. That's definitely too much for a first date.

"Do you have any siblings?" I ask, curious to learn more about her.

"No, just me," she says, twirling noodles around her chopsticks. "I always wondered what it would be like to have siblings. It must have been fun growing up with two brothers."

"It was—still is," I say. "They're my best friends, honestly. We've always been close, but more so these last few years."

"Tell me about them," she says, leaning forward slightly with genuine interest.

I smile, setting my food down. "Luke—he's the practical one, always has been. Even when we were kids, he was the voice of reason when Chase and I wanted to do something stupid." I chuckle, remembering countless childhood adventures. "He's got an amazing girlfriend, Bebe—she's become like family to us."

I carefully leave out how Bebe and her brothers had helped to save our family when the L.A. Chapter of The Keepers held us against our will. Best to leave that out—I want her to keep feeling safe around me.

"And Chase," I continue, smiling as I think of my youngest brother, "he's a total class clown, but scary smart. He has this ability to make you laugh until your sides hurt, but then he'll drop some profound insight that leaves you wondering where it came from. He's going to law school after graduation."

"That's incredibly impressive," she says. "Your family sounds wonderful," she says, setting down her chopsticks. "My childhood was... quieter. Being an only child meant a lot of time in my own head."

I notice a shift in her expression—a softening, like she's opening a door she usually keeps closed.

"I used to create these elaborate worlds," she continues, her voice taking on a nostalgic quality. "I'd spend hours in my room with colored pencils and sketch pads, designing houses for imaginary people or my dolls. Each one had a story—this one was for a marine biologist who studied dolphins, that one for a family with five children who needed separate spaces."

"So you always knew you wanted to go into architectural design?"

"I think so," she says with a smile. "When I wasn't drawing, I was building with Legos. My parents bought me this massive set for my ninth birthday, and I was obsessed. Not just following the instructions, but creating my own designs. I'd spend hours constructing these intricate structures—houses with small gardens, apartment buildings with tiny balconies. Each brick had to be perfect."

Her eyes take on a faraway look, and I lean closer, drawn in by the way she talks about her childhood passion.

"Sometimes I'd work on the same structure for days, adding small details, rearranging walls to get the flow right. The hardest part was always taking them apart," she continues. "I'd get so attached to each creation, but I only had one set. Every time I wanted to build something new, I had to dismantle what I'd already made."

"That must have been tough," I say, trying to imagine little Amelia reluctantly disassembling her creations.

She nods, tracing patterns on the blanket with her fingertip. "It was. I'd take pictures sometimes, but it wasn't the same."

"Have you ever drawn your dream house?"

Her face transforms instantly. She glows from the subside out with an enthusiasm that takes my breath away.

"Of course I have," she says, her voice animated in a way I haven't heard before. "Multiple versions. I've been designing it since I was twelve."

"Really?"

"It's changed so much over the years," she continues, gesturing with her hands as she speaks. "My first design was this ridiculous mansion with a movie theater and indoor pool —very twelve-year-old fantasy." She laughs, shaking her head at the memory. "In college, it became this ultra-modern, minimalist thing with concrete and glass everywhere."

"And now?" I prompt, captivated by the animation on her face.

"Now it's... evolving. More contemporary, clean lines, lots of natural light. As my life changed, my needs changed too. In college, I added a dedicated art studio. When I started at Wheeler & Marks, I redesigned the office space completely."

"Makes sense," I nod, picturing how her concepts would evolve with her. "I'm guessing it'll probably change a few more times before you're ready to build it."

"Definitely," she laughs.

"I'd love to see your designs sometime," I tell her, genuinely curious about this window into her creative mind. "The evolution of Amelia's dream house sounds fascinating."

She looks at me with surprise, then a shy smile spreads across her face. "Really? You would be interested in seeing them?"

"Absolutely."

She tucks a strand of hair behind her ear, suddenly looking almost bashful. "I've never actually shown them to anyone before. Not even—" Her voice softens. "He never thought we'd have the money one day to really build it—so he didn't care to see them."

Something protective stirs in my chest at the admission. *How could somebody not want to see what lights her up like this?*

"I'd be happy to show you," she says, reaching across the blanket to take my hand. "They're all digitized now, but I still have some of the original sketches."

Her fingers are warm against mine, and without thinking, I gently tug her toward me. "Come here," I murmur.

She moves with grace, allowing me to guide her into my lap. The food containers sit forgotten on the blanket as she settles against me, her back against my chest, her warmth seeping through both our clothes. I wrap my arms around her waist, resting my chin on her shoulder.

I breathe in the scent of her—a subtle floral perfume mixed with something uniquely her. My heart hammers against my ribs as I turn my face toward her neck, my lips barely grazing her skin.

She turns her head, our faces now inches apart. In the golden glow of twilight and candlelight, her eyes are luminous, searching mine with a question I don't need words to understand.

I close the distance between us, capturing her lips with mine. The kiss starts gentle, a tender exploration, but quickly deepens as she shifts in my lap to face me more fully. My tongue traces the seam of her mouth, seeking entry, and she responds immediately, opening to me with a soft sigh that sends heat coursing through my veins.

The candlelight flickers around us, casting dancing shadows across her face when we break apart for breath. Her eyes are dark, pupils dilated, lips slightly swollen from our kiss. She looks beautiful—in a way that steals my breath. Something shifts inside me as I look at her, something profound and terrifying in its intensity.

The realization crashes through me like a linebacker—I could fall in love with this woman. Easily. Completely. And maybe I *already* do.

Chapter Twenty

AMELIA

Warm arms suddenly encircle my waist from behind, and I catch Wes's reflection in the mirror, that lopsided smile making my heart skip. His chin comes to rest on my shoulder, his blond hair slightly mussed from sleep, though he's already dressed in his running clothes.

"Morning, Ladybug," he murmurs, his voice still carrying a sleepy roughness that makes my insides flutter.

I try to steady my hand as I reach for my second earring, the delicate gold hoop that matches the one in my left ear, then lean back against his chest, savoring his warmth. Though he hasn't slept over in the week since our date—he's come over early every morning to see me before work. The thoughtfulness of the gesture isn't lost on me.

"You don't have to get up this early just to see me off," I say.

"I want to," he replies simply, his eyes meeting mine in the mirror. "Besides, I need to go for my run before practices."

His lips find that tender area at the junction of my neck

and shoulder, sending shivers down my spine. His teeth graze lightly against my skin, and I tilt my head to give him better access. A soft moan escapes me as he works his way up to the sensitive spot behind my ear.

I turn my face, seeking his mouth with mine. Our lips meet in a slow, deep kiss that quickly ignites into something more urgent. His hands, which had been resting on my waist, wander upward until they cup my breasts through my silk blouse. My nipples harden instantly under his touch, and I arch into him, craving more contact.

"Wes," I breathe against his lips as his thumbs circle my peaks.

Those hands continue their exploration, sliding down my torso and over the swell of my hips until they're cupping my ass. His fingers squeeze appreciatively, and a low groan rumbles from his chest.

"God, Amelia," he murmurs. "Your ass in this skirt should be illegal. The way it hugs every curve..." He gives another gentle squeeze that makes my breath catch.

I can't help but smile at his appreciation. His hands suddenly gather the fabric of my pencil skirt, inching it upward along my thighs.

"What are you doing?" I ask.

His eyes lock with mine in the mirror, that mischievous glint I've come to adore dancing in their blue-green depths. "I can't hold back anymore; I need you—if you need me too. How about a quickie?" he asks simply, as if suggesting we grab coffee.

I glance at my watch, the responsible part of my brain still functioning despite the heat pooling between my legs. "I have five minutes before I need to leave."

He grins against my neck, his hands continue working my skirt higher. "That's enough time for you to come."

I smile at that—his word choice, said with a challenge. 'You'—not him. My orgasm. The fact that he's focused on my pleasure makes my knees weak. It's such a stark contrast to what I'd grown accustomed to with my late husband.

When the skirt is gathered at my waist, he looks at me through the mirror—silently asking for permission. I nod, and his fingers hook into the waistband of my white thong, slowly dragging it down my thighs. His fingers slide between my thighs, tracing the already slick pussy. A soft gasp escapes my lips as he finds me wet and ready for him.

"Someone's excited," he murmurs against my ear, his voice deepening with desire.

He nudges my feet apart with his own, widening my stance as I instinctively lean forward, bracing my hands on the cool marble of the bathroom counter. My face is toward the mirror now, and I see Wes's hungry expression behind me.

I watch his reflection as he tugs down his gym shorts, freeing his erection. My body clenches in anticipation, remembering exactly how those metal studs feel inside me.

He positions himself at my entrance, one hand gripping my hip while the other sweeps my hair to the side so he can see my face. Our eyes lock in the mirror as he pushes forward in a slow, deliberate thrust.

"Oh God," I moan, my fingers holding the edge of the counter as he fills me completely.

The sensation of him filling me is exquisite—the ridged metal of his piercings dragging against my inner walls with each movement. My eyes flutter closed as pleasure ripples through me.

"Look," he commands, his voice husky and deep. "Open your eyes, Amelia."

I obey, my gaze meeting his in the mirror. His rhythm shifts, each thrust becoming more purposeful, more intense. The slap of skin against skin echoes in the bathroom as he picks up speed.

"No, not at me," he says, his breath hot against my ear. "Look at yourself."

My eyes shift to my reflection—cheeks flushed pink, lips parted, eyes dark with desire.

"I want you to see what I see," he continues, his voice dropping to a growl. "How sexy you are when you take me like this."

His right hand slides up my torso, past my collarbone, until his fingers wrap gently around my throat. He doesn't squeeze—just holds his fingers there like the most intimate necklace, a possessive gesture that sends a thrill racing through me.

"Look at how beautiful you are," he urges.

My blouse has come partially unbuttoned, revealing the swell of my breasts. And the tiny gold hoop in my nose glints in the mirror—delicate, deliberate, defiant.

I am hot.

"That's it," he encourages, his rhythm never faltering. "See how fucking sexy you are when you're being fucked? How your eyes get all dark and dreamy?"

I've never seen myself like this before—flushed and wanting, my expression transformed by pleasure. The woman in the mirror isn't the put-together professional about to head to work. She's raw, uninhibited, consumed by desire. There's something intensely titillating about watching Wes's reflection behind me, his muscled body flexing with each thrust, while simultaneously seeing what he sees in me.

"I want you to say it." His voice drops even lower, his lips brushing against my earlobe. "Tell me what it's like to be fucked like this, bent over your bathroom counter when you should head to work."

His words shock me, but the thrill they send through my body is undeniable. The contrast between my professional appearance and what we're doing right now makes everything more intense.

"It feels... incredible," I manage between gasps.

"Not good enough," he says, his rhythm slowing to torturous, deliberate strokes. "Tell me exactly what you love about it."

My cheeks burn hotter. I've never been one for talking during sex, but something about how he's looking at me in the mirror, the raw desire in his eyes, makes me want to please him.

"I love how deep you go," I whisper, my voice growing bolder as I see his pleased expression. "The way you stretch me open, how full you make me feel."

His eyes darken with approval, and something inside me breaks free. Words I never thought I'd say spill from my lips.

"I love that you're taking me like this when I should head to work," I pant, watching his reaction in the mirror. "That I'll be sitting in meetings all day feeling where you've been, remembering how you bent me over this counter and fucked me until I couldn't think straight."

Wes groans; his pace quickens. "Fuck, Amelia. Keep going."

"I love how dirty it feels," I confess, shocking myself with my candor. "How you make me forget everything except how good you feel inside me."

"You're so beautiful," he murmurs, his eyes locked on mine in the mirror. "So fucking perfect."

I feel a new kind of power surge through me. This visual connection adds another layer to our intimacy—I can see exactly what he sees. The way my lips part with each gasp, how my eyes darken when he hits that exquisite spot inside me.

My hands grip the counter harder as I begin pushing back against him, meeting his thrusts with my own. The new angle makes his piercings drag exquisitely against my walls, sending sparks of pleasure racing up my spine.

"That's it, take what you need, Ladybug."

I watch my face as my orgasm builds—the way my mouth forms and 'o' shape in a silent cry. My eyes widen; my pupils dilate. The familiar pressure intensifies low in my belly, that delicious tightening that signals I'm close.

My orgasm crashes through me, wave after wave of pleasure radiating outward. I push back against Wes, seeking more, wanting him deeper, harder, as it peaks. My body trembles as I clench around him, milking his cock with each pulse of my climax.

"Good girl," he praises, his voice strained as his rhythm falters. "Such a good dirty girl."

His praise washes over me, intensifying the thrill as I continue to ride out my orgasm. His grip on my hips tightens, and I feel the sudden swell of him inside me. He groans, a deep, primal sound as he empties himself, his hot release filling me completely. The sensation of his warmth triggers another small aftershock of pleasure.

His movements slow gradually, his breath ragged against

my neck. When he finally stills, we're both panting, our reflections in the mirror showing flushed, satisfied faces.

He eases out of me and I feel a trickle of cum down my inner thigh.

I'm all smiles when he begins to pull my skirt back down like a perfect gentleman. His fingers smooth the fabric over my curves, taking extra time to caress my ass. I reach for the toilet paper roll, pulling a few squares free.

"What are you doing?" he asks, his voice still husky from our encounter.

"Getting something to wipe with," I explain, gesturing vaguely toward my thighs where I feel his warmth slowly trickling. "You know... to clean up."

He shakes his head, the mischievous glint returning to his eyes. "No. Leave it."

My eyebrows shoot up. "Leave it?"

His fingers smooth my skirt back into place, the fabric sliding against my bare skin. "I want you to let it dry and wear it to work."

"Wes! I have meetings today."

He steps closer, his hands settling on my hips as he pulls me against him. "That's what makes it so hot. You'll be sitting there in your professional clothes, talking about design concepts and budgets..." His lips brush against my ear. "And the whole time, you'll be feeling me between your legs. Thinking about what we did."

Heat rushes to my face—*and between my thighs*—at the thought. It's filthy, inappropriate, and somehow incredibly arousing. The idea makes me feel deliciously wicked, makes me want to do exactly what he's suggesting despite every professional instinct telling me not to.

"You're terrible," I whisper, but there's no conviction in my voice.

"You love it."

I bite my lip, unable to deny it. "You're going to make me late."

He chuckles, the sound vibrating through his chest against mine. Then, surprisingly, his expression softens. He puts his arm around my waist and leans in for a kiss that is sweet, completely unlike what we just did and what he suggested. His lips are gentle, almost reverent, touching me.

When he pulls back, his eyes are warm with something that makes my heart stutter. "Have a great day, Ladybug," he says softly. "I'll see you tonight."

I stand stunned as I watch him walk away, adjusting his shorts as he disappears from the bathroom. The tenderness of that last kiss compared to our passionate encounter leaves me breathless in a completely different way.

Chapter Twenty-One

AMELIA

I can't stop smiling as I zoom in on the 3D rendering of the Harding home. Adjusting the lighting to cast perfect shadows across the infinity pool, I bite my lip, trying to suppress the grin that keeps threatening to take over my face. It's not the project making me smile—though I am proud of how the design is coming together. It's the delicious secret I'm carrying between my thighs.

Wes's cum is still inside me, on my thigh, drying slowly against my skin throughout the morning. Every time I shift in my chair, I feel the slight stickiness, the phantom pressure of him filling me just hours ago. The memory sends a fresh wave of heat through my body, and I have to take a deep breath to focus on the screen in front of me.

I'm supposed to be finalizing this presentation for tomorrow's client meeting, not daydreaming about Wes bending me over my bathroom counter. But God, the way he looked at me in the mirror, the way he commanded me to watch myself and talk dirty...

"Earth to Amelia," a voice cuts through my thoughts.

I startle, looking up to find Gina leaning against my cubicle wall, arms crossed and eyebrows raised.

"Sorry, I was just focusing on this rendering."

"Wheeler wants to see you in his office. Now."

My stomach drops. "Did he say what about?"

"Nope. Just said to find you ASAP." She glances at my screen. "The Harding project looks great, by the way."

"Thanks," I mumble, saving my work before standing.

As I smooth down my pencil skirt, I feel the sticky reminder of my morning with Wes again.

"Good luck," she calls as I walk away. Something in her tone makes me nervous.

I proceed down the hallway, my heels clicking against the tile floors. Wheeler's office is at the end of the corridor, its glass walls offering no privacy—a design choice he claims promotes transparency but really just lets him monitor everyone.

He's on the phone when I arrive, but he waves me in without missing a beat in his conversation. As I settle into the chair across from his desk, I smooth my skirt over my thighs. Wheeler holds up one finger, signaling me to wait as he wraps up his call.

"Yes... We'll have those revisions to you by the end of day tomorrow... Perfect. Looking forward to it." He hangs up and turns his full attention to me, his expression unreadable behind his glasses.

"Amelia," he says. "I want to talk about the senior designer position with you."

My heart rate picks up. "Yes, of course."

Wheeler nods, a slight smile playing at the corners of his

mouth. "I'd like to discuss it over drinks tonight. The Union Club at seven."

I freeze, my throat suddenly dry. This again? The Union Club? That's not a casual business meeting venue—it's where executives take clients they want to impress—an upscale bar with fancy appetizers known more for its intimate atmosphere than business meetings.

"Oh, I..." I hesitate, my mind racing. *Why can't we discuss this here in his office during work hours?* "I have plans tonight. But Monday morning would be—"

Wheeler's eyebrows rise above his glasses. "Plans?"

"Yes, I'm attending a football game at Dalton University." As soon as the words leave my mouth, I realize how trivial it sounds compared to discussing my career advancement.

Wheeler leans back in his chair, steepling his fingers. "A football game." His tone makes it clear what he thinks of that excuse. "Amelia, we're talking about the senior designer position."

"I understand, but—"

"This role comes with a thirty percent salary increase," he continues, cutting me off. "Your own office, first pick of clients, and significantly more creative control." He removes his glasses, fixing me with a direct stare. "Is a college football game really more important than discussing that?"

I gaze at Wheeler. Thirty-percent salary increase. My private office. First pick of accounts. Everything I've worked for these past years. I think of the little life growing inside me, the future I need to secure—not just for myself anymore, but for my baby.

"When you put it that way..." I take a deep breath. "You're right. I can always go to another game. I'll meet you there."

Wheeler's face relaxes into a satisfied smile as he slides his glasses back on. "Excellent decision. I think you'll find this conversation well worth your time."

Something about his tone makes me uneasy, but I push the feeling aside. This is about my career, my future.

"I'll see you there," Wheeler says, already turning to his computer. "Don't be late."

"I won't," I promise, rising from my chair.

As I walk back to my desk, my hand instinctively moves to my stomach, though there's nothing to feel yet. Nine weeks pregnant. A baby who's going to need health insurance, a college fund, a stable home. A baby that will depend entirely on me.

Guilt washes over me as I think about canceling on Wes. He asked me to go to this home game last week on our date—said he's never asked someone to attend for him before. I grab my phone from my cubicle and step into an open conference room, closing the door behind me for privacy.

I dial Wes's number, my heart racing with nerves. He answers on the second ring.

"Hey there, sexy Ladybug," he purrs into the phone, his voice low and intimate. "Still feeling me between your legs?"

Despite everything, I can't help but smile, heat rushing to my cheeks. "Wes," I whisper, glancing at the glass walls to make sure no one is walking by. "You can't say things like that when I'm at work."

His laugh is warm and rich in my ear. "That's half the fun. I bet you're blushing right now."

My smile fades as I remember why I called. "Listen, I need to talk to you about tonight."

There's a brief pause on the line. "You don't sound excited. What's up?"

Taking a deep breath, I twist the hem of my blouse between my fingers.

"About tonight... I can't make it to the game."

There's silence. "Oh." Just a single syllable.

"Wheeler just called me into his office," I explain quickly. "He wants to discuss the senior designer position tonight— over drinks. I really need this promotion Wes."

"Amelia, it's okay," he interrupts, his voice softening. "I understand. This is important for your career."

"Are you sure?" I ask, relief washing over me even as guilt continues to gnaw. "I was looking forward to watching you play—in person."

"There will be other games," he says, though I can hear the slight disappointment beneath his reassurance. "This is a big opportunity for you. You should go."

I let out a breath I didn't realize I was holding. "Thank you for understanding. I'm sorry."

"Don't apologize."

I continue to bite my lip, already missing him despite having seen him this morning. "Do you want to stay the night tonight? After your game? I should be done with my meeting by nine, and we could—"

"Actually," he cuts in, "there's usually team parties— celebrations—after the games that run pretty late."

"Oh," I say, my voice small. The disappointment hits harder than I expected. Of course he has team parties. He's a college football star with teammates and a social life that revolves around campus events. Meanwhile, I'm a pregnant widow trying to secure a promotion to support my unborn child.

We're in completely different places in our lives. The reality of this hits me with sudden clarity. He's living the college experience—games, parties, teammates. I'm dealing with pregnancy, a career, and the aftermath of my husband's death.

"Right, of course." I force brightness into my voice.

There's an awkward pause, and I can feel the distance growing between us—not just physical space but life circumstances pulling us in different directions.

"Hey," he says. "What about this weekend? On Saturday, I'm free all day. We could do something then?"

"Yeah, this weekend sounds good."

"Great! I'll text you. And Amelia? Knock 'em dead at that meeting. You've got this."

"Thanks, Wes. Good luck tonight. I'll be cheering for you in spirit."

As soon as I get home, I rush through the door and head straight to my closet. Wheeler's invitation has left me feeling uneasy all afternoon, and I want to appear professional but not like I'm trying too hard. I settle on a navy blue cocktail dress that hits right above the knee—conservative enough for business but still elegant. I add a cream-colored cardigan to soften the look and slip into a pair of sensible heels.

Standing in front of the mirror, I smooth my hands over the fabric, pausing briefly at my stomach. There's no visible change yet, but knowing what's growing inside me makes every decision feel heavier these days.

"You can do this," I whisper to my reflection. "This promotion is for both of you now."

The drive to the Union Club takes fifteen minutes, and I spend it rehearsing what I'll say about my qualifications, my vision for the firm's design direction, and how I plan to bring in new clients. By the time I pull into the parking lot, I'd convinced myself this is strictly business—Wheeler's choice of venue was simply about privacy.

The Union Club's façade is all old-world elegance—dark wood, brass fixtures, and soft lighting. I approach the host, smoothing my dress one more time.

"Welcome to the Union Club," the hostess greets me, her smile practiced and perfect. "Do you have a reservation?"

"Good evening," I say, trying to sound confident. "I'm meeting Mr. Wheeler?"

She smiles warmly. "Of course. Mr. Wheeler and Mr. Marks are already seated. Follow me, please."

Wait—Marks is here too?

Relief washes over me instantly. This isn't some awkward one-on-one meeting after all. It's a legitimate business discussion with both of the firm's partners.

I follow the hostess through the dimly lit dining area, past tables of well-dressed patrons engaged in quiet conversation. The knot in my stomach unravels with each step.

I've been overthinking this entire situation.

Chapter Twenty-Two

Wesley

It's the middle of the fourth quarter, and I'm ready to end this misery.

The scoreboard shows Clemson 42, Dalton 10. Humiliating doesn't begin to cover it.

I wipe sweat from my brow and try to focus as Coach calls in the next play. My receivers look defeated, our offensive line is getting bulldozed, and I feel the weight of the stadium's disappointment pressing down on me. This was supposed to be my showcase game—scouts from at least six NFL teams are in the stands watching me implode.

I've thrown three interceptions tonight. Three. I haven't thrown that many in a single game since freshman year. My timing is off, my reads are sloppy, and my throws lack their usual precision.

"Dragon-right, Falcon-sweep on two," Coach's voice crackles in my helmet.

I nod and jog back to the huddle, where I'm met with

exhausted, frustrated faces. These guys deserve better than what I'm giving them tonight.

"Dragon-right, Falcon-sweep on two," I repeat, trying to inject some energy into my voice. "Let's make something happen here."

We break the group, and I scan the defense, immediately noticing they're showing blitz. I should call an audible, change the play, but my mind is foggy. All I can think about is the empty seat in section 103, row F—the seat that was supposed to hold Amelia before she canceled on me to go to whatever meeting she's having with her boss.

I don't want to admit it, but it's been eating at me all night. A "meeting" after work hours? Something about it feels off. But I don't dare say that to her and sound like an insecure "boyfriend" who doesn't trust her. I do trust her. It's him I don't trust.

But what do I know about corporate culture or what's normal in the business world? Maybe this is standard practice —discussing career advancement over drinks. Maybe I'm being paranoid because I'm twenty-one and she's... not.

"Hut, hut, hike!"

The football snaps to me and I drop back, my eyes scan downfield for an open receiver. The defense collapses around me, but somehow our offensive line holds just enough. I spot James breaking free on the right side, a sliver of daylight between him and the Clemson cornerback.

I launch the ball without thinking, muscle memory taking over where my distracted mind has failed all night. The spiral is tight; the trajectory perfect. For once, everything clicks. James leaps, snags it, and pirouettes away from the defender before sprinting the final twenty yards to the end zone.

Touchdown, Dalton University. Fucking finally.

My teammates erupt, slapping my helmet and shouting as we jog toward the sideline. Coach gives me a quick nod—the closest thing to approval I'll get tonight. The stadium announcer's voice booms overhead, and the crowd cheers, but it feels hollow. Empty.

I should be pumped. I should be fired up, ready to mount a comeback, no matter how unlikely. Instead, I feel nothing. This meaningless touchdown when we're down by twenty-five points is just that—meaningless.

Too little, too late.

Coach kicks the locker in frustration; my teammates and I keep our heads down in disappointment.

"This is unacceptable!" His voice booms through the room, echoing off the metal lockers. His face is flushed red with anger as he paces in front of us. "Forty-two to seventeen. Forty-two to seventeen! That's not just a loss; it's an embarrassment to this program!"

I stare at the floor, unable to meet his eyes or those of my teammates. The burden of this defeat sits squarely on my shoulders.

"Our execution was sloppy. Our defense couldn't stop a nosebleed. And our offense—" Coach stops directly in front of me, his voice dropping to something more terrifying than his yelling. "Our offense looked like they'd never seen a football before."

The silence in the locker room is suffocating. I can feel every pair of eyes flickering between Coach and me.

"I take full responsibility," I say, finally looking up. My voice sounds steadier than I feel. "My head wasn't in the game. Those interceptions were on me. The team deserved better leadership tonight."

Coach's expression softens slightly, but his disappointment is still palpable. "Damn right they did."

"Coach, I missed some key blocks," Jason speaks up from beside me.

"Coach, it was my coverage that fell apart in the second quarter," Tyler adds, his voice low but determined. "I lost track of their receiver on that big play."

"And I fumbled on the thirty-yard line," Rodney chimes in, rubbing his neck. "That was a momentum killer."

One by one, my teammates start speaking up, each taking blame for some aspect of our humiliating loss. I know exactly what they're doing—trying to shoulder some of the burden, distribute the weight of this failure. It's what good teammates do. But they shouldn't have to cover for me.

Coach holds up his hand, silencing the room. His eyes sweep across all of us, lingering on me for a beat longer than the others.

"Enough," he says, his voice calmer now but no less intense. "There's plenty of blame to go around. This isn't just about Sullivan's interceptions, missed blocks or blown coverage. This is about showing up prepared—mentally and physically." He taps his temple for emphasis. "And too many of you left your heads somewhere else tonight."

The truth in his words stings worse than any shouting could have.

He lets the statement hang in the air for a moment before his shoulders slump. "Hit the showers. We'll break down the film tomorrow morning. I know it's Saturday but I want you here at 6 AM sharp."

Without another word, he turns and walks out, the door closing heavily behind him.

The locker room erupts into subdued conversations as guys start peeling off their uniforms. I sit alone on the bench in front of my locker, still in my sweat-soaked uniform, helmet resting between my feet. My teammates have given me space, sensing I need time to process this disaster.

I rake my fingers through my damp hair. What the hell happened out there? I've never played this poorly, not even in high school when I was just learning the position.

Three interceptions. Countless missed opportunities. Plays I could make in my sleep suddenly beyond my grasp.

And I know exactly why.

Because instead of focusing on defensive schemes and receiver routes, my mind kept drifting to Amelia. To the empty seat in section 103. To the shady-sounding "business meeting" that couldn't wait until Monday morning.

"Get it together, Sullivan," I mutter to myself, slamming my fist against the metal locker. The sharp pain feels appropriate—a physical manifestation of my mental state.

This isn't you. You're Wesley Sullivan, star quarterback. Team captain. Future NFL draft pick. You win. You don't let personal distractions derail your game.

I wanted Amelia here tonight. I wanted to share my world, my passion, with her. But her absence just reminds me that we don't owe each other anything. We're not together, not officially. *We're just having fun, right?*

But that's a lie. We're not just having fun. At least, not for me.

The truth hits me like a blindside tackle, knocking the air from my lungs. I don't just want her at my games. I want her in my life—fully, completely, officially. I want to introduce her as my girlfriend, not my neighbor. I want to plan weekends around our schedules, take her to team events, and build something real.

Suddenly, the pressure or expectations I didn't want to put on the relationship because she's a recent widow, I now want defined. I need to know what this is.

"Fuck," I mutter, yanking off my jersey.

I stand abruptly, startling James, who's changing at the locker next to mine.

"You good, man?" he asks, concern etched across his face.

"No," I admit. "But I will be."

Chapter Twenty-Three

AMELIA

Wheeler stands first to greet me. "There she is. The woman of the hour."

Graham Marks, the other partner, remains seated, his expression unreadable, though I notice his eyes flicker down my dress before they return to his wine.

I smile anyway. That's what you do in rooms like this.

Marks is a fit, silver-haired architect in his early 60s, with a wardrobe that leans toward smart casual versus Wheeler's tailored suit look. Though age has added some lines to his face, there's a simple charm in his smile and an understated confidence that comes from years of success.

"Hope you're ready to celebrate," Wheeler says as he pulls out my chair.

My stomach flips. Was this *it*? The promotion?

"Wine?" Marks asks, already pouring before I can stop him.

"Sure. Thanks," I say, knowing I won't be drinking now that I know I'm pregnant. But I'm being polite.

Marks leans forward, forearms on the table. His tone drops slightly. "We've been watching you, you know."

"The Barlowe presentation was exceptional," Wheeler continues, his eyes never leaving mine. "Truly outstanding work. The way you transformed their outdated concept into something contemporary yet timeless? That's precisely the kind of vision we need at the senior level."

I try not to let my excitement show too obviously, but my heart is racing. "Thank you. I put a lot of thought into that redesign."

"It shows," Marks adds, swirling his wine. "Your attention to detail, the way you anticipated the client's needs before they even articulated them—that's rare, Amelia. Very rare."

Wheeler nods in agreement. "We've been discussing your trajectory. You've consistently exceeded expectations since you joined the firm."

"And your client retention rate is the highest in the company," Marks adds. "People request you specifically. That speaks volumes."

I take a small sip of water, leaving the wine untouched. "I appreciate that. I truly try to build relationships with clients that go beyond the immediate project."

I lean forward, feeling a surge of confidence. "I've been developing some ideas that I think could benefit the firm."

Marks's eyebrows rise with interest. "Oh? Tell."

"I've noticed a gap in our portfolio—sustainable luxury designs. The market is shifting that way, especially with younger affluent clients who want high-end aesthetics without the environmental guilt." I pause, gauging their reactions. Both men are watching me intently, so I continue. "I've already drafted concepts for an eco-conscious luxury line that could position us ahead of this trend."

"That's... actually quite insightful," Marks says, sounding genuinely impressed.

Wheeler exchanges a glance with Marks. "You've clearly given this considerable thought." He leans forward, lowering his voice slightly. "We see big things for you. Senior designer is just the beginning."

"The beginning?" I echo.

Wheeler swirls his wine. "You're more than ready, Amelia. You've outpaced everyone in your cohort. Your last presentation to Barlowe—impeccable. Honestly, we think it's time to make things official."

My breath catches. "You mean—"

"Senior architect designer," Marks confirms. "With full project autonomy and a seat in leadership meetings starting next quarter."

All the years of proving myself, of fighting to be taken seriously in rooms that liked me better silent—suddenly worth it.

"I don't know what to say," I say with excitement.

Wheeler raises his glass. "Say yes."

I laugh, slightly stunned, and clink my wine glass to theirs before pretending to take a sip.

Wheeler leans in more. "There's just one thing."

I don't like the way he said that.

"We like to keep leadership close-knit," Wheeler says, gaze steady. "It's about loyalty. Discretion."

I nod slowly, trying to follow. "Of course."

"And sometimes," he adds, resting a hand—warm and

deliberate—on my knee under the table, "we help each other through the hard times."

My body goes still. His hand doesn't move. His thumb strokes a line just above the hem of my dress.

"I lost my wife last year," he says, voice soft. "Work has been... a good distraction. But some nights are harder than others. You must be feeling the same way too."

I gasp under my breath. *Is this really happening?*

"I know exactly what you need, Amelia," Wheeler continues, his voice dropping lower. "We can help each other through this difficult time." His fingers inch higher on my thigh, barely, but enough to make his intention unmistakable.

I glance at Marks, hoping for some sign that this isn't what I think it is, but he's watching with the same unreadable expression, swirling his wine.

"We were just discussing how we can help you. No one should have to shoulder grief alone." Marks says, setting down his glass. "We'll take care of you."

The subtext is crystal clear. My promotion—my future— is being offered with strings attached. Strings that lead directly to their bedrooms.

"I appreciate the concern," I say carefully, my voice steadier than I feel. "But I'm managing my grief fine."

I feel sick. I think of Wes, probably on the field right now, completely unaware that I'm sitting here being propositioned by men twice my age who hold my career in their hands.

"What exactly would happen if I decline?" I ask, and I'm surprised my voice is steady despite the queasiness climbing up my throat. I move my leg away from Wheeler's touch.

The air in the room changes instantly. Wheeler's hand is withdrawn from my knee, but the warmth of where it had been lingers like a brand. His expression shifts subtly, the friendly mentor mask slipping just enough to reveal something harder underneath.

"Decline?" Wheeler repeats the word as if testing an unfamiliar taste. "Well, it would be disappointing."

Marks sets his wineglass down with a precise click against the table. "I think what he means is that the senior designer position requires someone who's... fully committed."

"To what exactly?" I press, anger beginning to burn through my shock. "Sleeping with my bosses?"

Wheeler's smile doesn't reach his eyes. "I think you're misinterpreting our intentions. We're simply offering you support during a difficult time."

"Support that comes with your hand on my thigh?" The words tumble out.

"Don't make this difficult. You're not a kid. You know how the world works," Marks says.

I stare at him. At both of them. They looked like they belonged on some glossy brochure for 'successful men who mentor the next generation.' But the way they were looking at me now? It was all leverage. Entitlement wrapped in power.

Wheeler lowers his voice. "We've got a suite next door. Two bedrooms. You wouldn't have to stay the night. Just... unwind. Have a drink or two. Celebrate."

My stomach turns. "You mean sleep with you."

I shift in my seat, trying to process what's happening. Wheeler's eyes flicker to Marks, and some unspoken communication passes between them.

"Let me be more direct," Wheeler says, leaning closer. "You can fuck either of us. Or both, if you're feeling... ambitious. The other is not opposed to simply watching." His lips curl into what I suppose he thinks is a seductive smile. "You make us happy, and we'll make you happy with a continued mutually beneficial arrangement. If you come with us to the hotel room tonight—we'll announce your promotion tomorrow."

My mouth goes dry. The restaurant suddenly feels too hot, too small. I glance around, wondering if anyone can hear this conversation, but the other patrons continue sipping their drink, having discussions, oblivious to what's happening at our table.

"It's a generous offer," Marks adds. "Many women would be grateful for the opportunity."

"Many women?" I repeat, finding my voice. "How many of your employees have you propositioned like this?"

Wheeler shrugs, unbothered by my question. "That's not relevant."

Marks folds his arms. "You're talented, Amelia. No one's denying that. But the senior designer position comes with trust, access... loyalty. It's not just about design."

I swallow hard. "I thought it *was* about my work."

Marks shrugs. "It's about how well you play the game. You scratch our backs—"

"And you'll ruin my career if I don't?" I ask, finally saying it out loud.

Marks sighs, as if I were being unreasonable. "You're not irreplaceable. But yes, we can have you blackballed from the industry."

I stand abruptly, my chair scraping loudly against the floor. "I quit."

Wheeler's expression shifts from shock to amusement, like I've just told the most ridiculous joke.

"Sit, Amelia," he says, his voice hardening. "You're being dramatic."

"I'm not being dramatic. I'm refusing to be sexually harassed by my employer." My hands are shaking, but my voice remains steady. "Consider this my resignation."

Marks let out a low laugh. "Not before you finish the Barlowe project."

I stare at him in disbelief. "Excuse me?"

"Your contract," Wheeler explains, all business now. "It specifically states you're required to complete all active projects before termination. Barlowe is three months from the deadline, and you're the lead designer."

"This is unbelievable," I say, my voice rising. "You propositioned me, threatened my career, and now you expect me to keep working for you?"

"It's not what we expect," Marks says coldly. "It's what you're legally obligated to do unless you want a lawsuit for breach of contract. And notification to every design firm in the tri-state area about your... unprofessional behavior. Which we'll also do if you breathe a single word about this conversation."

I stare at them both, rage and disgust burning through me like wildfire. The sheer audacity—to trap me with a contract after propositioning me. I notice my untouched wine glass, and for one dangerous second, I consider throwing it in Wheeler's smug face. But I remember I'm not one of those Real Housewives.

Instead, I grab my clutch from the table and turn on my heel.

"This conversation is over," I say.

I walk away, my heels clicking against the hardwood floor

with each determined step. Behind me, I hear Wheeler's voice, loud enough for nearby diners to turn their heads.

"See you Monday, Nine sharp!"

I don't turn back. My face burns with humiliation as I push through the heavy oak doors and into the cool night air. Only when I reach my car, do I allow myself to lean against the door, knees weak, breath coming in short gasps.

Three months. Three more months of working for men who just tried to coerce me into sex for a promotion. My stomach churns, and for a moment, I think I might be sick right here in the car.

I sit here for a long while, hands gripping the steering wheel so tightly my knuckles turn white. My whole body is shaking—with rage, with fear, with the sudden understanding of how vulnerable I am.

Tears pricked at the corners of my eyes. I fight them back, taking deep, shuddering breaths until the tightness in my chest eases slightly. My hand drifts instinctively to my still-flat stomach.

"It's okay," I whisper into the quiet of my car. "We're going to be alright."

The words hang in the air, meant for the tiny life growing inside me, but I hear the uncertainty in my voice.

Am I trying to convince the baby or myself? Both, probably.

Because right now, nothing feels alright. My career—the one I've worked so hard to build—is imploding around me. The men I thought were mentors see me as nothing more than a potential conquest.

"We'll figure this out," I continue, my voice steadier now. "I promise."

Chapter Twenty-Four

AMELIA

The tears don't stop coming during the drive home. I've cried so much this past hour that my face feels raw, my throat scratchy from sobbing. The humiliation of what happened at the Union Club keeps replaying in my mind—Wheeler's hand on my thigh, Marks's cold eyes watching me, their casual assumption that I would trade my body for a promotion.

And now I'm trapped—legally obligated to keep working for them for three more months while carrying a secret pregnancy no one knows about.

Wes. I glance at the clock on my dashboard. His game must be over by now. I wonder if they won, if he played well, if he's celebrating with his teammates while I'm falling apart.

I pull into my driveway and cut the engine with trembling hands. The house is dark and empty, a perfect reflection of how I feel inside. I lean forward, flipping down the visor to check my appearance in the tiny mirror.

God, I look terrible—exactly like what I am—a pregnant

widow who just had her career implode in front of her. My eyes are puffy and swollen, mascara smudged despite my attempts to clean it up.

With a deep breath, I grab my purse and step out of my Beetle, pressing the lock button on my key fob. The familiar chirp feels absurdly normal on a night when everything else has fallen apart.

The porch light is off—I forgot to leave it on this afternoon. I fumble with my key in the darkness, struggling to find the—

"Amelia."

I nearly drop my keys as a voice materializes from the darkness. My heart leaps into my throat as I whirl around, a startled gasp escaping my lips.

He's sitting in the corner of my porch, his large frame folded into the wicker chair I rarely use. In the shadows, I can barely make out his features, but there's no mistaking his voice.

"Jesus! You scared me half to death." My hand flies to my chest, feeling my racing heart beneath my fingertips.

He stands, moving into the faint glow from the streetlight. His expression is unreadable, but his eyes travel down my body, taking in my navy dress and heels.

"That's a nice outfit for a business meeting," he says, his voice oddly flat.

I shift uncomfortably, suddenly aware of how I must appear—dressed up for men who tried to coerce me into sleeping with them. The tears I thought I'd exhausted threaten to return.

"Why are you sitting here in the dark?" I ask.

He approaches, and now I can see his face clearly.

"Waiting for you," he says simply.

"I thought you'd be at the after party," I say, trying to hide the tremor in my voice while focusing on the lock.

"No party tonight. We lost." He steps closer, his eyes narrowing as he studies my face in the dim porch light. "Amelia, have you been crying?"

I turn away quickly, jamming my key into the lock with shaking hands. The last thing I want is for him to see me like this—mascara streaked down my cheeks, eyes puffy and red. I push the door open and step inside, leaving it open behind me as an unspoken invitation.

"What happened?" he asks, following me in and closing the door softly behind him. His voice is gentle but insistent.

I drop my purse on the entryway table and kick off my heels, buying myself time before I have to face him. The dress that had felt so appropriate now feels like a costume— something I put on to play a part I never should have agreed to.

"I didn't get the promotion," I say, blinking hard, trying to hold the tears at bay.

His expression shifts, his brows furrowing. "Wait, that doesn't make sense. Why would Wheeler ask you to meet him specifically to discuss the promotion if he wasn't going to give it to you?"

I meet his eyes, giving him a look that I hope conveys everything without me having to say the words aloud. One that says: *you know exactly why.*

Understanding dawns on his face, quickly replaced by anger. His jaw clenches and his hands ball into fists at his sides.

"That son of a bitch," he growls, his voice low and dangerous. "He didn't even talk about the promotion, did he?"

"Oh, he talked about it, Marks too," I say bitterly, moving toward the kitchen. I could use water. My throat is raw from crying. "They made it very clear what I'd need to do to get it."

He follows me, his footsteps heavy against the hardwood. When I turn from the sink with my glass, his face is thunderous.

"I'll kill them," he says.

"No, you won't," I reply, taking a long sip. The cool water soothes my throat. "I just need to figure out what to do now."

"Tell me what happened," he says, his voice gentler now but still tight with anger. He leans against the counter, his large frame tense like a coiled spring.

I set down my glass and take a shaky breath. "They made it sound like a dream come true, exactly what I've been working toward." I laugh bitterly. "They told me the promotion was mine."

He watches me intently, his eyes never leaving my face.

"Then Wheeler put his hand on my knee," I continue, the memory making me feel sick all over again. "Started talking about how he lost his wife and how they could help me through hard times."

His knuckles turn white as he grips the edge of the counter. "Both of them?"

I nod, wrapping my arms around myself. "Marks suggested we move the meeting to a hotel room." The tears fall again despite my best efforts. "Said if I went there with them tonight, slept with one or both, they'd announce my promotion tomorrow."

"Jesus Christ," he mutters.

"I tried to quit—right there. But they reminded me I'm legally required to finish the Barlowe project or they could take me to court for breach of contract. If I attempted to resign before completing it, they'd make sure I never worked in architecture again. They have connections to every major firm in the state. They'd blackball me completely."

Wes takes a step toward me, his eyes blazing. "They can't do that."

"They can, and they will," I reply, my voice breaking. "I'm completely trapped."

His expression is suddenly curious. "Wait—Barlowe? As in Russell Barlowe, the basketball player?"

I nod, wiping at my tears with the back of my hand. "You know him?"

"I've never met him, but I definitely know who he is. Everyone does—NBA legend."

"That's him," I confirm, leaning back against the counter. "His wife wanted to build this incredible mountain retreat, and I designed it. It's the biggest project I've ever handled." I drop my head into my hands. "And now I'm stuck there until it's done, which could be months, working for men who..." I can't even finish the sentence.

"Amelia," he says softly.

"My career is over," I whisper, fresh tears spilling down my cheeks. "Everything I've worked for, all those years of school, the late nights, the student loans... it's all for nothing."

He closes the distance between us and wraps his strong arms around me, pulling me against his chest. I collapse into his embrace, burying my face against his shoulder as the tears

I've been suppressing finally break free. His hand cups the back of my head, fingers threading through my hair as he holds me close.

"We'll figure this out," he murmurs, his breath warm against my ear. "I promise you, we'll find a way through this."

There's such conviction in his voice that for a moment, I almost believe him. I let myself be comforted by his strength, by the steady rhythm of his heartbeat against my cheek, by the gentle way his thumb strokes circles at the nape of my neck.

After a few minutes, I pull back. "Your game," I say, suddenly remembering. "You said you lost. What happened?"

His eyes drop away from mine, his jaw tightening. "It doesn't matter."

"It does to me," I insist, placing my palm against his cheek to guide his gaze back to me. "Tell me."

He sighs, his shoulders slumping slightly. "I was distracted. Kept making bad reads, missing open receivers."

"Why were you distracted?" I ask, studying his face. There's something he's not telling me.

He runs a hand through his hair and looks away, but I notice the muscle working in his jaw. "Because you weren't there," he finally admits, his voice soft. "I kept looking for you in the stands. I know it's stupid."

My heart constricts. "Wes, I'm so sorry. I wish I hadn't gone to that meeting. I should have been there for you instead."

"No, don't do that." He takes my hands in his, squeezing gently. "It's not your fault. This is my issue to work through. I've got to learn to focus regardless of who's watching."

But I can see it in his eyes—the way they are unable to quite meet mine, how his shoulders remain tense. This isn't just about missing a face in the crowd. There's something deeper here.

"Are you sure that's all it is?" I press, stepping closer. "Because it seems like you're in your head about."

His expression shifts, vulnerability flashing across his features before he can mask it. "Maybe I am," he confesses. "The truth is—" His voice catches, his eyes searching mine with an intensity that makes my breath hitch. "I've been trying to keep things casual, to give you space after everything you've been through, but I can't anymore."

I reach up, tracing the firm line of his jaw with my fingertips. "What are you saying?"

He captures my hand, pressing a gentle kiss to my palm that sends shivers racing up my arm. His eyes never leave mine as he speaks.

"I'm saying I want more than this, Amelia. I don't want to just be the guy next door or some casual fling." His voice deepens, grows more certain with each word. "I want to be with you—really be with you. I want to take you to dinner and hold your hand in public. I want to bring you to my games and introduce you to my family."

My heart skips a beat as his eyes lock with mine.

"I want us to be together. I know the timing is complicated. I know people will talk. But I don't care about any of that." He takes a shaky breath, his eyes so vulnerable it makes my chest ache. "I'm in love with you, Ladybug."

The raw honesty, the vulnerability in his voice—it's everything I've been afraid to hope for. Everything I want too. But there's something he doesn't know. Something that changes everything.

"I think I have been since the first time I saw you

unloading boxes from your car when you moved in," he continues. "And these past weeks, getting to know you, being with you... it's only made me more—"

I cut him off. The words tumble out before he can say anymore. Not that I don't want to hear them, but I might change my mind in saying what I need to say. "I'm pregnant."

Chapter Twenty-Five

WESLEY

"You're..." I start, then stop, my voice barely above a whisper. "Pregnant?"

Amelia nods, her lips trembling, eyes filling with fresh tears. "Nine weeks. I found out a few days ago."

The room seems to tilt on its axis. Pregnant. Her words echo in my head as if I'm underwater. Nine weeks. That means it's Nick's. Of course it's his.

Wait... what does this mean for us?

I take a step back, my hand falling away from hers. The timing hits me with brutal clarity—nine weeks means before Halloween, before Nick died, before she found out he was cheating. Before us.

"It's Nick's," I say, though it's not really a question. My voice sounds strange to my own ears, hollow and distant.

She nods, tears streaming down her face now. "I'm keeping it," she whispers, her hand moving protectively to her still-flat stomach. "I know the timing is terrible, and this changes things, but I have to—"

"Pregnant," I repeat, the word feeling foreign to my tongue. I stare at her stomach, trying to process that there's a life growing inside her. Nick's baby. The woman I love is carrying her dead husband's child.

My mind races through what this means—for her, for us, for any future we might have had. She's pregnant—keeping it. A child that will always connect her to him.

My legs feel rooted to the floor, but something inside me shifts. The initial shock subsides, making room for a different feeling—one I can't quite name yet. I take a deep breath and move toward her again, closing the distance I'd put between us.

"Can I..." My voice catches. I clear my throat and try again. "Can I touch you?"

My hand hovers uncertainly in the space between us, drawn toward her stomach by some inexplicable pull. I know there's nothing to feel yet—no bump, no movement—but something in me needs this connection, this physical acknowledgment of what she just told me.

Her eyes widen, a fresh tear slipping down her cheek. For a moment, I think I've said something wrong—crossed some invisible boundary. But then her expression softens, and she gives a small nod.

She takes my hand in hers and guides it to her belly. She puts her hand over mine, holding it there.

I press my palm gently against her, feeling the warmth of her body through the fabric of her dress. There's no physical evidence of the baby growing inside, but knowing it's there makes this moment feel sacred. My thumb moves in a small circle over the spot where her child is developing.

"I want this to work, Wes," she whispers, her voice breaking. "I want us to work. But I understand if you—"

A tiny life, innocent and unaware of all the complications surrounding its existence.

"I'm not going anywhere," I say, surprising myself with how much I mean it. "This doesn't change how I feel about you."

Her eyes shine with hope and uncertainty. "Are you sure? This is... this isn't what you signed up for."

"I'm sure." The words come out stronger than I expected, with certainty. "I meant what I said about falling for you. A baby doesn't change that."

A tremulous smile breaks across her face. "Really?" She whispers, as if afraid that speaking too loudly might shatter this moment.

"Really," I affirm, cupping her cheek with my free hand, the other still resting on her stomach. "I'm in this—all of it."

Tears spill from her eyes, but these differ from the ones she shed earlier. These glisten with joy, with relief, with something that looks like hope. They stream down her cheeks as she leans into my touch.

"I thought you'd walk away," she confesses, her voice catching. "I've been terrified to tell you. I kept thinking about your future, the NFL, everything you have ahead of you. Why would you want to be tied to someone with all this baggage?"

I brush aside her tears with my thumb. "Because you're worth it," I say, pressing my forehead against hers. "You're worth everything."

Amelia looks at me, her eyes still shimmering with tears, but something shifts in her expression. Her fingers grip my shirt tighter, like she's anchoring herself to me.

"I never expected this," she whispers and smiles through her tears. "I found something I never thought I'd have again—maybe something I never really had before. You gave me friendship when I needed it most. You respected me when I felt worthless. And then, somehow..." Her voice catches. "It turned into love."

My heart feels like it might burst. I pull her closer, wrapping my arms around her.

"We're going to face challenges," I tell her honestly. "People will talk. They'll judge. The timing isn't great. And with the NFL draft coming, I could end up anywhere in the country, but wherever it is, I want you there with me—if that's what you want too," I say, holding her close. "I'm not going to pretend this will be easy. And I can't promise I'll be perfect at this father-figure thing."

She pulls back slightly, her eyes searching mine.

"I've never been around babies much," I admit. "I don't know the first thing about changing diapers or warming bottles or whatever else infants need. But I want to learn. We can get those parenting books they have, and figure it out together."

A smile breaks through her tears, and then—unexpectedly—she laughs. It's a beautiful sound, bright and genuine amid everything.

"What?" I ask, smiling despite myself.

"Just picturing you with your big football hands trying to change a tiny diaper while reading Parenting for Dummies or whatever..." she says, wiping her eyes. "It's a good image."

I chuckle, relief washing through me at seeing her smile. "Hey, I have excellent hand-eye coordination. I'll master diaper changing in no time."

Her eyes are bright with a mixture of hope and determination. "I'll go anywhere with you, Wes. Wherever the NFL sends you," she says, her eyes shining with conviction. "Especially since I'll be jobless soon anyway. As soon as the Barlowe project is done, I'm out. I'll start fresh in a new city."

A sudden wave of protectiveness surges through me. Wheeler & Marks—those bastards. The way they tried to manipulate her, to use her talent, then demand more. My jaw clenches at the thought.

I might have a plan. But I hesitate to tell her what I'm thinking, not wanting to get her hopes up. The idea had come to me the moment she mentioned Russell Barlowe, but it's a long shot at best. I need to make a few calls.

"We'll figure everything out as it comes," I say, feeling oddly calm despite the enormity of what we're discussing. "One day at a time, right?"

Amelia nods, looking relieved. Her shoulders relax as if a weight has been lifted.

A sudden thought occurs to me, and I smile. "Hey, is the baby craving anything specific? I could order us a pizza, and we could watch more of those Real Housewives episodes you love. Take our minds off everything for a while."

Her face lights up immediately, eyes widening with excitement as she nods enthusiastically. "You mean, the Real Housewives show, you love?" she jokes, the most animated I've seen all night, a complete transformation from the broken woman who walked through the door earlier. "Pizza sounds amazing right now."

"Pepperoni and sausage?" I ask, already reaching for my phone.

"And extra cheese," she adds, wiping away the last of her tears. "Definitely extra cheese."

As I place our order, I watch her move around the living room, turning on lamps and grabbing the remote. There's a new lightness to her movements, as if our conversation has freed her from some invisible burden. She catches me looking and smiles—a genuine smile.

I'm struck by how different this night has turned out from how it began. Just hours ago, I was waiting on her porch, heart heavy from the game, worried about where things stood between us. Then she showed up, devastated from that awful meeting, and now...

Now we're planning our future together—with a baby.

I look at her, curled up on the couch, laughing at something ridiculous happening on the TV.

I'm excited about the possibility stretching before us. The woman I've wanted for so long is finally mine, and I'm about to become a father figure to her child. Not just any child—Nick's child. There's something poetic about it, in a way. The guy who never appreciated what he had, and me, who will treasure what he left behind.

"Thirty minutes," I say, joining her on the couch.

She immediately curls against me, and I wrap an arm around her shoulders and pull her closer.

My brothers are going to have a field day with this news. I can already picture Luke's raised eyebrows and Chase's stunned expression.

They'll probably think I've lost my mind.

Chapter Twenty-Six

AMELIA

"Hello Nick," I say to his gravestone with a sigh.

The cemetery is peaceful at this time of day. Golden light filters through the oak trees, casting dappled shadows across the manicured lawn. I kneel, my knees pressing into the soft earth in front of his headstone. His is still recent enough that the soil hasn't fully settled. The grass is just beginning to grow over where they buried him. The polished granite gleams in the sunlight, his name etched permanently into the stone: *Nicholas James Campbell. Beloved husband. Son. Friend.*

I place the bouquet of white roses at the base of the headstone, arranging them carefully so they fan out neatly against the dark granite. White for respect, for peace.

"I don't know why I'm here," I continue, my voice barely above a whisper. The cemetery is empty except for an elderly man several rows away, tending to a grave with careful attention. "Part of me still can't believe you're gone. Part of me remains angry."

My fingers trace the dates on the stone. So young. Despite

everything, it's still unfair that his life was cut so short. The wind rustles through the trees, sending a few early autumn leaves spiraling down around me.

"We had good times," I admit, remembering our honeymoon in Bali. Those two weeks of bliss, where we'd walked hand-in-hand along white sand beaches, swam in crystal-clear waters, and made love in our private villa overlooking the ocean. We were so young, so hopeful. I close my eyes, letting the memories wash over me.

"Remember high school? Those were the best times for us, weren't they?" I say, feeling a strange peace as I admit this aloud. "Before the pressures of adulthood. Before expectations. We'd drive around in your beat-up Camaro, windows down, music blasting. Everything seemed possible then."

I trace patterns in the dirt beside his grave, organizing my thoughts.

"I don't think you were ready to get married, Nick. Not really." The words feel liberating as they leave my lips. "Looking back, I believe you proposed because it was what everyone expected. Your parents had been dropping hints since junior year of high school. Mine weren't much better."

A squirrel darts across a nearby headstone, pausing to look at me before scampering up a tree. I smile faintly at the interruption.

"We rushed into it, didn't we? Following that perfect timeline. You were still figuring out who you were—but me— I knew I always wanted to be an architect."

A butterfly passes by and I follow it till it lands on a gravestone a few feet away.

"I wish I knew exactly where it went wrong between us.

I've spent so many nights replaying our marriage, looking for the turning point. Was it when you started staying late at the office? When I buried myself in my designs? Maybe it was always there, this disconnect, and we just didn't want to see it." I sigh, plucking a blade of grass from beside the headstone. "But I realize it doesn't matter. I'll never know the full truth, and honestly, it wouldn't change anything if I did."

The wind picks up, rustling through the oak leaves above me. It feels cleansing somehow, like it's carrying away the weight of unanswered questions.

"All I can do is move forward. That's what I'm trying to do, Nick." I take a deep breath, my hand instinctively moving to my still-flat stomach. "There's something else you should know. I'm pregnant. It's yours."

The words hang in the air between us—between me and a slab of granite that can't respond. Part of me had been hoping that saying it aloud here would make it feel more real, more resolved. Instead, it just emphasizes the strangeness of my situation—telling my dead husband about the kid he'll never meet.

"I'm keeping the baby," I go on, my voice "I've thought about it a lot, and despite everything that has occurred, this baby deserves a chance. Our child deserves to be loved."

A bird calls from a nearby tree, the sound breaking the stillness of the moment.

"I promise you this," I say, my voice steadier now. "No matter what happens between us—between my memory of you and the reality I discovered—I will never speak ill of you to our child. They deserve better than that."

The breeze stirs the roses I've placed near the bottom of his headstone, and I adjust them gently.

"My feelings toward you will probably change day by day for a long time. Some days I'll remember the good. Other days, I'll remember finding those messages, those pictures..."

I swallow hard, willing myself not to cry. This isn't about my pain anymore.

"But none of that will touch our child. They'll know you as their father—not the man who broke my heart. That's my promise to you, and to them."

A cloud passes overhead, momentarily dimming the golden light. In the distance, the elderly man stands and makes his way slowly down the path.

"And I should tell you something else," I add. "I've moved on, Nick. It happened faster than I expected, than anyone would think appropriate. But I'm... I'm happy."

The confession feels both wrong and right to say it aloud.

"I think... I think you'd want me to be happy. Despite everything. Maybe I can be loved the way I was meant to be loved. Maybe this is my second chance at happiness." I pause, swallowing past the tightness in my throat. "Even if it's with Wes—one of those 'loud college boys' you were always complaining about."

The memory of Nick rolling his eyes whenever Wes and his brothers were being rowdy next door brings a small smile to my face. He'd always mutter something about "college kids with no respect for working adults." The irony isn't lost on me.

"Wes is... he's a good man. He treats me with an honesty and openness that I didn't know I was missing." My fingers continue to trace patterns in the dirt as I speak. "When I told him I was pregnant with your child, he didn't run. He stayed. He's going to be drafted into the NFL soon." I shake my head.

"And yet he's promised to be there for me—for us. For your baby."

I inhale deeply, feeling something shift inside me—a weight lifting.

"I've been holding onto so much anger. A great deal of resentment and pain. It's been weighing me down. Every morning I wake up and feel it—this heaviness in my chest."

The cemetery remains quiet around me, with only the occasional rustle of leaves breaking the silence. It feels right to be here now, saying these words.

"But I can't carry it anymore. Not with our baby growing inside me. Not with the future I'm trying to build." My voice grows stronger with each word. "So I'm letting you go. I'm letting go of the pain, the betrayal, the sadness—all of it."

I place my palm flat against the stone, feeling its solidity beneath my hand. "I forgive you, Nick. Not because you deserve it, but because I deserve peace. Our child deserves a mother who isn't consumed by the past."

A sense of lightness spreads through me, starting in my chest and flowing outward to my fingertips. It's like something that's been knotted inside me finally unraveling.

"Thank you," I continue, surprising myself with how much I mean it. "For the good times we had. For this baby. Despite everything that happened between us, you've given me a gift."

I stand, brushing the dirt from my knees. The sun breaks through the clouds, warming the spot I'm standing on.

"Goodbye, Nick."

Chapter Twenty-Seven

WESLEY

I crouch low behind a half-busted plywood wall, chest heaving and sweat trickling down the inside of my mask. Paint is splattered all around me, green and yellow, some still fresh and dripping. I peek from the corner. Nothing but trees, a barrel, and maybe—yep. There it was. A flash of red moving close to the edge of the bunker.

"Left side, ten o'clock!" I shout. "Luke, he's flanking."

"I see him."

A burst of paint flies over my head, pelting the wall. I duck, roll, and sprint to the next cover—a stack of rusted barrels—landing hard but intact. "Chase, where are you?"

"Pinned near the tower. Guy in camo's camping me."

Great. Our baby brother, stuck again. But to his credit, he'd been holding that spot like a stubborn badger.

"Hang tight," I say. "We'll pull him."

I flick a signal to Luke from across the clearing. He nods, then stands tall like an idiot and fires a few loud, obvious shots to draw fire. The red-band team takes the bait.

With their focus shifted at Luke, I sprint left, looping around to the back of the tower. I catch movement—just a sliver of fabric—and fire twice. One hit. The guy goes down with a resounding "Damn it!" and raises his marker in surrender.

"Chase, move now!" I call.

He pops out from his hiding spot, with a huge grin like he'd just been rescued from a gorilla. He shoots off three rounds and takes out the camper who'd pinned him before bolting to my side.

"Thanks, bro," he pants.

"Thank Luke. I'm just the distraction to the distraction."

"Move it," Luke yells. "Two left. I'm pushing center."

We charge as a unit—Luke through the middle, Chase and I taking the flanks. Paint flies everywhere, chaos and adrenaline mixing with the sound of rapid fire and shouts. One guy stands and surrenders after Chase nails him in the leg. Luke gets the last one with a clean shot right to the chest—bright blue color exploding across the guy's vest.

The whistle blows.

Game over. We win.

We head back to the staging area, riding the high of our victory. I pull off my mask, running a hand through my sweat-soaked hair as Chase recounts his last shot with theatrical enthusiasm.

"Dude, did you see that last one? Right between the shoulder blades as he was turning. Perfect shot!"

"Yeah, yeah, we were all there," Luke says, but he's grinning too. We're all covered in paint splatters—evidence of near misses and direct hits alike.

I grab our gear bag and lead the way to the parking lot. The afternoon sun is beating down hard now, and my t-shirt sticks to my back as I pop open the Jeep's tailgate.

"Man, I needed that," I say, tossing my mask and marker into the bag. "There's nothing like getting shot at with paint to clear your head."

Luke chuckles, gulping down water from his bottle before passing it to Chase. "Coach would kill you if you got injured though."

I pull my water bottle from the cooler and drain half of it in one go. The cold liquid feels amazing after two hours of running, diving, and ducking. I wipe my mouth with the back of my hand and glance at my brothers.

"Next time we should bring Bebe," I state, tossing the empty bottle back into the cooler. "She's actually pretty good at this. Remember when she got those three guys in a row?"

Luke nods, stretching his arms over his head. "Yeah, give her a couple more weeks to recover."

"What about Amelia?" Chase asks, leaning against the Jeep. "You think she'd be into paintball?"

"No—she's pregnant," I blurt out, without thinking then freeze.

My brothers' heads snap toward me in perfect unison, their eyes wide with shock.

Shit. I didn't mean to say that out loud.

"Uh, what did you say?" Luke asks slowly, his water bottle suspended halfway to his mouth.

I swallow hard, feeling like I just stepped on a landmine. "Yeah, uh, Amelia's pregnant. About nine weeks."

Luke sets his bottle down. "Nine weeks means it's not yours."

"It's Nick's," I confirm. "Wasps' baby."

Chase's mouth hangs open. "Holy shit, Wes."

"Are you okay with that?" Luke asks, his voice carefully neutral, but I notice the concern in his eyes.

I lean back on the Jeep, suddenly feeling the exhaustion from the game catch up with me. "I love her." The words come out more easily than I expected. "She's been dealt a bad hand, and I'm trying to help her through this."

"The baby?" Chase asks.

I shake my head. "Not even that or her dead husband, but the shit her work is putting her through. Her bosses are complete assholes. They dangled this promotion in front of her, then told her she'd need to sleep with them to get it."

"The fuck?" Luke's jaw tightens.

"Yeah, it's bad," I continue. "She's currently designing Russell Barlowe's new home at her firm. Like *the* Russell Barlowe."

Chase's eyes widen. "No way. That's legit."

"It's her biggest project yet. And these assholes are holding it over her head, saying she has to finish it before she can leave."

Luke's expression shifts from shock to something more calculating. "You're thinking of reaching out to Barlowe, aren't you?"

"He's one of us—a Keeper," I admit. "If he knew what was happening to the designer of his wife's dream house, maybe he could help somehow. Pull the project; take it to another firm with Amelia... I don't know."

Chase looks skeptical. "You think an NBA superstar will get involved in some architecture firm's HR problems?"

"It's a long shot, but I'm going to try," I say, shrugging. "What's the worst that can happen? He ignores me? I've got nothing to lose, and she has everything to gain."

Luke crosses his arms, studying me with that analytical look he gets when he's thinking several steps ahead. "Does dad know about any of this? Amelia, the baby, your plan?"

"No," I admit, shifting uncomfortably. "I haven't told him yet."

"You should," Luke says. "Before you go charging in like a knight in shining armor. And Wes," he adds, his expression serious now, "when you meet Barlowe—if you get that far—wear a suit. An actual suit with a tie. Look like someone he'd take seriously, not some frat boy in jeans and a Dalton U hoodie."

Chapter Twenty-Eight

WESLEY

"Mr. Barlowe will see you now."

I follow the woman in her crisp navy pantsuit through what has to be the most impressive home I've ever set foot in. The ceilings soar at least twenty feet high in the entryway, with floor-to-ceiling windows offering panoramic views of Los Angeles. Modern art pieces that probably cost more than my parents' house line the hallway.

"This way, Mr. Sullivan," she says, her heels clicking against the marble floors. Her posture is perfect—back straight, shoulders squared—as she leads me deeper into Russell Barlowe's home.

I adjust my tie nervously. It's the one Luke urged me to put on, claiming it made me look like someone worth listening to.

"Mr. Barlowe rarely takes meetings with college players," she says over her shoulder, her voice professional but not unfriendly. "You must have made quite an impression on him."

I nod, trying to keep my cool despite the nerves fluttering in my stomach. "I appreciate his making the time."

We pass through what resembles a living room with furniture that appears to have never been sat on, then down another hallway lined with framed jerseys and memorabilia from his playing days. Thunder, Rockets, Lakers—the history of his career displayed like a museum exhibit.

The woman stops at a heavy wooden door and knocks twice before opening it. "Mr. Barlowe, Wesley Sullivan Junior," she announces, stepping aside to let me enter.

I walk into what must be Barlowe's home office, though it's larger than most people's living rooms. Floor-to-ceiling bookshelves line one wall, a massive desk dominates the center of the room, and behind it stands the man himself.

Mr. Barlowe rises from his leather chair, and immediately I notice the distinctive silver band on his right hand, the same design I've seen countless times on my father's hand, and soon, I'll have one of my own. The Keeper ring.

"Mr. Sullivan," he says, extending his palm across the desk. "I was intrigued when I got your call."

I shake his hand firmly, feeling the cool metal of his ring press against my fingers.

"Thank you for seeing me, Sir," I manage, attempting to keep my voice steady.

He gestures to the chair across from his desk. "Have a seat. Can I get you anything? Water? Coffee?"

"No thank you, Sir. I'm fine." I straighten in my chair, feeling the fabric of my suit pull across my shoulders. The formal clothes might feel foreign on my body, but I remind myself why I'm here. For Amelia.

Barlowe settles back into his seat, studying me with the intense focus that made him legendary on the court. "So, Wesley Sullivan Junior," he says, emphasizing my name. "What can I do for the son of Wesley Sullivan Senior?"

The mention of my father sends a jolt of confidence through me. Dad might be overbearing and controlling, but his position on The Keeper's council gives me an in that few others would have. Barlowe and my dad are connected through the secret society that's bound our families for generations.

"I'm here about your mountain retreat project," I say, leaning forward slightly. "Specifically about the architect who designed it."

Barlowe's expression shifts subtly—a slight narrowing of the eyes, a tightening around the mouth. "Amelia Campbell," he says. "Talented woman. What about her?"

I take a deep breath. "She's being sexually harassed— forced out of her firm by the partners— Wheeler and Marks," I explain, the words coming easier now. "After your project is complete, they're planning to terminate her because she refused certain... inappropriate demands."

Mr. Barlowe sits straighter in his chair, his eyes narrowing. The casual demeanor disappears instantly, replaced by the intensity he's famous for on the court.

"They told her if she quit before finishing your project or reported the incident, they'd make sure she never worked in architecture again," I state. "With their connections, she's convinced they could do it too."

I swallow hard, thinking about how devastated Amelia was that night, how helpless she felt.

"She doesn't deserve any of this," I continue, my voice growing more passionate. "Her husband recently died in an accident. And she..." I hesitate, unsure if I should share such personal information, but decide honesty is my best approach. "She recently found out she's pregnant with his child."

Barlowe's expression darkens further. He stands abruptly, turning to look out the windows at the view. His hands are clasped tightly behind his back.

"A pregnant widow," he says quietly, almost to himself.

After a long moment, Barlowe turns back to face me, his expression unreadable. "What exactly are you asking of me, Mr. Sullivan?"

I shake my head suddenly unsure. I've been so focused on getting this meeting that I hadn't fully thought through what I wanted from him. "I'm not exactly sure, Sir. Maybe... maybe you could pull your project from the firm?" I suggest, the words coming out less confidently than I'd hoped. "You could continue working with Amelia directly instead."

Barlowe's eyebrows rise. He returns to his chair, leaning back as he studies me. "You realize I've already invested a significant amount of money into this project, don't you? There are signed contracts, schedules, and commitments." He taps his fingers against the desk. "If I pulled the project now, I'd lose out on a lot of money. Not to mention the delays it would cause."

My heart sinks. Of course there are contracts. Of course it's not that simple. I should have known better than to think I could waltz in here with my half-baked plan and save the day.

"I understand," I say, trying to hide my disappointment. "I just thought—"

"I didn't say I wouldn't do it," Barlowe interrupts, his voice measured. "I said it would cost me money. The question is whether it's worth it."

He sits again, studying me with renewed interest. "Tell me something, Wesley. What is Amelia Campbell to you?"

"She's everything to me," I say without hesitation, the words pouring straight from my heart. "I love her."

Barlowe's expression shifts subtly, his eyes narrowing as he surveys me more intently.

"Love," he repeats, testing the word. "That's a strong claim from someone your age."

I don't flinch from his scrutiny. "I know how it sounds. College football player, NFL prospects ahead of me, why would I tie myself to a pregnant widow? But it's the truth. I've been in love with her since she moved in next door two years ago."

Barlowe leans forward, resting his elbows on his desk. "And does she know you're here? That you're asking me to potentially break contracts worth millions of dollars?"

"No," I admit. "She doesn't know. She doesn't even know I'm a Keeper."

"You're taking quite a risk. For someone who doesn't know the full truth about you."

"If I can help her and her baby, then seeing the look on her face will be worth it." I pause, picturing Amelia's face when I tell her she's free from Wheeler & Marks. "She's lost so much already. Her career is the one thing she has left." My hands tremble slightly, so I clench them into fists on my knees where Barlowe can't see them.

Barlowe sighs heavily, running his hand over his close-cropped hair. His expression softens, the intensity in his eyes giving way to something more compassionate.

"No woman should have to go through what she's experiencing," he says quietly. "Especially not in her condition." He taps his Keeper ring thoughtfully against the polished surface of his desk. "Sexual harassment, pregnancy, widowhood—it's a heavy burden for anyone to bear."

My heart leaps with hope. He's considering it. I can see it on his face.

"I appreciate your passion, Wesley. I do," he continues. "But I'd feel more comfortable moving forward with the blessing of The Keepers. Your father's blessing specifically. Wesley Sullivan Senior has considerable influence within our ranks. This isn't just about breaking contracts. There are certain protocols, certain ways we handle these matters within our brotherhood."

The hope that had been building in my chest deflates. "My father doesn't know I'm here either," I admit, my voice lower now. "And honestly, he wouldn't help with this. He'd see it as interfering in business affairs that don't concern us. He's always been about connections and leveraging relationships for gain, not... this."

The silence stretches between us, heavy with disappointment.

"I'm sorry, Wesley," he finally says, his voice genuinely regretful. "Without the backing of a senior Keeper, your father —my hands are tied. There are protocols within our brotherhood that must be respected."

I nod, trying to hide the crushing dejection I feel. "I understand."

"For what it's worth," Mr. Barlowe adds, "I admire what

you're attempting to do for this woman. It speaks to your character."

I stand, straightening my tie—the one Luke insisted would make me look professional. Now it just feels like it's choking me. "Thank you for your time, Sir. I appreciate your hearing me out."

Chapter Twenty-Nine

WESLEY

With plan A failed, I'm moving to plan B.

I drive to my parents' house, my mind racing with a new strategy. I need to try a different approach since Barlowe wouldn't help without my father's blessing. It's time to go straight to the source.

The familiar neighborhood feels smaller, like I've outgrown it. I park in the circular driveway and stay for a moment, gathering my courage. This conversation won't be easy, but I have to try.

I find my dad in the backyard mowing the lawn. He notices me standing there and cuts the power. I move to sit on a patio chair as mom comes out to place three lemonades on the table like a typical Keeper housewife.

"This is a surprise," Dad says, wiping sweat from his brow. "I didn't expect to see you today."

Mom leans in to kiss my cheek. "Everything okay, honey? You look stressed."

"I need to talk to you both," I say, taking a sip of the lemonade. It's tart and sweet, just like she always makes it.

Dad sits across from me, his Keeper ring glinting in the sunlight. "Is this about the NFL scouts?"

"No," I say, setting the glass down with more force than necessary. "It's about a woman."

His eyebrows shoot up, and he exchanges a quick glance with mom. "A woman?" he repeats, leaning forward in his chair.

"I'm in love," I say bluntly, deciding to just put it all out there. "And she's being sexually harassed at her workplace."

Dad's expression immediately shifts, his lips curling into a knowing smirk that makes my blood boil. "Let me guess," he says, his tone condescending. "Some slutty sorority girl who caught wind of your NFL prospects and is now clinging to you for dear life? Using this 'harassment' story to get your sympathy?"

"Wesley!" Mom gasps, but he waves her off.

"What? It's a legitimate concern," Dad continues. "These college girls see dollar signs when they look at Wes. They'll say anything—"

"She's not a college girl!" I snap, feeling my temper flare. "She's older than me—she's an architect with her own career. She doesn't need my money—she has her own."

Dad's eyebrows rise, his smirk fading slightly.

"She's designing Russell Barlowe's mountain retreat right now for Wheeler & Marks," I continue, my voice getting louder. "But those partners are sleazy as hell. They're sexually harassing her, threatening to blackball her from the industry if she doesn't sleep with them. Both of them."

Mom's hand flies to her mouth. "That's terrible."

Dad's expression shifts; his interest is clearly piqued at the mention of Barlowe. "Russell Barlowe? The basketball player?"

"Yes," I say, leaning forward. "I already went to see him, tried to convince him to pull his project from the firm."

"You did what?" Dad's voice rises sharply. "Without consulting me first?"

"I don't need your permission to help someone I care about," I shoot back.

His face darkens. "When it involves approaching another Keeper on your own, you absolutely do," Dad says, rising to his feet. "You've overstepped, Wes. What were you thinking?"

"I was thinking about helping someone I love!" I'm standing now too, my hands clenched at my sides. "Barlowe seems willing to help, but he said he needed your blessing first."

Dad scoffs. "Of course he did. That's protocol—respect between brothers."

"Then give it to him," I plead, my voice softening. "Dad, please. This woman means everything to me. She's pregnant, and her husband just died—"

"Pregnant?" Dad interrupts, his eyes widening. "And widowed? How old is this woman?"

"Thirty," I admit.

Dad throws his hands up. "For God's sake, Wes! A pregnant widow? This is exactly why I need to be involved in these decisions. You're throwing away your future for some—"

"Don't," I warn, my voice dropping dangerously low. "Don't say another word about her."

Mom steps between us. "Wesley, please calm down," she

says, putting a hand on Dad's chest. "This is clearly important to your son."

Dad takes a deep breath, visibly trying to control his temper. "Look, Son. I understand you think you're in love, but you're twenty-one. You have your entire future ahead of you. The NFL. A career. There are plenty of suitable Keeper girls who would—"

"Keeper girls?" I repeat with disbelief.

I've heard enough.

"Where are you going?" Dad calls after me as I stride toward the house. "Wes! We're not finished here!"

I spin around, the anger I've been working to contain finally boiling over. "Why is it so damn hard for you to be supportive?" I shout, my voice echoing across the perfectly manicured lawn. "Why can't you actually listen to what your kids want from their lives instead of trying to force us into your perfect Keeper mold?"

Dad's face reddens. "Don't take that tone with me, young man. I've done everything for this family—"

"No, you've done everything for The Keepers," I say, the words bursting out of me like they've been trapped for years. "Luke doesn't even want to take over the family business! He quit pursuing baseball professionally—for you."

Dad's face goes slack with surprise, clearly not expecting me to bring my brothers into this.

"And Chase?" I continue, unable to stop now that I've started. "You're dictating which law schools he can apply to, which branch he should study. He wants to practice environmental law, dad, not corporate. But that doesn't fit your impeccable Keeper plan, does it?"

"Those decisions are for their own good," Dad sputters.

"And me? I can't even get my own sports agent without you interfering! Coach told me you've been hounding him for the scouts' contact information. What were you planning to do? Call them yourself? Set up meetings without my knowledge? You're controlling us," I yell. "We can be Keepers and still participate in society in our own ways. We can leave our own mark without your micromanagement. The world is changing, Dad. The Keepers need to change with it."

"The traditions have worked for generations," he argues.

"And what about what I want?" I ask, my voice softening as I see genuine confusion in his eyes. "Do you ever think about that?"

Dad's expression falters. Briefly, I see something vulnerable beneath the stern Keeper patriarch facade—uncertainty, maybe even hurt.

"I love you, dad, I do," I state, the words coming from somewhere deep and honest inside me. "But sometimes I wish you would just listen and genuinely want your kids to be happy. It would be nice if you'd support us through everything—our successes and our failures."

Mom steps closer to dad, placing her hand on his arm. His shoulders stiffen, but he doesn't pull away.

"Wes..." he begins, but I shake my head.

"I will be a parent soon," I tell him, my voice steady despite the emotion growing heavier in my chest. "And I swear I'll never treat her child the way you've treated me. I'm going to show up for this kid—really show up. I'll listen. I'll support their dreams, whatever they are."

Dad's face pales. He opens his mouth to speak, but nothing comes out.

"I'll find another way to help Amelia without you."

I turn and walk away, my footsteps heavy against the stone patio. Behind me, I hear mom call my name, but I don't stop. I've said what needed to be said for years now. My chest feels lighter, like I've finally set down a weight I've been carrying since I was a kid.

Dad doesn't follow me. I didn't expect him to either.

As I slide into my car and start the engine, I catch a glimpse of my parents in the rearview mirror. They're still standing in the yard, mom's hand on dad's arm, both of them watching me leave. For a moment, I think I see something like regret on his face, but I'm probably just seeing what I want to see.

I pull out of the driveway, hands gripping the steering wheel so tight my knuckles turn white. Pride swells in my chest for finally standing my ground, for speaking up not just for myself but for my brothers too. It's been a long time coming.

But as the adrenaline fades, reality crashes back in. I'm still no closer to helping Amelia. Barlowe won't act without Dad's blessing, and dad is... well, dad.

Chapter Thirty

AMELIA

"I'm pregnant."

I witness the shock register on the surrounding faces. My mother gasps, her hand flying to her mouth. My father straightens in his seat, his eyebrows shooting up toward his hairline. Nick's parents—Catherine and Robert—sit frozen on the opposite couch, their expressions unreadable at first.

"You're... pregnant?" Mom repeats, her voice barely above a whisper. Her eyes light up, the shock transforming into joy. "I'm going to be a grandmother?"

I nod. "Nine weeks along. The doctor confirmed it."

My father leans forward, his initial surprise melting into a broad smile. "That's wonderful news, sweetheart."

Across from us, Catherine makes a small sound— something between a gasp and a sob. Tears well in her eyes, spilling over before she can wipe them away. Robert puts his arm around her shoulders, his own eyes glistening.

"Nick's baby," Catherine whispers, her voice breaking. "A part of him is still here."

The weight of her words settles over the room, heavy and profound. I swallow hard, watching their faces as they process the news. For a moment, I'm transported back to the cemetery, kneeling before Nick's grave, making promises to him—promises I intend to keep.

My mother rises from her seat and crosses the small space between our couches to hold Catherine in a tight embrace.

"We're going to be grandmothers together," she says, her voice thick with emotion.

Catherine returns the hug fiercely, both women clinging to each other as they cry and laugh simultaneously.

My father stands and extends his hand to Robert, who takes it firmly. Instead of the formal handshake I expected, they pull each other into a bear hug, clapping each other on the back.

"Congratulations, Grandpa," dad says with a watery smile.

"You too, old man," Robert replies, his voice gruff with emotion.

I watch them all celebrating, their faces alight with joy and anticipation. The grandparents-to-be are hugging and crying, their delight palpable in the small living room of my childhood home. I'd chosen to drive to Auburn for the day and tell them here, in person, thinking the familiar setting might soften the news.

"Oh, we need to plan!" my mother exclaims, pulling away from Catherine but keeping hold of her hands. "A baby shower, of course. We could host it at our place—the backyard would be perfect in spring."

Catherine nods enthusiastically, wiping tears from her cheeks. "It should be coed, so that all of Nick's friends and family can attend."

"And gifts!" My mother's excitement builds. "We should coordinate so that everyone doesn't buy the same things. We need to start a registry. I still have your old crib in the attic, Amelia. Your father can refinish it."

Dad agrees with a nod. "I'd be happy to."

"You know," Catherine says, turning to me. "You shouldn't be alone during this time. Especially with everything you've been through."

Mom immediately nods in agreement. "Absolutely not. You need support. I'm thinking that maybe I could come stay with you for a few weeks, then Catherine could take over. We could rotate—"

"Yes!" Catherine interjects, leaning forward with growing excitement, "The house is so empty—"

Okay, stop right there... I'm about to ruin the moment.

"There's... more," I say.

My mom pulls back from Catherine, searching my face.

"I've started seeing someone."

The silence this time is colder. Thicker. Like walking into a room where the fireplace had just gone out.

Mom blinks. "I'm sorry, what?"

"I'm seeing someone," I repeat, firmer. "It's... new. And it's real. His name is Wes, and he knows about the baby."

"You're pregnant with my son's child," Robert says, his voice tinged with disbelief, "and you're seeing another man?"

"Yes," I say. "I didn't plan any of this. God knows I didn't expect to fall for someone else. I didn't think I even could. But grief doesn't follow rules. And neither does healing."

Dad shakes his head. "It's just... so soon."

"We haven't even made it through the first year without him," Catherine says.

"I know," I say gently. "I understand it probably feels like I'm betraying him. But I'm not."

I am definitely not.

Tears well in Catherine's eyes again, but now they are different—conflicted, hurt.

I take a deep breath and lean forward, looking directly at Catherine and Robert, trying to bridge the growing distance between us. "I promise you both that this baby will understand exactly who their father is. They'll know Nick through stories, photos, through both of you. This child will know they had a father who would have loved them."

Catherine's lips press into a thin line as she stares at me.

"And Wes..." I continue, my voice softening, "He will be wonderful with them. He's already talking about reading parenting books, about being there for every appointment, every milestone. This is my reality now, and I'm trying to build something good from all this pain."

Catherine rises to her feet, her movements stiff with barely contained emotion. She swipes at her tears with the back of her hand, attempting to compose herself.

"I think we should go," she says to her husband, her voice wavering slightly. She pauses, then adds with visible effort, "But... would you send me the sonogram pictures when you get them? I'd like to see my grandchild."

"Of course I will," I promise. "I have an appointment next week."

Robert stands beside her, his expression still closed off, jaw tight with disapproval. He places his hand on Catherine's lower back, guiding her toward the door without another word to me.

My father walks them out, murmuring something I can't

quite hear. When he returns to the living room, his expression is troubled.

"Well," my mother begins after a moment of heavy silence, "that could have gone worse."

"Could it?" I ask, sinking back into the couch. "They're hurting. I understand that."

Mom sits beside me, reaching for my hand. "Tell me about him," she says. "This Wes person. Is he good to you?"

I inhale deeply, relieved by her gentle tone. "He's wonderful, mom. Kind and thoughtful and..." I trail off, suddenly aware of how this might sound. "he's one of the college guys next door. The football player."

Mom's eyebrows shoot up, and I watch a series of emotions cross her face in rapid succession—surprise, concern, and finally something like resignation mixed with forced acceptance. She's trying to look supportive, but I see the disappointment in her eyes.

"One of the Dalton U boys?" She repeats carefully. "The ones Nick used to complain about?"

"Yes," I admit with a small laugh. "Wes Sullivan. He's twenty-one."

Mom presses her lips together, nodding slowly. "I see."

"He's not what you think," I blurt. "He's confident, makes me laugh and smile. He communicates with me and he listens. He has ambition and drive. The NFL is scouting him. He's got a real future ahead of him. When I told him about the baby, he didn't run. He stayed. He wants to be part of this."

Mom's gaze softens. Her hands twist nervously in her lap, but I tell see she's trying. For me.

233

"I hope he's as good a man as you believe him to be," she says finally, her voice gentle but cautious.

"He is," I reply with more certainty than I've felt about anything in months.

I take a deep breath, deciding now is the time to lay all my cards on the table. "There's one more thing you should know. I'll probably be leaving Wheeler & Marks, after I finish the Barlowe project."

Dad, who has been quietly listening from his armchair, leans forward. "What? Why? I thought you loved that firm."

"I did," I say carefully, choosing my words. "But it's... not a good fit for me anymore. The environment has changed."

I don't mention Wheeler's hand on my knee or Marks suggesting we continue our "meeting" in a hotel room. I don't tell them about the ultimatum or the threats to blackball me. They don't need to know the details.

My mom looks at me with a particular blend of worry and love that only mothers seem capable of.

"Sweetheart, this is a lot of change all at once," she says. "A new baby, a new relationship, potentially a new job... I just want to make sure you're not overwhelmed."

I squeeze her hand back and offer a small smile. "I know it is, Mom. But, I'm actually looking forward to all of it." I place my other hand on my stomach, still flat but holding so much promise.

Dad clears his throat, his eyes a little misty. "As long as you're happy, that's what matters to us."

"I am," I assure them both. "And besides, you two should be excited too. You're going to be grandparents!" I deliberately lighten my tone, wanting to shift the mood. "Have you thought about what you want the baby to call you?"

The question works its magic. Mom's face immediately brightens, her concerns momentarily forgotten.

"Oh! I hadn't," Mom says, her eyes lighting up with excitement. "What do you think, Richard? Grandpa? Grandad?"

Dad makes a face, scrunching his nose. "Grandpa makes me sound ancient. How about Papa?"

"Papa," I repeat, testing it out. "I like that. Simple but sweet."

"And I could be Nana?" Mom suggests, her head tilting thoughtfully.

Catherine would probably want to be Grandmother," I say, remembering Nick's mother's formal nature. "Very proper."

"That sounds exactly like her," Mom agrees with a small smile. "Though Robert might surprise us. He seems like a 'Pops' to me."

"Or maybe Pawpaw," Dad suggests with a mischievous grin.

I burst into laughter at the thought of serious, buttoned-up Robert Campbell asking a toddler, "Come give Pawpaw a hug!" The mental image is so absurd that I can't contain myself.

Mom joins in, her laughter mingling with mine. "Could you imagine? Or what about Grampy?"

"I would like the name G-money," Dad says, looking a little too serious.

Mom and I look at each other and tell him no—laughing. The synchronicity of our response makes us laugh even harder, dad's bewildered expression only fueling our amusement.

"What's wrong with G-money?" Dad asks, looking genuinely confused, which sets off another round of laughter.

"Dad, you are not having my child call you G-money," I say, wiping tears from my eyes. "That's just... no. Absolutely not."

"Fine," he huffs, though I see a smile tugging at the corners of his mouth. "Papa it is, then."

Chapter Thirty-One

AMELIA

"Amelia," Wheeler says, his voice carrying false warmth, "would you mind grabbing me a black coffee from the kitchenette? I can't focus without my caffeine."

The conference room freezes as I stare at him across the polished mahogany table. His lips curl into what others might mistake for a casual smile, but I recognize the predatory gleam behind it.

A week. It's been seven days since he had his hand on my thigh at the Union Club, since he and Marks made it clear what a "promotion" would cost. I've spent days avoiding eye contact in hallways, taking strategic bathroom breaks whenever I sensed either of them approaching my desk.

And now this.

Twelve pairs of eyes dart between Wheeler and me, then quickly away, studying notepads, laptops, the ceiling—anywhere but the sudden tension crackling between us. Marks watches with barely concealed amusement from the head of the table.

Everyone knows that getting coffee isn't my job. Everyone should know what this is.

Evan shifts uncomfortably in his seat. I catch his sympathetic glance before he, too, looks down at his notepad. No one will speak. No one will object. Not to Wheeler.

"I'm sorry," I say, my voice steadier than I feel, "but I'm not an assistant, Mr. Wheeler. I'm a designer."

Someone—Gina, I think—draws in a sharp breath.

"We're all team players here, aren't we?" he says, leaning back in his seat. "No one's too important to pitch in. Especially those still proving their commitment to the firm."

I stand, my chair rolling on the tiled floor. Everyone's watching me now, their gazes burning into my skin as I walk deliberately toward the kitchenette in the corner. My heels click with each step, marking the seconds of my humiliation.

This isn't about coffee. It's about power.

I reach for the carafe, my hand surprisingly steady despite the rage boiling inside me. The dark liquid streams into the mug— one of those branded ones with the firm's sleek logo. I stare at each drop as it falls, wishing I could poison it with my thoughts alone.

I hope it burns your tongue.

I hope it stains your perfect white shirt.

I hope it gives you heartburn for a week.

The conference room remains deathly quiet. Not a single paper rustles, not a keyboard clicks. They're all watching this power play unfold, all complicit in their silence.

I finish pouring, set down the carafe with a soft clink, and walk the mug over to Wheeler. His eyes follow me the entire way, that smirk never leaving his face.

"Your coffee, Mr. Wheeler," I say, my tone neutral but my

eyes holding his for a second longer than necessary—long enough for him to see that this changes nothing.

I place it in front of him on the table.

"Thank you, Amelia," he says, voice dripping with false gratitude.

I turn and make my way back to my chair, sliding into it with as much dignity as possible. Before I get the chance to even open my portfolio, Marks clears his throat.

"I'll take one as well," he says with a smirk, leaning back in his chair as he looks at me expectantly.

My stomach drops. Of course. Why stop at one humiliation when they can make it a double feature?

I grip the edge of the table, my knuckles whitening as I prepare to stand again.

"Actually," Evan interjects, rising from his seat. "I was about to get myself a coffee anyway. I'll grab yours too, Mr. Marks."

Relief washes over me as he gives me a subtle nod, and I offer him a grateful smile.

"How thoughtful," Marks replies, his disappointment barely concealed. This wasn't part of their script. His power play was interrupted by basic human decency. "Black, two sugars."

While Evan busies himself at the kitchenette, Wheeler taps his pen against the table, the rhythmic clicking filling the uncomfortable silence. When Evan returns with Marks' coffee, Wheeler clears his throat and continues the meeting as if nothing happened.

"Now, where were we? Ah yes, the Calloway referral." He shuffles through some papers. "We received an excellent recommendation based on the Sanderson project from last year."

My ears perk up. The Sanderson project was one of my designs—a complete renovation of a historic brownstone that made a feature in an architectural magazine spread. The clients had been thrilled, promising to recommend me to all their friends.

"Excellent opportunity," Marks states.

"We're assigning it to Peggy," Wheeler announces, not even bothering to look at me.

The air leaves my lungs in a silent rush.

Peggy Morgan, who sits across from me, straightens in her chair, her expression carefully neutral though I catch the slight flash of satisfaction in her eyes.

"In fact," Marks chimes in, setting down his coffee mug, "we have another announcement to make. After careful consideration of all candidates, we're pleased to announce that Peggy will step into the senior designer position, effective immediately."

The conference room erupts in applause. I force my hands together; the sound of my own clapping hollow in my ears. My smile feels stretched and brittle across my face as she accepts congratulations from around the table.

"Thank you all," she says, her voice steady and professional. "I'm looking forward to taking on this new role and continuing to build on the exceptional work we do here."

Peggy is smiling with quiet triumph while I wonder if she knows what that "exceptional work" really costs.

Did they invite her to the Union Club too? Did she go back to their hotel room?

My eyes drift to her left hand, where a platinum wedding

band gleams under the fluorescent lights. Two teenage sons at home and a husband of twenty years, according to the family photo on her desk. I'm feeling suddenly ill. Are Wheeler and Marks ruining families now too? Or did Peggy simply play their game better than I could—smiling and deflecting until they decided the chase wasn't worth it?

I want to hate her, but all I feel is a sort of pity. Whatever she did or didn't do to get the promotion, she's still trapped in this toxic ecosystem. We all are.

"Moving on to assignments," Wheeler continues. "Jan, you'll take the lead on the Westside Commercial Center. Brandon, the Franklin residence needs someone with your eye for detail."

One by one, every designer at the table receives an assignment—everyone except me. I wait for my name, expecting some mundane bathroom remodel or closet reorganization, but it never comes. When Wheeler closes his laptop with a decisive snap, I realize I've been completely overlooked.

And honestly? I'm relieved.

Three months, two weeks, and four days. That's how long until the Barlowe project wraps.

Three months, two weeks, and four days of enduring this humiliation before I'm able to walk away clean.

The meeting finally adjourns, and everyone gathers their things. I slip my portfolio into my bag, eager to escape to my cubicle where I can at least pretend to have some dignity left.

"Amelia," Marks calls out as people file through the door. "A word before you go."

I freeze in place, watching as my colleagues avoid eye contact while leaving me behind—sacrificed to whatever new humiliation awaits. Evan gives my shoulder a supportive squeeze as he passes—the smallest gesture of solidarity, but I cling to it like a lifeline.

And then it's just the three of us.

"Sir?" I remain standing rather than sitting back down.

"We have a situation," Marks says, his voice all business despite the gleam in his eyes. "The janitorial service contacted us. Their employee assigned to our floor called out sick today."

I stare at him, waiting for the point of this conversation.

Wheeler gestures toward the hallway. "The bathrooms need cleaning before tomorrow's new client meeting. We want you to handle it."

For a moment, I think I've misheard him. "Excuse me?"

"The sanitation supplies are in the utility closet," Marks continues as if I hadn't spoken. "Make sure you get under the rims of the toilets. That's where the buil—"

Something inside me snaps. A surge of rage so powerful it feels like electricity coursing through my veins. I step toward them, my finger jabbing the air between us.

"No."

Both men blink in surprise, clearly not expecting resistance.

"Excuse me?" Wheeler's voice drops dangerously low.

"I said no. I will not be cleaning your bathrooms." My voice doesn't waver. "I'm an architect with a master's degree, not your personal maid service."

Marks recovers first. "I'm sorry?" he says, as if I've told a joke he doesn't quite understand.

I step forward, my heart hammering in my chest but my voice steady. "You need me for the Barlowe project. You said it yourself—I'm contractually obligated to finish it. And Russell Barlowe specifically requested me as his designer."

Wheeler's jaw tightens. "We can easily reassign—"

"Can you? Really?" I laugh, the sound harsh and unfamiliar even to my own ears. "You think Barlowe, who's paying seven figures for this project, will be happy to learn his hand-picked architect was removed because she wouldn't scrub your toilets? Go ahead, make that call."

The men exchange glances, and for the first time, uncertainty flashes across their faces.

"You know what I think?" I step closer. "I think you're both pathetic. Two middle-aged men who can only feel powerful by humiliating women. You abuse your positions because deep down, you know that's the only way you could ever get a woman's attention. God knows neither of you probably knows how to actually please a woman without paying for it or holding her career hostage."

Wheeler's face flushes a deep crimson while Marks's mouth drops open in shock.

"How dare you—" Wheeler starts, but I cut him off.

"No, how dare YOU." My voice rises.

Wheeler's hand clenches into a fist at his side. "You're fired."

"No, I'm not," I say with a calm I don't entirely feel. "Contract, remember? But don't worry—I won't be alone with either of you ever again. And if you try to make me clean bathrooms or fetch coffee or anything else outside my job description, I'll be happy to explain to a lawyer—exactly why you're retaliating against me."

I turn and walk toward the door. Neither man speaks as I reach for the handle. They didn't expect this—a woman who refuses to be broken, who knows her worth beyond what they've tried to reduce her to.

I don't look back. I don't need to see their faces to know I've won this round.

The hallway stretches before me, and I force myself to maintain my composure until I'm safely inside the women's restroom—the very one they wanted me to clean. Once the door locks behind me, I lean against it, my legs suddenly weak as adrenaline courses through my system.

"Oh my God," I whisper to my reflection in the mirror.

Did I really just do that?

I place a protective hand over my still-flat stomach. "We did it," I murmur. "We stood up to them."

I called their bluff.

They need me. As much as Wheeler and Marks want to punish me for rejecting them, they need me to finish the Barlowe project more than they need to satisfy their bruised egos.

I look at myself in the mirror again, straightening my shoulders. Three months, two weeks, and four days. I can endure this. Every minute will be torture—the sideways glances, the whispers, the calculated humiliations they'll still try to inflict. But I'll weather it all if it means keeping my name and career intact.

Because that's what this is about now: survival. Not just for me, but for my baby. For our future.

Chapter Thirty-Two

WESLEY

I slam my economics textbook shut and rub my eyes. I've been sitting at this dining table for three hours, and all I've accomplished is highlighting random passages that I'll probably need to re-read later.

The package that arrived this morning sits on the edge of the table, taunting me. I've been stealing glances at it between failed attempts to memorize economic theories.

"Screw it," I mutter, reaching for the box.

I tear open the brown packaging and pull out the book I ordered two days ago: *What to Expect When You're Expecting*.

The cover shows a silhouette of a pregnant woman, her belly a perfect round curve against a soft yellow background. I run my fingers over the glossy surface, feeling strangely nervous.

This isn't even my baby, technically speaking. Yet here I am, buying pregnancy books like some excited first-time dad.

I flip to the table of contents, scanning through chapter titles:

First trimester, second trimester, third trimester. Week by week development. Pregnancy symptoms. Labor and delivery. I pause at a chapter called "When Things Go Wrong" and quickly flip past it.

I turn to the section on the ninth week—where Amelia is now. There's a diagram showing the embryo is about the size of a cherry or a grape. Something that small, causing so much change.

"Holy shit," I mutter, scanning a graphic description of what happens during childbirth. The words "tearing," "episiotomy," and "stitches" jump out at me, making me wince. I quickly flip to a different section.

The chapter on morning sickness seems more manageable. I read about ginger tea and saltine crackers, creating mental notes. She hasn't complained much, but I've noticed how she sometimes goes pale at certain smells.

I find myself absorbed in a part about the baby's development—how its heart is already beating, how tiny buds that will become arms and legs are forming. It's fascinating in a weird, sci-fi kind of way.

The doorbell rings, pulling me from my reading. I close the book but leave it on the table as I head to the entryway. When I open the front door, it's dad—standing there in his pressed khakis and button-down shirt.

"Dad," I say, genuinely surprised. "What are you doing here?"

He clears his throat. "May I come in?"

"Yeah, sure." I step aside, allowing him to enter.

I lead him back to the dining table, hastily gathering my scattered papers. "I was just studying. Econ midterm next week."

He nods, but his eyes have already locked onto the pregnancy book sitting prominently on the table. His expression tightens slightly, but he doesn't comment on it. Instead, he stands awkwardly, hands in his pockets, looking around the house.

"What's up?" I ask, striving to keep my voice casual. We haven't spoken since I stormed out of his house the other day, and now he shows up unannounced?

Dad shifts his weight from one foot to another. "Where are your brothers?"

"They took Bebe shopping. Trying to get her out of the house for a bit."

Dad nods, his gaze still lingering on the pregnancy book. He pulls out a chair and sits down heavily. His fingers drum nervously against the table as he looks everywhere but directly at me.

"Wes," he finally says, his voice unusually hesitant. "I've been doing a lot of thinking since our... conversation."

I lean against the counter, crossing my arms. "Yeah?"

He takes a deep breath before meeting my eyes. "I owe you an apology. You and your brothers."

I blink, not sure I heard him correctly. In twenty-one years, I can count on one hand the number of times Wesley Sullivan Senior has apologized for anything.

"I know I can be a little controlling," he continues.

I raise my eyebrows, giving him a look that clearly communicates exactly what I think of that understatement.

Dad clears his throat. "Alright, fine. I can be a lot controlling." He runs a hand over his face. "It's who I am, Wes. Sometimes I can't control my controlling." A rueful smile plays on his lips. "Your mother says it's my worst quality."

"Mom's right," I say, but there's no heat in my voice. I'm too shocked by this unexpected vulnerability.

"After you left," Dad continues, "I couldn't stop thinking about what you said. About your brothers... and you." He glances at the pregnancy book. "And about this woman you're willing to fight so hard for."

I sit across from him.

"I want you to know," he says slowly, "I think it's admirable what you're doing—wanting to take on a father role for this child." His voice is gruff but sincere in a way I rarely hear from him. "Not many young men would step up like that."

I stare at him, unsure how to respond to this unexpected praise.

"I was blessed to have three sons," he continues, a warmth entering his tone. "And I took that responsibility seriously. Being your father has been the greatest privilege of my life."

"Too seriously sometimes," I mutter.

To my surprise, he chuckles. "Fair enough." His expression grows more solemn as he looks at me. "But I need you to understand something, Wes. My proudest moments— the ones that matter most—have nothing to do with The Keepers or business or status. They're about being a father. Watching you boys grow up, become men."

There's a vulnerability in his eyes I've never seen before.

Dad glances toward the hallway, then back at me. "Speaking of families... I wanted to tell you I've been getting to know Bebe a bit."

This catches me off guard. "You have?"

He nods, his expression softening. "After everything the Laurent family did for us—I feel indebted to them." He taps his fingers thoughtfully on the table. "But beyond that obligation, I've found Bebe to be quite... pleasant."

"Pleasant?" I repeat, unable to hide my surprise.

"Yes," Dad says with a hint of defensiveness. "She's intelligent, well-spoken, and clearly cares deeply for this family." A small smile tugs at his lips. "And I see how Luke looks at her."

I sit back in my chair, processing this unexpected revelation. "I didn't know you'd noticed."

"I notice more than you boys give me credit for. And I realize now," Dad says, his voice softer than I've ever heard it, "that I've been so focused on what I wanted for my sons that I haven't been listening to what you want for yourselves."

I shift in my seat, uncomfortable with this new version of my father—vulnerable, reflective, almost... human.

"I spoke with Russell Barlowe this morning," he continues, and my head snaps up. "About the situation with Amelia Campbell."

My heart pounds against my ribs. "You did?"

Dad nods. "I did some digging into Wheeler & Marks after our conversation. Their reputation... well, let's just say yours isn't the first complaint about their behavior toward female employees."

"So you believe me?" I ask, still not quite trusting this sudden change.

"Of course I believe you." He looks genuinely hurt that I would question it. "I may be stubborn and controlling, but I raised you to be honest. If you say this woman is being harassed, I believe you."

I wait, barely breathing, for him to continue.

"Russell and I may have come up with a solution that wouldn't require him to lose his investment in the project. Wheeler and Marks will not be happy about it."

Chapter Thirty-Three

AMELIA

Evan's voice fades in and out like a badly tuned radio as I pick at my turkey sandwich. Something about HR restructuring and potential layoffs, but I can't summon the energy to care.

"Amelia? Hello? Earth to Amelia?" He waves his hand in front of my face. "Did you hear what I said about Jessica from accounting?"

"Sorry," I mumble, forcing myself to look up from my lunch. "Just a little distracted today."

"Morning sickness is still bad?" he asks, his voice dropping to a sympathetic whisper. As the only person at work who knows I'm pregnant, Evan has appointed himself my unofficial caretaker.

I shake my head. "Actually, it's getting better. I kept breakfast down this morning." A small victory, but one I'll happily take after weeks of running to the bathroom every morning. My aversions seem to be only toward breakfast foods.

"That's progress!" He beams, then leans forward conspiratorially. "So if it's not the baby making you zone out, what is it?"

Gina appears at our table, slightly out of breath.

"Amelia," she says urgently, "The partners need you in the conference room right now. Mr. Barlowe is here."

My stomach drops. "Barlowe? Today?" I wasn't expecting him until next week. I have nothing prepared to show him."

I straighten and push away from the table, gathering my notes and tablet with trembling hands. My mind races as I smooth down my blouse, suddenly conscious of how it fits over my barely there baby bump.

"Good luck," Evan whispers as I hurry off.

Mr. Barlowe showing up unannounced can't be good.

Is he pulling the project?

I pause outside the glass doors, take a deep breath and put on my most professional smile.

Show time.

I push through the doors with confidence I don't feel. Russell Barlowe stands as I enter, his imposing six-foot-three frame commanding the room. Wheeler and Marks remain seated at the table, their expressions unreadable.

"Mr. Barlowe," I say warmly, extending my hand to him directly. "What a wonderful surprise to see you today." I deliberately avoid even glancing at Wheeler and Marks, focusing all my attention on our client.

"Mrs. Campbell," he responds with a firm handshake and a genuine smile that crinkles the corners of his eyes.

I notice another man standing quietly behind Mr. Barlowe. Older, distinguished-looking, with familiar blue-green eyes I'd recognize anywhere.

"Amelia, I'd like you to meet Wesley Sullivan Senior," Mr. Barlowe says, gesturing to the man. "He's joining us today to notarize some very important paperwork."

What is Wes's father doing here? Is this a bizarre coincidence?

My heart races as I try to process this unexpected development. Of all the people to appear in this conference room, he is the last one I expected.

"Mrs. Campbell, it's a pleasure to meet you," Mr. Sullivan says, extending an arm. His voice carries the same confident tone as his son's.

I take his hand, acutely aware of how clammy mine must feel. His grip is firm, authoritative. His eyes—so eerily similar to Wes's—scan my face with careful assessment.

Does he know who I am?

"Likewise, Mr. Sullivan," I manage to say, trying to keep my voice steady.

Mr. Barlowe gestures to the conference room table. "Let's all have a seat and get down to business, shall we?"

I nod, grateful for the direction, as my legs feel suddenly unsteady. Mr. Barlowe takes the head seat at the table, radiating the confidence of a man accustomed to controlling rooms. I slide into a chair directly across from the partners, who haven't said a word this whole time. Their faces are carefully blank, but I catch the tension in Wheeler's jaw, the way Marks keeps swallowing nervously. Something significant is happening, and they know it.

"Let's cut right to it," Mr. Barlowe says, folding his hands on the table. "My first order of business today involves this firm's relationship with my project."

Mr. Sullivan reaches into his leather briefcase and

extracts a crisp document, sliding it across the polished conference table toward Wheeler and Marks. "This is a formal notice of project withdrawal," he explains in a measured tone. "It releases the Barlowe project from Wheeler & Marks, effective immediately, with no early termination penalties."

Wheeler's face drains of color as he stares at the document. Marks sputters, "Mr. Barlowe, surely we can discuss—"

"There's nothing to discuss," Mr. Barlowe cuts him off firmly. "I've made my decision."

He's withdrawing his project.

All my work, all those hours of designing and redesigning, all those late nights perfecting every detail of what would have been my career-defining project... gone. I grip the edge of the table to steady myself, trying to keep my expression neutral despite the panic rising in my chest.

Mr. Sullivan places an elegant fountain pen in front of the partners. "Your signatures, gentlemen."

Wheeler's hand trembles as he takes the pen, his signature shaky but legible. Marks follows, his face a mask of contained fury. Once the document is signed, Mr. Sullivan takes it back, stamps it with his notary seal, and adds his own signature.

"Now, the second order of business," Mr. Barlowe says as Mr. Sullivan extracts another document. "This acknowledges Mrs. Campbell's resignation letter, which has been backdated for two weeks, making today officially her last day at Wheeler & Marks."

My mouth falls open. *Resignation letter?* I never submitted one.

The partners both turn to glare at me.

"Gentlemen," Mr. Sullivan says sharply, "I'd appreciate it

if you wouldn't look at Mrs. Campbell. Your attention should be on the paperwork in front of you."

They reluctantly shift their gaze back to the document Mr. Sullivan has placed before them. I'm still trying to process what's happening.

Mr. Sullivan produces a third paper, sliding it across the table.

"This final document," Mr. Barlowe says, his voice deliberate and clear, "transfers all creative ownership and all monies for the Barlowe Mountain Retreat project from Wheeler & Marks to Ladybug Designs, LLC."

I gasp, my hand flying to my mouth. Wes—he's behind this—he's saving me. My mind races back to that night when I told him about Wheeler and Marks, how he'd gone quiet when I mentioned Russell Barlowe's name. He must have called in a favor through his father.

Mr. Barlowe's eyes meet mine with understanding. "This paper allows you to continue working on the project with me since you are no longer employed at this firm."

I sit in my seat, focusing on my breathing. *In and out. In and out.* The room seems to tilt slightly as the magnitude of what's happening washes over me.

Wheeler's face contorts with rage. "This is preposterous! You can't just—"

"I can and I am," he interrupts, his voice carrying the authority. "You've messed with the wrong people. There are consequences for those who try to manipulate and sexually harass their employees," he continues. "My wife's best friend had a similar experience at her last law firm. I made sure that company never landed a major contract in the industry. Here —you're getting a second chance. Mrs. Campbell and I walk away, and you stay in business as long as it doesn't involve propositioning another woman again."

Wheeler's face pales even further, and Marks looks like he might be sick. I sit perfectly still, hardly daring to breathe as I watch this unfold.

"You're lucky I'm not pursuing legal action," he adds. "Though the option remains on the table if either of you ever speaks a word against Mrs. Campbell or attempt to interfere with her future in this industry."

Mr. Sullivan slides the final document toward the partners. "Your signatures, gentlemen. This recognizes the transfer of the project to Ladybug Designs, with all related intellectual property and compensation."

Wheeler's hand shakes so badly he can barely hold the pen. "This is extortion," he hisses through clenched teeth.

"No," Mr. Sullivan replies calmly. "This is justice... sign the paper."

They sign, one after the other, their signatures jagged with suppressed rage. Mr. Sullivan slides the paper to me next. I take the pen, its weight suddenly significant in my hand. This is it—the moment everything changes. I sign my name with a steady hand, feeling the weight of my power for the first time in my professional life.

Mr. Sullivan collects the signed document, notarizes it, and hands me a copy. "It's official, Mrs. Campbell. Ladybug Designs is now the firm on record for the Barlowe Mountain Retreat."

Mr. Barlowe stands and gestures toward Wheeler and Marks. "Gentlemen, we're done here. You can go."

The two men rise stiffly, their faces twisted with barely contained rage. Wheeler opens his mouth as if to say something, then thinks better of it. They gather their things and walk out without another word, the glass door swinging shut behind them with a soft click.

As soon as they're out of sight, the emotions I've been holding back burst free. Tears well up and spill down my cheeks, my shoulders shaking with relief and disbelief. I press my hands to my mouth, trying to muffle the sound of my sobs.

"I... I don't know how to thank you both," I manage between breaths, looking from Mr. Barlowe to Mr. Sullivan. "What you've done for me..."

Mr. Barlowe's expression softens as he watches me struggle to contain my emotions.

Mr. Sullivan sighs, sliding a Kleenex box across the table to me. "Pack your things, Amelia. Your future is starting now, and there's no time to waste."

I take a tissue, dabbing at my eyes while trying to process everything. In fifteen minutes, I've gone from employee to business owner. From trapped to free.

"I—I don't even know where to begin," I stammer, looking around the conference room that suddenly feels like it belongs to someone else's life.

"Start by collecting your personal items and everything related to Mr. Barlowe's project," Mr. Sullivan says, checking his watch. "I've arranged for movers to arrive at three o'clock to transfer all project materials to your new office space."

"New office space?" I repeat, feeling like I'm several steps behind in a conversation moving too quickly.

Mr. Barlowe nods. "Mr. Sullivan has secured you a temporary workplace in his building downtown. Sixth floor, excellent natural light. It's yours for six months, rent-free, while you establish Ladybug Designs and figure out where you're going next."

An hour later, I'm standing in the middle of my cubicle, staring at the desk where I've spent countless hours for the past two years. The surface is bare now, wiped clean of all traces of me. My plants, design sketches, my framed degree that used to sit by my computer—all packed away in a small cardboard box that Evan insisted on carrying for me.

"So," he says, leaning against the cubicle wall, "are you going to tell me what happened in that conference room? Because Wheeler stormed out looking like he was about to murder someone, and Marks was practically in tears."

I smile, still processing everything myself. "It's a long story. And one day, I'll tell you."

His eyes are brimming with questions, but he respects my privacy enough not to push.

As we make our way through the office, I feel the stares of my now-former coworkers. Word has already spread like wildfire—Amelia Campbell has quit, or been fired, or some incident happened involving Russell Barlowe himself. The whispers follow us down the hallway.

Evan presses the elevator button. When the doors slide open, he hands me my box.

"You've got this, Amelia," he says with surprising seriousness. "Go build something beautiful."

"I will," I promise, stepping into the elevator.

He tells me good luck, and the door closes.

When I make my way out the glass doors of the building, it's like déjà vu.

Wes is leaning against his Jeep parked at the curb, arms crossed over his chest, aviator glasses on, that familiar lopsided smile playing on his lips. His blond hair catches the afternoon sunlight, giving him an angelic glow. He's wearing jeans and a simple blue t-shirt that makes his eyes look even more vivid. My heart stutters in my chest.

I place my box carefully on the ground and run—actually running toward him. His arms open as I launch myself at him, wrapping my legs around his waist as his strong arms catch me. Our lips find each other instantly, desperately, saying everything words can't express. His mouth is warm and familiar against mine, tasting faintly of coffee and mint. His hands grip me tightly, one at my waist, the other tangled in my hair as he deepens the kiss.

Chapter Thirty-Four

WESLEY

I burst through the front door with Amelia, our bodies colliding the moment we're inside, unable to keep our hands off each other. My heart is hammering against my ribs, desire burning through my veins.

"I need you," I growl against her mouth, my fingers fumbling with the buttons of her blouse while she tugs at my shirt. "Right now."

"Show me how much," she gasps between kisses, her fingers sliding under my shirt, nails scraping lightly against my skin.

We stumble down the hallway, shedding clothes like breadcrumbs—the shirt I was wearing by the entryway, her top near the kitchen, my belt abandoned in the hall. Each discarded item brings us closer to what we both desperately want. I can't get enough of her—the taste of her lips, the softness of her skin, the little sounds she makes when I touch her just right.

By the time we reach her bedroom, we're both half-naked

and breathing hard. She steps back, her eyes never leaving mine as she unzips her skirt and lets it pool at her feet. She stands before me in nothing but her matching lace bra and thong, her skin glowing in the soft light filtering through the curtains. My breath catches at the sight of her.

"You're so beautiful," I whisper, reaching for her to run my fingers along the curve of her waist.

She backs toward the bed, a seductive smile playing on her lips. When her legs hit the mattress, she sinks onto it and reclines, her hair fanning out across the pillows.

I'm over her in an instant, my body covering hers as our lips meet in a desperate kiss. Her hands tangle in my hair, pulling me closer as our tongues dance together. I'm completely consumed by her taste, her scent, the feel of her body under mine.

I break the kiss to trail my lips down her neck, savoring the soft moans that escape her. My hands slide behind her back to unclasp her bra, freeing her perfect breasts. I take one nipple in my mouth, circling it with my tongue before sucking gently. Amelia arches beneath me, her fingers digging into my shoulders.

"Wes," she gasps, her voice breathy with need, her body arching toward mine. I slide my lips down the valley between her breasts, trailing kisses across her ribs, down to her stomach.

I pause there, my hands tenderly cradling her hips. My eyes meet hers as I drop my head, pressing my lips softly against the smooth skin where her child grows. Something shifts inside me as I place this tender kiss—something profound and protective. This tiny life that's part of her.

She watches me with wide eyes, her breath catching—eyes glistening with emotion.

Her fingers find my hair, stroking softly as I continue my journey downward. I hook my fingertips into the delicate lace of her thong, slowly dragging it down her thighs. She lifts her hips to help me, and I slide the rest of the way, tossing it aside.

I settle between her, my hands gently spreading her legs wider. I take in the sight of her completely exposed to me, her pink pussy glistening with arousal. She's perfect—swollen and wet, waiting for me. My mouth waters at the sight, and I feel a primal hunger consume over.

"God, you're beautiful," I murmur, lowering my face between her thighs.

I lower my head and taste her with a long, slow lick that makes her gasp. Amelia is sweet and tangy and absolutely intoxicating. I dive in like a man starved, savoring her. Her back arches off the bed with a soft whimper. Her hands find my hair, fingers tangling in the strands, not pushing or pulling, just holding on as if she needs something to anchor her.

"That's it," I breathe against her delicate flesh. "Be a good girl and come on my mouth, Ladybug. Let me taste all of you."

Her breath catches at my words, her thighs trembling on either side of my head. I return my attention to her pussy, working my tongue deeper inside her while my thumb finds her clit, circling the sensitive bud with firm, steady pressure. She's getting closer, her muscles tensing beneath my hands, her breathing becoming more erratic.

I increase the pressure, flicking my tongue faster against her clit as I sense her tense. The combination of my tongue plunging inside her and my thumb working her clit sends her over the edge.

She comes undone with a sharp cry that echoes through the bedroom. Her body tenses completely before a flood of warmth rushes against my mouth. I greedily drink it all in, not wanting to waste a single drop of her pleasure. Each time my tongue passes over her, she jerks slightly, oversensitive but not pushing me away.

When the last waves of her orgasm subside, I pull back and wipe my lips with the back of my hand, my eyes never leaving hers. Her face is flushed, hair wild against the pillows, chest rising and falling with ragged breaths. She's never looked more beautiful.

I crawl up her body, trailing kisses along her stomach, between her breasts, up her neck until I reach her mouth. I capture her lips with mine, letting her taste herself on my tongue.

I gently grasp her wrists, gathering both in one hand as I pull them above her head. Her eyes widen with surprise at my dominance and desire as I pin her hands against the pillow. The trust in her gaze makes my heart pound even harder.

"Is this okay?" I whisper, needing to be sure.

"Yes," she breathes, arching her body toward mine. "Please, Wes."

I shift my weight, using my knees to spread her thighs wider, positioning myself between them. My cock throbs painfully, aching to be inside her.

With my free hand, I guide myself to her; the head sliding through her slick pussy.

"Look at me," I command softly.

Her eyes lock with mine as I push forward in one smooth

thrust. The sensation is indescribable—hot, wet, tight perfection enveloping me completely. Even after her orgasm, she's deliciously snug around me, her inner walls gripping my pierced shaft like a glove.

"Christ," I groan, my eyes nearly rolling back at the exquisite pressure. "You feel incredible."

I begin to move, establishing a rhythm that has us both gasping. Each thrust drives me deeper, the metal studs of my piercings dragging against her. Her legs wrap around my waist, pulling me even further in. I release her wrists, bracing myself on either side of her head, fisting the sheets as I pick up the pace.

"God, Amelia," I groan, watching her face contort with pleasure beneath me.

I thrust harder, faster, my body claiming hers with a primal need I've never felt before. The metal barbells of my piercings create an exquisite friction against her inner walls, making her cry out with each deep stroke. I'm consumed by her—the way she feels around me, the sounds she makes, the trust in her eyes as I take her.

"More," she pleads, her nails digging into my back. "Please, Wes. Harder."

Something inside me snaps at her words. I grab her hips, lifting them slightly to change the angle, and begin pounding into her. The headboard slams rhythmically against the wall as I drive into her again and again, the wet sounds of our bodies meeting filling the room along with our mingled moans.

Her inner walls clench around me, fluttering and pulsing in that telltale rhythm that signals she's about to break. Her eyes widen, lips parting in a silent 'oh' as pleasure overtakes her.

"That's it," I encourage, maintaining the punishing pace she begged for. "Come for me again, Ladybug."

She shatters beneath me, her body arching off the bed as she cries out my name. Her pussy grips me like a vise, squeezing and milking my cock with each pulse of her orgasm. Seeing her coming undone—eyes glazed with pleasure, face flushed, legs trembling—pushes me past the point of no return.

"Fuck, Amelia," I groan, my rhythm faltering as my release builds.

I manage a few more erratic thrusts before the pressure becomes overwhelming. With a final deep plunge, I bury myself to the hilt and let go. My orgasm hits me like a freight train, pleasure exploding through every nerve ending as I empty myself inside her—each hot pulse as I fill her.

The thought crosses my mind as I'm still buried inside her —if Amelia wasn't already carrying Nick's child, she might be carrying mine now. My seed, exactly where nature intended it to be, and there's something primal and possessive about knowing a part of me remains within her.

I ease myself out gently, watching with fascination as my release follows, a pearly stream trickling from her onto the dark sheets. It's oddly beautiful—intimate.

I can't help myself. Instinctively, I reach down and trace my fingers through the warm wetness, gathering what's dripped out, and slowly push it back into her. My fingers slide in easily, still slick with our combined arousal. Once deep inside, I curl them upward, finding that spot that causes her to gasp.

"Wes," she whispers, her eyes widening with surprise and renewed desire.

"I enjoy seeing you filled with me." I murmur, working my fingers deeper.

Her walls clench around my fingers, still sensitive from her orgasms. I watch her face as I continue the gentle massage, her lips parting with each breath.

"Does that feel good?" I ask, my voice husky.

She nods, unable to form words as her hips move against my hand. I add a second finger, stretching her, watching as her body accepts me again.

I wonder if someday it will be my baby growing in her stomach, a life we created together.

"What are you thinking about?" she asks, my fingers still working inside her as I stare at her stomach.

"The future," I admit. "Our future."

She props herself on her elbows, her gaze questioning. "Yeah?"

"Yeah." I press tight circles over her clit, causing her to gasp. "I was thinking about this baby, and maybe... someday... one that's ours too."

Her eyes widen, and for a moment I worry I've said too much too soon. But then her expression softens, her gaze holding mine with such tenderness it makes my chest ache.

"Wes," she whispers. "I would be honored to carry your child."

There's sincerity in her voice, absolute certainty in her eyes. Everything I've ever wanted, everything I never knew I needed until her, crystallizes in this perfect moment. My heart feels too big for my chest, too full of every emotion I have for this woman.

I withdraw my fingers slowly and bring them to Amelia's lips, mesmerized by the way her eyes darken with understanding. Her lips part immediately, welcoming, eager. When her mouth closes around my fingers, her tongue swirling around them coated with our combined essence.

"Fuck," I whisper, watching her suck my fingers clean.

Her eyes never leave mine as she takes them deeper, cheeks hollowing. Watching her taste herself, taste us together, sends a fresh wave of heat straight to my groin. My cock twitches with renewed interest despite having just emptied inside her.

When she finally releases my fingers with a soft pop, her lips are wet and glistening. She licks them slowly, deliberately, savoring our flavor.

"We taste good together," she murmurs, her voice husky with satisfaction.

I lean in to capture her mouth with mine, tasting the lingering saltiness. The kiss is slower now, gentler, but no less intimate. My hand slides to cup her face, thumb stroking her flushed cheek.

"I love you," I whisper.

I collapse beside her, overwhelmed by emotion, and pull her in for a long, deep kiss. When we finally break apart, both breathless, I rest my forehead against hers.

"For now," I murmur, grinning against her lips, "we'll just have to practice."

Her laughter bubbles up between us, bright and beautiful, filling the room with its melody. The sound wraps around my heart, squeezing it tight.

Chapter Thirty-Five

AMELIA

I wake up to the feeling of warmth against my back, muscular arms wrapped securely around my waist like an anchor keeping me from drifting away. For a moment, I simply exist in this bubble of contentment, savoring the weight of him against me, the safety I feel in his embrace.

The afternoon light filters through the curtains, casting the bedroom in a soft golden glow. I glance at the clock on my nightstand—6:00 PM. We must have fallen asleep after having sex—twice, our bodies exhausted.

I turn carefully in Wes's arms, trying not to wake him. He makes a small sound in his sleep but doesn't stir, his grip loosening enough to let me shift to face him. In this unguarded moment, I'm struck by how young he looks—his features relaxed, hair tousled, long eyelashes resting against his cheeks, mouth slightly parted. The usual intensity that animates his face is gone, replaced by a peaceful vulnerability that makes my chest ache with tenderness.

One of his eyes cracks open, bright blue and drowsy,

catching me staring. The corners of his mouth turn into that lazy, lopsided smile that always makes my heart skip.

"See something you like?" he mumbles, voice still thick with sleep.

Heat rises to my cheeks at being caught, but I don't turn away. "Just admiring the view," I admit softly, reaching to trace the line of his jaw with my fingertips. "You look so peaceful when you're sleeping."

He makes a low, contented sound in his throat, somewhere between a hum and a growl. His arm tightens around my waist, pulling me closer until our bodies are flush against each other, the heat of him seeping into me.

"Come here," he whispers, then his mouth is on mine.

The kiss is different from our earlier urgency—slow, tender, unhurried. His lips move against me with gentle precision, as if we have all the time in the world. There's no rush, no desperate need, just a sweet exploration that makes my insides melt. I melt into him, my hand coming up to rest against his chest where I can feel his heartbeat, steady and strong beneath my palm.

When we finally break apart, he doesn't go far, just enough to look into my eyes.

His eyes are so blue in this light, so tender as they look at me, that the question tumbles from my lips before I can think better of it.

"Are you going to tell me what you did?" I ask softly, running my fingertips along his collarbone. "About my job, I mean. How did you get me out of it?"

His expression shifts immediately. The lazy contentment vanishes, replaced by something more guarded. He brushes a strand of hair from my face, his fingers lingering against my cheek. I watch as he swallows hard, his Adam's apple bobbing with the motion.

"There's something I need to tell you," he says, his tone suddenly serious. "About how that all happened."

I feel a chill run through me despite the warmth of his body against mine. The gravity in his tone makes me push myself up slightly, propping my head on my hand so I can see his face more clearly. I nod, steeling myself for whatever's coming.

"I'm listening," I say, trying to keep my voice steady.

He sits, the sheet pooling around his waist as he runs a hand through his hair. His eyes search mine, and I notice he's struggling with whatever this is. I'd assumed that maybe his father and Barlowe were friends or business associates—that Wes had pulled some strings through family connections. But the look on his face tells me there's more to it than that.

"There's a brotherhood," he says, looking directly into my eyes. "That's been attached to Dalton University for over a century. When certain men graduate, they maintain networks throughout the country—in business, politics, sports, everywhere. Russell Barlowe is a member. My father is a member." He pauses, his gaze unwavering. "And so am I."

I sit up fully now, pulling the sheet around me as I watch his face. "A brotherhood? Like a fraternity?"

"No, not like a fraternity," he says, shaking his head. "It's much more... structured. They help each other, support each other's businesses, and create opportunities."

"A secret society," I whisper, my sociology courses from college rushing back to me. "I studied groups like this—networks that operate behind the scenes, maintaining power structures."

His eyebrows lift, surprised by my immediate understanding. "Yes, exactly. Though we prefer the term 'private organization.'"

"Do they... do bad things?" I ask tentatively, wrapping the sheet tighter around me.

"No," he says immediately, his voice firm. "Nothing like that." He shifts on the bed, turning to face me more fully. "But that doesn't mean there aren't bad people in it," he adds, his expression serious. "Just like any organization, we get people who join for the wrong reasons or abuse their connections. We do our best to weed them out—revoke their status."

I observe his face, trying to process this revelation. A secret brotherhood with ties throughout the country, powerful enough to help me escape Wheeler & Marks' clutches.

He winces suddenly, as if remembering something unpleasant. "We wear these cheesy robes though," he admits, looking slightly embarrassed. "For ceremonies and meetings. They're ridiculous—all navy blue with this silver embroidery around the edges."

A laugh bubbles out of me at the mental image of Wes— tall, athletic Wes—wearing some kind of ceremonial robe. The contrast is too much.

"So what, are there blood sacrifices too?" I joke, but his expression suddenly goes serious. My smile falters as I watch his expression darken, his eyes narrowing.

His face breaks into a huge grin. "Got you."

I let out a mock gasp of outrage and reach for the nearest pillow, swinging it at his smug face. "You jerk!" I laugh, but his reflexes are too fast. His hand shoots out, catching the pillow mid-swing.

"Too slow, Ladybug," he teases, tossing it aside.

I let the sheet fall away from my body as I move closer to him, no longer concerned with covering myself. His arm automatically wraps around me, pulling me in. The cool air raises goosebumps on my skin, but the heat in Wes's eyes as his gaze travels over me makes me feel anything but cold.

"So," I say, my voice softer now as I place my hand on his chest, feeling his steady heartbeat beneath my palm. "A secret brotherhood with special robes and connections all over the country. That's... different."

He watches me carefully, like he's waiting for me to freak out or pull away. Instead, I lean in and press a gentle kiss to his shoulder.

"I'm grateful they helped me," I continue, meeting his eyes. "If this brotherhood is important to you, then I'm okay with it. I trust you."

The relief that washes over his face is beautiful to witness. His gaze softens, and he cups my cheek with his palm.

"I love you, Amelia," he says, his voice low and raw with emotion.

My heart swells in my chest, the words I've been holding back finally finding their way to my lips. "I love you too, Wes."

The instant the syllables leave my mouth, I watch his eyes transform—the clear blue darkening with desire, pupils dilating as he gazes at me. Without warning, he moves, gently pushing me back against the pillows. His body covers mine, warm and solid as he hovers above me.

"Say it again," he whispers, his lips brushing against my neck.

"I love you," I repeat, the words coming easier now, like they've been waiting to be spoken.

He makes a sound deep in his throat, almost a growl, before capturing my lips in a kiss that steals my breath. When he pulls away, his eyes are still dark with that intense hunger that makes my pulse quicken.

He trails kisses down my neck, across my collarbone, until his mouth closes around my nipple. I gasp, threading my fingers through his hair to hold him there. The warm, wet suction sends electricity racing through me.

"God, you make me feel so good," I breathe, my head falling back against the pillow.

He moves his attention to my other breast, and wince a little as I shift beneath him, a delicious ache between my thighs reminding me of our earlier activities.

"Mmm, wait," I murmur, gently pressing against his shoulder. "As much as I want you again, I'm a little sore."

He immediately lifts his head, concern replacing desire in his eyes. "I'm sorry, Ladybug. I should have been more gentle."

"No, no," I reassure him, combing my fingers through his hair. "Don't apologize." I smile shyly. "I loved every second."

His expression softens, and the mischievous glint I adore returns to his gaze. "That's okay," he says, pressing a kiss to my sternum. "I'm hungry anyway."

He moves down my body, trailing kisses across my ribs, lingering for a moment over the slight curve of my belly where my child grows. My breath catches as I realize his intention. There's something so tender in the way he acknowledges my pregnancy, something that makes my heart swell.

"Wes, you don't have to—"

"Shhh," he whispers against my skin, his firm hands gently easing my legs apart. "Let me take care of you."

The first brush of his mouth is electrifying, a jolt of pure pleasure that causes my back arch off the bed. He traces my pussy with his tongue with exquisite patience, his touch so gentle yet deliberate that I can barely breathe. When he finds the sensitive bundle of nerves, I gasp, my fingers tangling in his hair.

"Wes," I whisper, his name a prayer on my lips.

His blue eyes flick up to meet mine, watching my reaction as he continues his sweet torture. The sight of him between my thighs, so dedicated to my pleasure, sends another wave of heat through me. His strong hands hold my hips steady as I tremble.

I close my eyes, surrendering to the sensation. In this moment of pure bliss, gratitude washes over me—for finding him, for the life growing inside me, for this second chance I never expected. I was a grieving widow discovering my husband's betrayal. Now I'm here, loved completely by this extraordinary man who wants not just me, but my child too.

"Let go," he murmurs, his breath hot against my most sensitive place. "I've got you."

I've got you.

Three simple words that somehow contain all I need to hear. It resonates deep within my soul as pleasure builds inside me.

Wes may be saying them in this moment, but I'm thinking about everything. My life. My future. My child.

The orgasm crashes through me in waves, pulling sounds from my throat I didn't know I could make. He holds me steady as I shudder beneath him, his touch both gentle and firm, keeping me grounded as I soar.

Tears prick at the corners of my eyes. Not from the physical sensation, though that's overwhelming enough, but from the realization that for the first time since Nick died—maybe even before that—I feel completely safe. Protected. Cherished.

"Hey," he whispers, crawling back up my body when he notices my tears. His thumb gently brushes one away. "Did I hurt you?"

I shake my head, unable to find words for a moment. "No," I finally manage, my voice thick with emotion. "Just the opposite."

He settles beside me, pulling me into his arms, my back against his chest. His lips press against my hair, hold tightening around me.

"What is it then?"

"When you said 'I've got you'..." I pause, feeling emotions rising inside me. "It just hit me how much I needed to hear that. How much I needed someone to be there, to catch me." My voice cracks as fresh tears spill down my cheeks.

"Oh, Amelia," he murmurs, turning me gently in his arms so he can see my face.

"I'm sorry," I say, dabbing at my eyes with the back of my hand. "I don't know why I'm crying so much. It's just—oh God," I say with a watery laugh, wiping at my face. A strange realization washes over me as I feel the intensity of my emotions—how they seem to crash through me like waves, overwhelming and all-consuming. "I think these are pregnancy hormones. I'm sorry I'm such a mess."

Wes's face softens as he reaches up to brush away a tear I missed. "Don't apologize. Not for this. Never."

His hand moves from my cheek to rest gently on my stomach, the warmth of his palm seeping through my skin. "It's me and you now." His eyes, so blue and earnest, hold mine as his lips curve into a gentle smile. "And soon it'll be us."

"Us," I repeat, my voice thick with emotion. The word feels both simple and profound at the same time. Us. A family.

His thumb traces gentle circles on my stomach as his eyes hold mine with unwavering intensity.

"I know you're scared, Amelia," he says softly. "And I understand why. Everything's happened so fast between us, and with the baby, and all the changes in your life..." He pauses, his expression earnest. "But you should know something—you're the strongest woman I've ever met."

I start to shake my head, about to protest, but he continues.

"You are," he insists. "Think about everything you've survived. Losing Nick. Discovering his betrayal. Building a new life for yourself. Being harassed. And now this pregnancy." His voice lowers to a whisper. "You've faced it all with so much grace and courage. It's one of the things I love most about you."

"I don't feel strong," I admit, vulnerability making my voice tremble. "Most days I feel like I'm barely holding it together."

"That's exactly what strength is," he says, tucking a strand of hair behind my ear. "It's not about never feeling scared or overwhelmed. It's about feeling all of that and still moving forward." His eyes crinkle slightly at the corners. "And you never have to do it alone again. I promise you."

"Thank you," I whisper, turning my face to kiss his palm. "For seeing me that way. For being here."

"Always."

Chapter Thirty-Six

WESLEY

I've never been good at waiting. Not for game day, not for Christmas morning, and definitely not for this—sitting in a doctor's office about to see my child for the first time.

Well, not biologically mine. But mine in all the ways that matter.

My knee bounces as I flip through a tattered parenting magazine, not absorbing a single word. Next to me, Amelia sits perfectly still, her hands folded protectively over her stomach, which still looks flat beneath her loose sweater. Ten weeks pregnant, and you'd never know by looking at her.

I clasp her hand. "Everything's going to be fine, Ladybug."

Her lips curve into the smile I love, the one that appears whenever I use my nickname for her. She leans against my shoulder, and I breathe in the scent of her shampoo— something floral and familiar that grounds me.

The waiting room is crowded with other couples. Women in various stages—some with barely-there bumps, others looking ready to pop any second. I'm probably the youngest guy here by a decade.

"Amelia Campbell?" A nurse in blue scrubs calls out from a doorway.

I jump to my feet immediately, then freeze, suddenly uncertain. Am I supposed to follow her back there? She asked me to come to the appointment, but now I'm realizing I don't know what all she meant by that. Does she expect me to wait here?

Amelia rises more gracefully beside me, gathering her purse. She must notice my hesitation because she smiles and reaches for my hand.

"You can come back if you want," she says softly. "I'd like you to."

Relief washes over me. "Yeah, of course."

We follow the nurse down a hallway lined with framed photos of babies—hundreds of them. The evidence of this doctor's work displayed like trophies. It's both reassuring and intimidating.

"First time dad?" she asks.

I open my mouth to correct her, to explain our complicated situation, but something stops me. Instead, I nod, feeling a strange warmth spread through my chest at being called "dad."

The nurse leads us into a small exam room with mint green walls and gestures toward the examination table covered in paper.

"Amelia, I'll need you to undress from the waist down," she says, pulling a folded paper drape from a drawer. "You can leave your top on and cover up with this. Dr. Martinez will be in shortly."

"Wait," I blurt. "I thought we were doing a sonogram today? To see the baby?"

The nurse smiles. "We are. At this stage of pregnancy, we typically use a transvaginal ultrasound wand."

"A what?" I ask, my voice coming out higher than intended.

"A transvaginal ultrasound," she repeats patiently. "It's a special tool that goes into the vagina to get closer to the uterus. Don't worry, it's completely safe for both mom and baby."

My jaw drops. "Inside? Like... all the way inside?"

Amelia laughs. "Wes, it's okay. I knew about that part."

The nurse nods. "Most first-time parents are surprised. The traditional abdominal ultrasound will probably be for her next appointment, when the baby's a bit bigger." She gives me a reassuring smile. "I'll step out while you get changed."

As the door closes behind her, I turn to face the wall, giving Amelia privacy. I hear the rustle of fabric, the crinkle of paper as she settles onto the examination table.

"You can turn around now," she says softly.

When I do, she's sitting on the edge of the surface, a paper gown draped across her lap, looking small and vulnerable. I move to stand beside her, taking her hand in mine.

A soft knock makes us both jump slightly. The door opens and a woman in a white coat walks in, followed by the nurse. The doctor is shorter than I expected, with dark hair pulled back in a neat bun and warm brown eyes that crinkle at the corners when she smiles.

"Hello, I'm Dr. Martinez," she says, extending a hand to Amelia, then to me. "And you must be dad."

There it is again—that word. *Dad.* It sends a strange thrill through me.

"Wes," I say, shaking her hand.

The doctor nods, her smile genuine. "Well, Wes, today we're going to do some measuring and get our first pictures of your baby."

The nurse dims the lights while the doctor wheels a machine closer to the examination table. She pulls on gloves and picks up what must be the ultrasound wand, squeezing clear gel onto its tip.

"This might be a little cold," she warns Amelia gently, and suddenly I'm feeling like I'm intruding on something intensely private.

Amelia squeezes my hand tight as the doctor moves the instrument beneath the paper drape.

I keep my eyes fixed on the screen. The monitor shows a grainy black-and-white image that I can't quite make sense of. Then she holds the wand steady on a particular spot.

"Ah, there we are," she says, pressing a button on the machine.

Suddenly, the room fills with a rapid, rhythmic sound—swoosh-swoosh-swoosh—fast and insistent like a tiny galloping horse.

"That's your baby's heartbeat," Dr. Martinez says to Amelia. "And it's very strong—exactly what we want to hear at this stage."

I look at Amelia, and our eyes lock. There are tears welling in hers, and I'm surprised to feel moisture in my own. A wide smile spreads across my face, and I squeeze her hand tighter.

"That's our baby," I whisper, the words feeling both strange and completely right on my lips.

Dr. Martinez lets us listen for another moment before turning off the sound. "Now I'll take some measurements and capture a few keepsake photos for you to take home," she explains, moving the wand slightly.

I watch in fascination as she freezes the picture on screen, using digital calipers to measure. My eyes struggle to make sense of the grainy image, to find the shape of a baby in the swirls of black and white.

"Is that... a baby?" Amelia asks.

"Yes, it is." Dr. Martinez traces the outline with her finger on the screen. "See this curve here? That's the head. And this little fluttering area is the heart we just heard."

Now that she's pointing it out, I can see it—the distinct shape of a tiny person forming. It's surreal, like looking at a weather radar, except instead of storm clouds, it's showing us our future.

"Everything looks completely normal," Dr. Martinez continues, moving the wand a little to get different angles. "The measurements are right on track for ten weeks. Strong heartbeat and good placental attachment."

Amelia's grip on my hand relaxes, and I realize how tense she's been this whole time.

"So the baby is healthy?" she asks, her voice small but hopeful.

"Very healthy," Dr. Martinez confirms with a reassuring smile. "You're doing everything right, Amelia."

The doctor takes a few more measurements, explaining each one as she goes. I try to absorb it all.

"I'll print some pictures for you," she says, clicking a few buttons on the ultrasound machine. The printer whirs to life, spitting out several glossy black-and-white photos.

Dr. Martinez finishes the exam, gently removing the wand.

"Everything looks perfect. Your baby is developing right on schedule."

The nurse hands us the small photos. They're grainy, but there it is—a tiny bean-shaped figure with what's clearly a head and the beginning of limbs.

"Congratulations to you both," Dr. Martinez says with a warm smile. "I'll see you back here in a month for your next checkup. Take your time getting dressed and you can check out up front."

She and the nurse leave us alone, the door clicking shut behind them. I move closer, perching on the edge of the exam table beside her. For a moment, neither of us speaks. I'm staring at the photos in my hand, tracing the outline of the tiny person we saw on screen.

"That's our baby," I whisper, my voice thick with emotion. "Look at that little head."

"I can't believe it's real," she says softly. "Hearing that heartbeat..."

I wrap my arm around her shoulders, pulling her close as we both stare at the images. "It's beautiful," I finish, staring at the photo in my hand. "A little blurry blob with a heartbeat."

Amelia laughs quietly, leaning her head against my shoulder. Her finger traces the outline of our baby's head in the sonogram picture. *Our baby.* The words still feel surreal in my mind, but increasingly right.

Her expression softens as she studies my face. There's something in her eyes I can't quite read—wonder, maybe, or disbelief. She takes the photo from my hand and places it carefully on top of the others before turning to face me fully.

"Wes," she says, her voice suddenly serious. "I need to tell you something."

My heart skips a beat. "Is everything okay?"

"Everything's perfect." She nods quickly, placing her hand on mine. "I love you. I just... I want you to know that. What you're doing for me—for us—" she gestures to her stomach, "it's more than I ever could have hoped for."

My throat tightens with emotion. "Amelia..."

"No, please let me finish." She takes both my hands in hers, her eyes never leaving mine. "You didn't have to choose this. You could have walked away when I told you about the baby. Most men would have. We haven't known each other that long, and this is... complicated. But you stayed. You're here, holding my hand, looking at sonogram pictures of another man's child like it's the most precious thing you've ever seen."

I swallow hard, trying to find the right words. The truth is, walking away never felt like an option. Not really. From the moment she told me she was pregnant, something inside me just... knew. This was where I was meant to be.

"I didn't choose you despite the baby," I tell her, squeezing her hands. "I chose both of you. Together—because my life is better with you in it. That's all there is to it."

She blinks rapidly, tears spilling onto her cheeks. I wipe them away with my thumb.

As I look at her now, holding those photos of our baby—because that's how I think of it now, our baby—I can't imagine any other choice. The alternative would have been a dark, empty life without her. The thought of not being here, of having walked away, makes my chest constrict painfully. I would have missed this moment—hearing that tiny heartbeat, seeing that blurry little bean on the screen, feeling this overwhelming surge of protectiveness and love.

"I love you too," I tell her, my voice rough with emotion. "More than I knew I could love anyone. And I already love this baby." I place my hand gently on her stomach. "Our baby."

Her eyes widen at my words, fresh tears spilling down her cheeks.

"You mean that?" she whispers. "You really think of the baby as ours?"

"Completely," I say without hesitation. "Biology isn't what makes a family. Love is. And I love this little raspberry-sized human."

Amelia laughs through her sobs, the sound warming me from the inside out. She leans forward, pressing her forehead against mine.

I look at the sonogram picture again, at that tiny miracle. My throat tightens as I imagine not being part of this journey —not getting to see her belly grow, not feeling those first kicks, not being there for the birth.

"My heart has never felt so full," I whisper, surprised by the raw honesty pouring out of me.

Her eyes fill with fresh tears, but her smile is radiant. "You mean that?"

"With everything I am."

Epilogue

WESLEY

A year and a half later...

I hear a soft coo from the back seat and glance in the rearview mirror. Willow's tiny face lights up when our eyes meet, her chubby cheeks dimpling as she gives me a gummy smile that melts my heart every single time.

"Almost home, princess," I say, my voice automatically shifting to that higher pitch parents naturally adopt. "You had fun with daddy and his friends today, didn't you?"

She responds with an excited babble, her little hands waving in the air. God, she's perfect. She turned one last month and is already developing such a personality. Sometimes I catch glimpses of Nick in her features—the shape of her eyes, the curve of her nose—but her smile is all Amelia.

My phone rings through the Range Rover's Bluetooth, and Luke's name flashes on the display. I tap the button on my steering wheel.

"Hey, man."

"Hey big brother." His voice comes through the car's speaker. "What's up?"

"Not much. Heading home after spending the afternoon with Willow and some guys from the team."

The sunlight streams through the windows of my SUV as we cruise down the tree-lined streets toward home. Today was perfect—my first real father-daughter day with the team. Coach surprised everyone by announcing a family day during the off-season, and I finally got to show her off to all the guys. The way she charmed everyone, especially the offensive line, had me bursting with pride. Those massive dudes were practically fighting over who got to hold her next.

"How're the little quarterback's hands?" Luke asks, and I hear the smile in his voice.

"Getting stronger every day," I laugh. "She's got a grip. Almost pulled my ear off yesterday."

I glance in the rearview mirror again. Willow is fascinated by the colorful dangling toys attached to her car seat, batting at them with focused determination.

"So, how's the road trip with Bebe going?" I ask, switching lanes as I take the exit toward our neighborhood. "My old Jeep giving you any trouble?"

"She said yes, man," Luke says, his voice cracking with emotion.

My face breaks into a huge grin remembering Luke told me that he was planning to propose to Bebe this summer and possibly stop in Vegas on the way back from their road trip to get married. "Of course she said yes! Congratulations, Luke. I'm so happy for you both."

"Thanks, bro," he says, and I can picture him running his hand through his hair the way he always does when he's emotional. "Listen, we'll be in Vegas tomorrow night—we've booked a chapel and everything. I already called mom and dad, Chase, and Bebe's brothers. Everyone's coming out. Really hoping you, Amelia and the little princess will be there."

"We'll be there, just send me the details," I promise, feeling my excitement build. My little brother is getting married. Wow. "I'll talk to Amelia as soon as I get home."

"Listen, Wes..." Luke's tone shifts suddenly, the excitement draining from his voice. "Have you talked to Chase lately?"

I tap my fingers on the steering wheel. "Here and there. Text messages mostly. Why?"

"I'm worried about him," Luke says with a sigh. "The last couple times I called, he barely said two words. I don't know, man. He's not himself. Becoming withdrawn and distant. Hiding out in his room—sleeping a lot. Bebe noticed it too."

"He's probably just going through a rough patch after what happened with Vanessa," I say, referencing his girlfriend —or ex-girlfriend now. "Finding out she was cheating probably did a number on him."

"Maybe," Luke says, but he doesn't sound convinced. "I've never seen him this... detached."

"Look, I'll talk to him at the wedding tomorrow, okay?"

"Thanks, man, see you tomorrow."

"See you tomorrow. Congrats again!" I end the call as I pull into our driveway. The two-story house in Las Vegas I've come to call home over the past year is bathed in golden afternoon light. It's amazing how much has changed in the last eighteen months. The draft was a blessing I never expected— keeping us close to family while starting my NFL career.

I glance behind at Willow as I put the car in park. Her eyelids are drooping, fighting sleep the way she always does after a big day of excitement. I grab the diaper bag from the passenger seat before getting out and opening the back door to unbuckle her.

"Come here, princess," I murmur, lifting her carefully from the car seat. She immediately nestles against my chest, her little head finding that perfect spot on my shoulder. The weight of her in my arms still amazes me—this tiny person who's completely changed my life.

The front door opens as I'm walking up the path, and there's Amelia—my wife, backlit by the warm light from inside.

She's a vision standing there in the doorway, in a simple sundress that hugs the gentle curve of her belly. At twenty weeks pregnant, she's absolutely radiant—her skin glowing, her hair falling in soft waves around her shoulders. My breath catches at the sight of her. Carrying our child has only made her more beautiful.

"My two favorite people," she says as she steps forward to meet us.

Willow stirs against my shoulder, lifting her head when she hears her mother's voice. "Mama," she mumbles sleepily, reaching out with one chubby hand.

She kisses Willow's fingers first, then rises on her tiptoes to press her lips against mine. The softness of her mouth, the familiar scent of her perfume—it centers me instantly, like coming home after a long journey.

"How was daddy-daughter day?" she asks, taking the diaper bag from me.

"Amazing. She had the entire offensive line wrapped around her little finger," I say, following Amelia inside.

"That's my girl," she says with a proud smile.

"I think someone's ready for a nap," I say, noticing how Willow's eyes are struggling to stay open against my shoulder. "All that charming is exhausting business. Let me go put her down."

"Perfect timing," she says, brushing Willow's dark curls with gentle fingers. "I just finished some design work on our dream home and was about to take a break. I'll be in our room."

I carry Willow upstairs to her nursery, the room Amelia decorated with such care—soft mint green walls with a hand-painted mural of a meadow and ladybugs on flowers. I laid her in her crib, observing as her eyelids flutter closed immediately.

"Sweet dreams, princess," I whisper, leaning down to press a kiss to her forehead.

I stand here watching her for a few moments, still amazed that I get to be her dad. Though she's not biologically mine, she's my daughter. From the moment I first held her in the hospital, I knew I'd do anything to protect her.

My eyes fall on the silver frame sitting on her dresser— Nick staring back at me with that confident smile of his. Amelia placed it there when we first decorated the nursery, keeping her promise that Willow would always know who her biological father was. I trace my finger along the edge of the frame, feeling a strange mix of emotions I've come to accept as part of our unique family story.

I respect Amelia for how she's handled this—making sure Willow knows Nick while still allowing me to be her dad. We've agreed that Willow doesn't need to know the uglier parts of their relationship. She'll have a clean image of her father, one carefully preserved through photos and the better memories.

Catherine and Robert have been incredible grandparents too, despite their initial hesitation about me—including my intentions to officially adopt her. They visit often, bringing stories and little keepsakes that belonged to Nick. It's important that Willow has a connection to her roots, to the Campbell side of her family.

Looking at his photo, I find myself doing something I never expected—silently thanking him. For this beautiful little girl who's completely stolen my heart. For the incredible woman who became my wife. For the life we're building together.

"Thank you," I whisper, so quietly it's barely a breath.

I adjust her blanket before turning on the baby monitor and quietly close the door behind me.

When I walk into our bedroom, I stop dead in my tracks. My wife is standing by the bed wearing only a black lace thong set and matching stilettos—highlighting the fullness of her breasts and the beautiful roundness of her belly where our child grows.

"Wow," I breathe, unable to form coherent thoughts as I take in the sight of my gorgeous wife... my body responds instantly.

She saunters toward me, a seductive smile playing on her lips. Her confidence is intoxicating—the way she embraces her changing body, proud of the life we created together.

"You like?" she asks, her voice low and sultry as she places her hands on my chest.

"Like is an understatement," I manage, my palms automatically finding her hips, fingers tracing the delicate lace.

She pushes me gently, guiding me backward until my legs hit

the edge of the bed. I sit, looking at her in awe as she stands between my knees. The afternoon light filtering through our curtains bathes her in a golden glow, making her look almost ethereal.

"I missed you today," she whispers, her fingers trailing down my chest, over my stomach, until they reach the waistband of my shorts.

My breath catches as she slowly lowers herself to her knees in front of me, her eyes never leaving mine. The room feels suddenly hot as she undoes the button, then slowly drags the zipper down. The sound seems impossibly loud in the quiet room.

I lift my hips as she tugs at my shorts and boxer briefs, helping her slide them down my legs. My cock springs free, already hard and aching. The cool air of the bedroom makes me shiver slightly, but then her warm hand wraps around my shaft and all other sensations fade away.

"God, I've been thinking about this all day," she murmurs, her eyes locked with mine as she slowly strokes me from base to tip.

My breath catches in my throat as she lowers her head, maintaining that intense eye contact that drives me wild. The first touch of her mouth against my sensitive head sends electricity racing up my spine. She swirls her tongue around the tip, teasing me with light, playful licks before taking me fully into her mouth.

"Fuck," I groan, one hand instinctively moving to cradle the back of her head while the other grips the edge of the mattress for support.

The wet heat of her mouth is exquisite as she takes me deeper with each bob of her head. My pierced shaft slides between her lips, and I know the metal barbells are creating extra sensation for her.

My eyes roll back, but I force them to stay open, not wanting to miss a second of this view. The warmth, the perfect pressure of her tongue as it traces the underside of my cock—the piercings—it's exquisite torture.

"I need to be inside you," I groan, unable to contain myself any longer. My hands grip her shoulders gently. "Now, Amelia."

She releases me from her mouth with a wet pop, her lips red and swollen, eyes dark with desire. Seeing her on her knees, pregnant with my child, wearing nothing but black lace and heels—it's almost enough to push me over the edge.

I scoot back on the bed, settling against the pillows as she rises gracefully to her feet. Even with her baby bump, she moves with a sensuality that takes my breath away. She climbs onto the bed, crawling toward me with predatory grace.

"Let me," she whispers as she straddles my thighs, taking my cock in her hand.

She's already pushed the thin material of her thong aside, and I can feel how wet she is as she positions herself above me. Our eyes lock as she slowly sinks down, enveloping me inch by delicious inch until I'm fully sheathed inside her.

"God, Wes," she moans as I grip her hips, helping guide her movements as she rides me. Her body moves in a slow, hypnotic rhythm that has me mesmerized. The sight of her pregnant belly, round and perfect, makes my heart race even faster. There's something primal and intensely erotic about making love to my wife while she carries our child. Her breasts are fuller, her skin glows, and the way she moves—more deliberate, more sensual—drives me wild.

I think about how after she delivers our baby, I'll want to see her like this again soon. Maybe wait a few months and then put another child in her. If I had my way, she'd always be carrying our children—one after another until we had enough for an entire football team. The thought alone makes my cock throb inside her.

I grip her hips tighter, thrusting up to meet her movements. My piercings drag against her inner walls, making her gasp and throw her head back, exposing the elegant line of her throat.

"You're so fucking beautiful like this," I growl, one hand moving to caress the swell of her belly. "Carrying my baby."

Her eyes flutter open, meeting mine with such raw emotion that it steals my breath. Her movements become more desperate, more urgent as she rides me. She throws her head back, her long hair cascading down her back. The Vegas sunlight streaming through our bedroom window bathes her in golden light, highlighting every curve, every inch of her perfect body. My wife—pregnant with my baby—riding me like she was made for this. For us.

I never imagined this life for myself. In college, my goals were simple—party, paintball with my brothers, play football, make it to the NFL. I had no idea what I was missing. I never saw myself as a family man, never thought I'd find this kind of happiness. But watching my wife now, her body joined with mine, carrying our child—I couldn't have imagined that I could feel this complete. I'm overwhelmed by how lucky I am, how one moment of kindness extended to a grieving widow— changed everything.

If someone had told me two years ago that I'd be here, married to the most amazing woman I've ever known, raising her daughter as my own and with another baby on the way—that my greatest joy wouldn't be draft picks or touchdowns—I would have laughed. But now, watching my wife, her eyes half-closed in pleasure as she takes me deeper, I know this is everything—I can't imagine any other life.

I think about all the paths not taken, all the decisions that led us here. The regrets I might have had in another life—going to a different college, pursuing a different career—none of them matter now. I wouldn't change a single thing about how we found each other, about how I found my happiness with my Ladybug and our family.

The end.

About the Author

Lulu Hart

Lulu Hart is a passionate storyteller who has been fascinated by the written word since childhood. From the whimsical worlds of Disney and Dr. Seuss to the thrilling adventures of Goosebumps and Sweet Valley High and the literary classics studied in high school. While in college, she dabbled in poetry, eventually publishing a collection that captured her creative spirit.

Lulu decided to bring her own love stories to life and share them with the world. Her debut novel, *Punches & Pirouettes*, marks the beginning of an exciting chapter in her writing journey. With its emotional depth, unforgettable characters, and engaging storytelling, this love story will keep lovers of contemporary romance captivated and yearning for more.

Lulu is a full-time professional in administrative healthcare and lives in Las Vegas, Nevada, with her loving husband and adorable daughter. In her free time, she finds fulfillment in watching horror movies, reading romance novels, and celebrating the joy of the holidays—Christmas being her favorite.

Also by Lulu Hart

The Fitzpatrick Clan

Punches & Pirouettes

Whiskey & Wine

Interludes with Insects

The Killer Bee

Ladybug Designs

TBD Book 3